A CATERED
CAT WEDDING

Books by Isis Crawford

A CATERED MURDER
A CATERED WEDDING
A CATERED CHRISTMAS
A CATERED VALENTINE'S DAY
A CATERED HALLOWEEN
A CATERED BIRTHDAY PARTY
A CATERED THANKSGIVING
A CATERED ST. PATRICK'S DAY
A CATERED CHRISTMAS COOKIE EXCHANGE
A CATERED FOURTH OF JULY
A CATERED MOTHER'S DAY
A CATERED TEA PARTY
A CATERED COSTUME PARTY
A CATERED CAT WEDDING

Published by Kensington Publishing Corporation

A Mystery with Recipes

A CATERED CAT WEDDING

ISIS CRAWFORD

KENSINGTON BOOKS
www.kensingtonbooks.com

Longely is an imaginary community, as are all its inhabitants. Any resemblance to people either living or dead is pure coincidence.

KENSINGTON BOOKS are published by

Kensington Publishing Corp.
119 West 40th Street
New York, NY 10018

All Kensington titles, imprints and distributed lines are available at special quantity discounts for bulk purchases for sales promotion, premiums, fund-raising, educational or institutional use.

Special book excerpts or customized printings can also be created to fit specific needs. For details, write or phone the office of the Kensington Special Sales Manager. Kensington Publishing Corp., 119 West 40th Street, New York, NY 10018. Attn.: Special Sales Department. Phone: 1-800-221-2647.

Library of Congress Control Number: 2018932862

ISBN-13: 978-1-4967-1496-1
ISBN-10: 1-4967-1496-2
First Kensington Hardcover Edition: October 2018

eISBN-13: 978-1-4967-1498-5
eISBN-10: 1-4967-1498-9
First Kensington Electronic Edition: October 2018

10 9 8 7 6 5 4 3 2 1

Printed in the United States of America

To my cousin, Joan.

Prologue

Susie Katz knew that everyone in Longely thought she was crazy. She knew that everyone hated her, but she really didn't care. That was the thing with having serious money— you got to do what you wanted when you wanted—and she wanted this wedding.

For a moment, she stopped making her list and looked at Boris, losing herself in the deep green depths of his eyes. Those eyes. She could write a poem about those eyes. Then Boris blinked, and the spell was broken. Susie came to her senses and returned to the task at hand.

"Boris, what do *you* think?" she cooed. "The Royal Ossetra, at ninety-five dollars an ounce, or the Ossetra President, at two hundred and fifty dollars an ounce?"

Boris tilted his head and said nothing.

"No, no," Susie said, drinking in his face. "Of course that's not good enough. What was I thinking of, my sweetums? For my baby boy, only the best, the freshest will do."

She leaned forward, stretched out her hand, and began rubbing his belly. It was so soft. Like velvet, really. She closed her eyes, enjoying the sensation. A minute went by. Then two. By the third minute, Boris had had enough. He let out a loud mew, flexed his claws, and dug them into Susie's skin. She screamed and jerked her arm away. Four spots of blood appeared where none had been before.

"Bad Boris," Susie scolded the cat as she took a tissue from the box on the desk that she kept for such occasions and dabbed at the scratches. She turned to Natasha. "Your fiancé is a naughty, naughty boy," she told her.

Natasha ignored Susie and began a bout of intense grooming as she watched Boris flick his tail back and forth. A minute went by. Finally, she couldn't resist. She pounced. Boris hissed. Then he jumped down from the desk, padded over to the armchair in front of it, jumped up, and curled himself up in a ball.

Susie knew she should be mad at him as she reached for the tube of Neosporin she always kept on hand and dabbed it on her arm. He'd really gotten her good this time, but she couldn't be angry with her baby boy. She loved him too much. Of course, she loved Natasha, too, but Boris was special. He had that indefinable star quality that set him apart from all the other kitty cats.

Susie watched him for a moment, enjoying the way the desk lamp illuminated the steel-blue color of his fur. Then she sighed and got back to what she'd been doing—planning Boris and Natasha's wedding. She wanted something elegant, something unusual, something that would make her guests eat their hearts out, and something that the cats would enjoy. That was a given.

She'd use the good china for everyone, as well as the Waterford crystal. Wineglasses for the people, and cut-crystal bowls for the cats. What was the point of having that stuff if you couldn't use it? She especially wanted to make that point to her guests. Susie tapped her pen, a Montblanc, against her yellow legal pad while she thought. The noise attracted Boris and Natasha's attention, and they pricked up their ears. Then Susie went back to writing, and the cats closed their eyes and went back to sleep.

Susie wrote the heading *table decorations* and underlined it. Beneath it, she wrote the word *pom-poms*, followed by a question mark. Blue, of course, to match Boris's and Natasha's coats. Or maybe she'd use big bows? Or little silver mice? Where had she seen them? *Tiffany*, she thought. Well, she still had a little time to decide.

She continued with her list. She had to call Gertrude Van Trumpet (*the* person to go to when it came to officiating cat weddings) and discuss the content of the wedding ceremony, as well as write Boris and Natasha's vows and firm up the menu with the Simmons girls. They could do the wedding cake, as well. Oh. And the save-the-date cards. She couldn't forget those! She had to get those hand lettered in copperplate style and out right away. Maybe something like *Save April 10 for the Purrfect Wedding*.

"What do you think, sweetie pie?" Susie asked Natasha, putting down her pen.

Natasha opened an eye, meowed, and coughed up a hair ball.

"I see," Susie said as she cleaned it up. "Maybe you're right, snookums. Maybe it is a little too cute."

Having made her point, Natasha meowed again. Then she stretched and jumped off the desk and onto the chair Boris wasn't occupying.

Susie looked at both of them. "It's going to be a wonderful event," she assured them. "You're going to love it."

Neither cat looked impressed. They started to lick themselves. Susie was just about to offer them a treat of freeze-dried Copper River salmon when her cell phone rang. She picked the phone off the desk, looked at the number, and then put the phone down. No need to answer it. She knew what Charlene was going to say.

I mean, good God. More sob stories about her damned birds. Not that that would be her problem soon. None of it would be. Susie tapped her fingers on her desk. *If she is so concerned about their getting killed, don't put feeders out.* It was as simple as that. She was sorry about the birds, but cats had been killing birds since the beginning of time.

Anyway, it wasn't her fault if her cats got out on occasion. It was her niece's and nephew's. They couldn't manage the simplest tasks without screwing them up. For a moment, Susie thought about calling Charlene back and telling her what was going to happen, about the consequences of complaining to the zoning board about her, but after a moment's reflection, she decided against it. The conversation would just turn into a time suck, and she had better things to do. Charlene would find out soon enough. Susie picked up her pen again and took up where she'd left off.

She had to rent the tent and the tables and chairs, as well as get Natasha measured for her veil and Boris measured for his tux, in addition to having matching diamond-studded collars made for them. *Or maybe not diamonds.* She tapped her pen on her chin while she thought. *Possibly crystals? Or sapphires? Yes. Sapphires would be nice.* They'd pick up the blue color scheme she was thinking about. Susie sighed. She also had to decide what the bride's and the groom's parties were going to wear.

She wove her pen back and forth between her fingers. So much to do and only four months to do it in. Four months sounded like a lot of time, but it really wasn't. Especially for a wedding.

Take the vaunted Mrs. Gertrude Van Trumpet. Just thinking about her and her hoity-toity airs brought a smile to Susie's face. The lady was normally booked for a year in advance. But she, Susie, had gotten her to fit Natasha and Boris's wedding in. And how had she done it? The way she always did. By knowing things, secret things, things that people didn't want anyone to know. It had worked for her in the finance game, and it was working for her now. Some people would call it blackmail, but she called it being well informed.

She thought about her successes for a moment, and about where she had started and where she was finishing; and then she thought about her will and the changes she would be making to it, before turning her attention to the gift registry. Should she or should she not have one? Would it be too much? What was too much? Was there any such thing as too much?

Susie was in the middle of debating those questions with herself when the doorbell rang. She looked at her watch. *Three o'clock.* Bernie and Libby Simmons were right on time. *Good.* Because if there was one thing she couldn't abide, it was people who weren't prompt. At least, Susie thought as she yelled for her nephew Ralphie to answer the door, she could get the menu nailed down. That would be one thing crossed off her list.

Chapter 1

Bernie and Libby looked around the Connor estate as they drove through the gate. It had been at least eight years since the sisters had been there, and they could see what all the fuss in the town was about. The estate, which was situated on a hill, was located on the outskirts of Longely, in a wealthy neighborhood called the Pines. The Pines was known for its classic brick colonials, rolling lawns, brooks, restrained landscaping, and house-proud owners. The Connor estate, now officially known as the Katz estate, had changed that algorithm. With a vengeance.

"Wow," Libby said, pointing to the eight-foot-high pink neon cat still decorated with Christmas lights, a cat that would have been at home in front of a roadside diner in Vegas but was definitely out of place in this neighborhood. "That's certainly . . ."

"Visible," Bernie said, finishing her sister's sentence for her. She gestured to the other five cats, each in a different garish color, dotted around the immaculate lawn. "They remind me of strippers at a DAR meeting. I can understand why Constance is upset," Bernie continued. Constance was one of Susie Katz's neighbors and a regular at

A Little Taste of Heaven. (One large coffee with room for cream and a toasted corn muffin, no butter.) "I wouldn't be happy if I had to look at those out my living room window, either."

"Well, she's in good company," Libby informed her sister. "I heard Charlene Eberhart went to the town board about them. Those cats aren't cheap, you know," Libby added.

"No, I didn't." Bernie slowed Mathilda down. The road had become a series of sharp turns, and she didn't want to end up on the lawn. "How much?"

Libby named a figure. She'd gotten the lowdown from one of their customers who had a sister who served on the board.

Bernie whistled. "I'm impressed."

"And that doesn't include the hefty donation Susie Katz made to the town coffers to have Charlene's complaint go away."

"I'm shocked, simply shocked," said Bernie, parroting a line from *Casablanca*. "I guess when you have that much money, you get to do what you want," she observed as she continued up the road that led to Susie Katz's house. "She could probably buy the whole town if she wanted to."

"Thus it was, and thus it will ever be," Libby replied.

Bernie glanced over at her sister. "You're getting cynical in your old age," she remarked.

Libby laughed. "I learned it from you."

A moment later, the sisters arrived at their destination. Bernie parked next to the house, and she and Libby got out.

It was a gray afternoon in early January, and a cold wind had sprung up off the Hudson. It blew up the valley and wound itself around the hills before creeping under the Simmons sisters' upturned coat collars.

"It's colder than I thought," Bernie remarked as she and

Libby walked up to the entrance of Susie Katz's house and rang the bell. They stamped their feet to keep warm as they waited to be let in.

"I wish we were catering a wedding," Libby said.

"We are," Bernie observed as she jammed her hands into her pink peacoat and wished she'd brought gloves with her.

Libby put the hood of her old parka up, noting the frayed edges as she did. "For people."

"This will be easier," Bernie told her.

"That's not the point," Libby objected. She blinked her eyes. The wind was making them tear.

"Maybe this will bring us more business."

"Great. Just what I want us to specialize in. Pet weddings," Libby grumbled.

"It could be lucrative."

"I don't care. I don't want to bake dog biscuits."

"I'm talking about Susie, Libby. Maybe this could be our foot in the door."

"She doesn't entertain," Libby objected. The catering community was small, and everyone knew what everyone else was and wasn't doing.

"But she used to," Bernie replied. "Maybe she will again."

"I'm not sure I want our foot in the door, Bernie. I hear Susie's pretty weird."

"Eccentric," Bernie answered. "If we were living in an English village, she would be called eccentric."

"*Catcentric* in this case," Libby corrected. "But we're not living in an English village. We're living in Westchester." She pointed to the pictures of cats Susie had had painted on the shutters and the door of the stately hundred-year-old brick colonial. The effect, Libby reflected, was like adding hot fudge sauce to *pommes soufflées*. "I mean, why buy a house like this and do this to it?" Libby asked, gesturing to the painted cats and statues.

Bernie shook her head. She didn't have an answer.

Libby sneezed. She hoped she wasn't getting sick. "She changed her name, you know."

"I do." Bernie had read Susie Katz's bio in *People*, too.

The headline had proclaimed SUSIE, LARGER THAN LIFE, which she was, in all senses of the word. According to the article, Susie Katz, née Susie Abrams, had made a killing on Wall Street, after which she'd retired, moved up to Longely, bought the old Connor estate, and become a semi-hermit. The movers and shakers of Longely had expected a slew of parties once she'd settled in—she'd been the hostess with the mostess when she'd lived in New York City—but according to local gossip, the only people she saw on a regular basis now were her niece and nephew and her staff.

A moment later, Susie's nephew Ralph Abrams opened the door. Bernie judged him to be in his early thirties. He was tall and skinny, with a thatch of light red hair, a prominent Adam's apple, and thick glasses that magnified his eyes. He was wearing a pair of jeans held up with a pair of red suspenders, and a tucked-in flannel shirt with a dusting of cat litter around the cuffs.

"Sorry it took so long," he told them after introducing himself. "I was feeding some of the cats."

"I can hear them," Libby said.

Ralph smiled. "Yes, they do have a lot to say." Then he added, "Susie will be here in a minute. It just takes her a while to locomote."

"No problem," Bernie said as she and Libby stepped into the hallway.

When she and her sister had been here eight years ago to cater an engagement party for Mr. and Mrs. Harriman's daughter June, the walls had been painted a pale green, the furnishings had been Stickley, the paintings on the walls had been landscapes, and the floor had been black-and-white marble tile.

The floor was the only thing that remained the same. Now the walls were a bright electric blue and were covered with cat portraits, while the furnishings were midcentury modern. Intensive redecorating had also occurred in the living room. If the Harrimans' furniture had looked as if it had come directly from the showroom, Susie Katz's looked as if it had come from a grad student's apartment. The armchairs were sagging, the sofa had a blanket thrown over it, and the tables were scratched and dented.

And then there were the cats. They seemed to be everywhere, perched on the living-room chairs and sofas, lounging on cat trees, sniffing at Bernie's and Libby's heels, or watching them from a suspension bridge made of rope that hung a foot below the ceiling.

"Neat, isn't it?" Ralph said, referring to the bridge. "My aunt had it specially made."

"How many cats are there?" Bernie asked over a loud meow.

"Why? Do you think there are too many?" said a deep female voice behind her.

Bernie and Libby spun around. It was Susie Katz herself, standing before them in all her glory.

Chapter 2

As Bernie studied Susie Katz, she reflected that she moved very quietly for such a big woman, and *big* was the operative word here. She was as wide as she was tall, but that wasn't the only notable thing about her. Her hair was fire-engine red and fought with the green eye shadow and the pink lipstick Susie had applied, as well as the orange bandanna she'd tied pirate-style around the top of her head. Her jeweled green and yellow caftan glittered in the light as she extended her arms to Bernie and Libby. This, Bernie reflected, was a woman who was clearly not afraid of color.

"So," Susie said. "I repeat my question. Do you think I have too many cats?" The expression on her face made the answer she expected clear, and Libby gave her what she wanted.

"Of course not," Libby lied. "After all, you are a breeder."

"It's like little black dresses," Bernie added. "You can never have too many of those either."

Susie frowned and pointed to herself. "I wouldn't know about that. The word *little* isn't in my vocabulary."

Bernie tried to redeem herself. "You know what they

say? A cat a day chases the blues away." Now where had that come from? She didn't have a clue. "In fact," Bernie continued, "we have a cat ourselves."

Her interest piqued, Susie smiled. "What kind?"

Bernie wrinkled her forehead. "Kind?"

"What breed?" Susie asked impatiently, drumming her fingers on her thighs.

"None, as far as I know," Bernie replied. "She's just a cat."

Susie sniffed her disdain. It was obvious to Bernie that she'd just lost the points she'd scored.

"I have nothing against the non-breeds," Susie told her, an obvious lie, "but I prefer my Russian blues and Burmese." As if on cue, a grayish blue cat wound itself around Susie's ankles. Susie picked him up and scratched behind his ears. "This is Serge. He's going to be Boris's best cat."

Libby reached out a hand to pet him, but Serge growled at her, and she quickly drew her hand back.

"The poor dear is a little cranky," Susie informed her. "He didn't sleep well last night. Nightmares, you know."

"I didn't know cats had nightmares," Libby said.

"Of course they do," Susie said indignantly. "Everyone knows that!"

Libby apologized. She wondered if their cat dreamt. Somehow, she doubted it. Cindy did snore from time to time, but that wasn't the same thing.

Susie handed Serge to Ralph, instructing Ralph to feed Serge in the kitchen. "And make sure you chop the liver up fine enough. He doesn't like big pieces," Susie told her nephew, raising her voice.

"Yes, Auntie," Ralph replied, a look of resentment flashing across his face.

"See that you do, Ralphie," Susie said, reiterating her point. She shook her head. "I have to remind him of everything," she confided to Bernie and Libby before Ralph was out the door. She shook her head again, a gesture intended to convey pity, Bernie decided. "If he weren't my nephew, I would have fired him a long time ago." Bernie watched the back of Ralph's neck redden. Then Susie waved her hand and changed the subject. "This year I'm going to win," she said.

"Win what?" Libby asked politely, trying not to sneeze. Even though the place was spotless, the cats were beginning to get to her.

"Best in show at the CFA Extravaganza, of course," Susie answered in a tone that proclaimed the self-evidence of the response. She pointed to a clear spot on one of the shelves. "That's where I'm going to put the trophy." She sniffed. "And then that will be the final proof. The cherry on the sundae, if you will. Then no one will dare question my lineages."

"Lineages?" Bernie asked.

Susie explained as she continued her march forward. The sisters tagged along behind her, zigzagging this way and that to avoid tripping over the cats sauntering across their paths, rubbing up against their legs, and just generally getting underfoot. It was like walking through an obstacle course that moved, Libby reflected.

Finally, the three of them arrived at the teak-paneled study. Although the sisters had never been in this room, looking around, Bernie could surmise from the built-in bookshelves that this room had once functioned as a library. But not anymore. Susie had converted the room into a museum for everything feline.

The shelves were filled with porcelain Hello Kitties, Japanese cat prints, Egyptian statues of the cat goddess Bastet, cat mugs, cat and dog salt and pepper shakers, and cat T-shirts. The selection ranged from extremely expensive to dollar store, and as far as Bernie could see, no attempt had been made to sort anything out.

Susie laughed as she followed Bernie's and Libby's gaze. "One of these days, I'll get around to organizing this lot." She waved her hand dismissively. "But not now. Take a seat," she said, gesturing to the ones in front of her desk, the ones Boris and Natasha were lounging on.

The cats gave Bernie and Libby the evil eye.

"Here are the lovebirds now," Susie sang. She introduced them. "Natasha Abramova and Boris Spectorski, this is Libby and Bernie. They are the people who will be catering your wedding."

Natasha licked her paw, while Boris just stared.

"They don't look impressed," Bernie noted.

"They're a little standoffish with new people," Susie explained. "Just scooch them off the chairs," Susie told the sisters.

Bernie and Libby scooched. The cats stayed where they were. After the sisters' third failed scooching attempt, Susie took over.

"Bad kitties," she crooned. "Naughty, naughty, naughty. Mommy wants to speak to the nice ladies." Nothing. She clapped her hands. The cats stared at her. "Snookums want a treatie?" Susie sang.

Boris's and Natasha's ears perked up. Bernie watched as Susie moved a pink folder decorated with a picture of Grumpy Cat to one side, unscrewed the top of a cat-shaped Wedgwood cookie jar, took out two fish-shaped treats, and held them out. Both cats got up ever so slowly, stretched, then gave Libby and Bernie baleful glares before they jumped down off the chairs, collected their treats, and retreated to the Oriental rug on the other side of the room.

"Aren't they sweet?" Susie crooned.

"Darling," Bernie said as she and Libby sat down.

Susie gave her a suspicious glance, but Bernie just smiled at her. Assuaged, Susie sat down and started rummaging through the papers on her desk.

"Boris and Natasha are very rare, you know," she informed Bernie and Libby while she looked. "Their bloodlines go back to the czars."

Libby tried to look interested.

"I was lucky to get them." A moment later, Susie found the yellow legal pad she was searching for and handed it to Libby. "The menu is on top," she informed her.

"Very Russian," Libby said after she'd scanned the menu and handed it to Bernie. Bernie raised an eyebrow as she read.

"That's the idea," Susie said, pleased that Libby had understood what she was after.

"You want to serve this menu to both groups?" Bernie asked when she was done. It was almost all caviar; raw, smoked, and poached salmon; and a variety of pâtés.

"Naturally," Susie replied. "That's the whole idea." She frowned and fiddled with her pen. "Although, Grace and Ralphie will probably be too busy to eat. It's the caviar I'm concerned with," Susie continued, changing subjects. "Who's your supplier?"

Bernie named theirs.

"No. No. No." Susie waved her hands in the air. "They won't do at all!"

"Why not?" Bernie asked. "They're extremely reputable. We've never had any problems with them."

Susie put her pen down and leaned back in her chair. Boris jumped up on her lap, and she began to pet him. "They handle salted caviar."

"All the caviar we get here is salted," Libby pointed out. "Lightly salted, but salted nevertheless."

"Not the kind I want," Susie said. "Salt is not good for

my babies." She leaned down and kissed Boris's head. The cat yawned.

"Okay," Bernie said, leaning forward in her chair, not sure where the conversation was going.

Susie took back her yellow pad, wrote a name at the bottom of the top page, and put the pen down.

"Here," she said, tearing the bottom quarter of the page off and handing it to Bernie. "I want you to call him. I've already talked to him. He's absolutely trustworthy. After all, he got me Boris and Natasha."

"I don't understand," Libby protested. "What's this guy going to do that our guy can't?"

"He'll supply you with pure sturgeon eggs, eggs that have never been salted or processed. I want only the best for my babies."

"And these eggs are coming from?" Bernie asked.

"Russia, of course!" Susie exclaimed, the shock emanating from her voice, underlining her amazement that anyone could even ask a question like that.

"Won't the roe spoil?" Libby asked.

Susie snorted. "Would I do this if that was the case?" she asked. Then she answered her own question. "Of course I wouldn't. The eggs will be overnighted from Russia to here on the day of the wedding, and they'll be delivered to your shop."

"My God, how much is this going to cost?" Bernie asked.

Susie named the price.

Bernie couldn't help it. She gasped. She wasn't shocked by much, but she was shocked by this.

Susie shrugged. "What's the point of money if you can't do what you want with it?"

"I suppose," said Libby. This was not a problem she anticipated having. Ever. She cleared her throat.

"Yes?" Susie said in a voice that didn't encourage questions.

"About the wedding cake," Libby said.

"What about it?" Susie asked.

"It just seems to me that actual fish-head decorations are a bit . . ."

"A bit what?" Susie demanded.

"Nuts," Libby wanted to say. What she said instead was, "A bit people unfriendly."

Susie picked up the pen that was sitting on her desk and began weaving it through her fingers. "People eat fish heads in Asia," she informed the sisters.

"But not so much here," Bernie observed. "Maybe we could go in a different direction?"

"I see," Susie said. She paused for a moment before continuing. "Do you know why I was so successful in business?" she asked Bernie and Libby.

The sisters shook their heads.

"Do you want to know?"

Neither Bernie nor Libby wanted to, but Bernie said yes, anyway.

"I was successful because I came up with the concept and let my subordinates implement it. Now, if you don't think you're up to the challenge . . ." Susie's voice drifted off.

"We'll figure something out," Bernie assured her.

"Given the price I'm paying, I assume you will," Susie said as she pulled out her checkbook and wrote them a check. "A third now, a third before the event, and the last third after the event. I assume that's satisfactory," Susie asked, although it wasn't really a question.

Libby and Bernie both nodded.

"Good," Susie said, handing the check to Libby.

Libby looked at the check before folding it up and putting

it in her wallet. *Money*, she decided, *can, despite what people say, make up for a lot of things.*

"Can you find your own way out?" Susie asked, putting her yellow pad and checkbook back in the desk drawer.

"Not a problem," Bernie said as she and her sister rose.

They were almost out the door when Susie called them back. "I forgot to mention that I want ice sculptures—four of them. For the caviar," she explained when neither sister said anything. "Two for each table. Swans," Susie added. "I think swans would be nice," she told them, then dismissed them with a wave of her hand.

"What are we going to do about the cake?" Libby asked once they were outside the house.

"I have no idea," Bernie told her. "But we have four months to figure it out."

It had started to snow, and white snowflakes clung to the neon cats, softening their colors, making them look almost pretty as the sisters climbed back in the van.

"It must be nice to have that much money," Libby said as Bernie put the key in Mathilda's ignition and turned it. The van spluttered and coughed and finally started up.

"It would be nice to have enough money to get a new van," Bernie observed.

As Bernie started driving back down the road, a car zipped by them in the opposite direction. It was going so fast, it missed one of the turns and slid onto the grass. The driver paused for a moment, reversed, and sped off. When the vehicle reached the front of the house, it screeched to a halt.

Bernie stopped the van to watch. A woman emerged from the car. Marie Summer. She adjusted her studded leather pants and tossed her long, gray braid over her shoulder and bounded up the stairs.

"I should have known," Libby said. "I guess her safe-driving course hasn't helped much."

"Evidently not," Bernie said, thinking that she'd be seeing her this coming Friday, when she came into A Little Taste of Heaven to buy her usual: two pounds of red ginger chicken, a pound of pea, rice, and artichoke salad, and two linzer tarts.

"She looks really pissed," Libby observed as she watched Marie bang on the door. A moment later, the door flew open and Marie stomped inside. "I wonder what that was about?" Libby mused as the door slammed behind Marie.

Bernie hazarded a guess as she started the van back up. "Probably cats." Marie was a breeder, too, as well as a part-time librarian and a full-time menace on the road. "You can ask her when she comes in," Bernie suggested as she looked at her watch. If they hurried, they could get to the bank before it closed. She knew she could scan the check in, but she didn't quite trust that technology. Some things she preferred to do the old-fashioned way.

"That's okay," Libby said, leaning back in her seat. She really wasn't that interested.

Chapter 3

April tenth dawned bright and clear. The weather forecast was for a sunny, seventy-degree day, with a slight breeze from out of the east. It was perfect, thought Libby as she and Bernie drove onto the old Connor estate. They could see the wedding tent from the gate. It was one of those expensive ones that people rented for fancy affairs.

"It reminds me of a marshmallow," Bernie observed as they parked next to it. "A large marshmallow."

Libby didn't reply. Instead, she looked at her watch. It was now one o'clock, and the wedding wasn't scheduled to start until three. Which left them plenty of time to decorate the tables and take care of the food—not that there was a lot to take care of in this case. All she and her sister had to do for the first course was open the jars of caviar packed in ice that had arrived at the shop that morning and carefully place the roe in the carved ice swans (which had been residing in Susie Katz's freezer since yesterday), set out the caviar's accompaniments—chopped egg, onion, and sour cream—and reheat the blini they'd made earlier in the day.

The second course was equally easy. Pâté on toasted

baguettes, accompanied by cornichons, spiced green olives, and plumped sultana raisins. Then came the salmon. There was salmon tartare, which they were serving on a bed of greens shot through with catnip for the cats, and with an arugula and avocado mélange for the humans, after which came Copper River salmon served two ways: poached and sautéed. They were garnishing the humans' plates with two classic French sauces, cucumber and rémoulade, as well as new potatoes and green peas, while the cats' plates were decorated with more sprigs of catnip and strips of quickly seared tuna.

Suddenly Libby had a vision of eight stoned cats running amok. "I hope we didn't overdo the catnip thing," she said as she and Bernie got out of their van.

"It'll be fine," Bernie reassured her, although she didn't have the slightest idea if that was the case or not. The catnip had been one of those "seems like a good idea at the time" thoughts.

Libby rebuttoned the middle button of her white shirt. Susie had insisted both she and her sister wear white blouses and black pants—something they usually did, anyway. "Maybe we should just go with a sprig of catnip," Libby said as the sisters walked into the tent.

"Maybe we should go with a good stiff drink," Bernie observed, stopping to get the lay of the land. "I'm thinking bourbon and branch water. Whatever that is."

The altar where the wedding was going to take place was on the right, while the tables for the banquet were on the left. A wide space separated the two areas. Garlands of pussy willows, dandelions, lion's tail, and tiger lilies were draped over the backs of the chairs for the guests and over the dais where the wedding was going to be performed, while large potted ferns lined the sides and the entrance to the tent.

"Pretty," Bernie commented.

"And there's plenty of room for everything," Libby observed. "More than enough room, actually, when one considers the guest list."

"Such as it is," Bernie said as she began rummaging through the box of decorations Susie had left for them. "Cats definitely outnumber the people."

"Which is what's worrying me," Libby said as she folded the Irish linen napkins they'd brought with them into flowers.

An hour and a half later they were done. Well ahead of schedule. Bernie was in the midst of deciding how long after the ceremony began she should bring out the ice swans when Susie's niece Grace passed by. She was slightly shorter than her brother but just as skinny, and she had the same strawberry blond hair.

"Hey, Grace," Bernie called out. "Nice job with the decorations."

Grace grunted.

"Is everything okay?" Libby asked.

Grace pointed to the dress she was wearing. "Would you be happy in this?"

"Heavens no," Bernie responded. It looked like a pink bubble with large white polka dots. The dress started slightly above the knees and ended with cutout sleeves and a high collar. It was the kind of dress that flattered no one, and Bernie couldn't imagine who could have designed something like that. "It's hideous."

Grace nodded. "Exactly. I look like a giant pink bonbon with legs."

"It's not that bad," Libby said, trying to be diplomatic.

"Yeah. It is," Grace retorted.

"Okay. You're right. It is. Where did you get it?" Libby asked. She couldn't imagine anyone actually selling it.

"My aunt had it specially designed for me."

"Good God," Bernie said, truly appalled.

"She says it makes me look cute."

"*Cute?*" Bernie repeated. "Not the word I would have used."

"No. *Pregnant* is," said Grace. "The only bright spot is that none of my friends are going to see me in this. I'd never live it down." She gestured to the three guests moving to take their seats in front of the altar. "Although having those women see me is bad enough."

Libby pointed to Marie Summer. "The last time I saw her, she was banging on Susie Katz's door."

"Yeah. She was definitely steaming that day," Grace remarked.

"About what?" Libby asked.

Grace shrugged. "It had something to do with the cat show they both entered."

"What?" Libby asked.

"I think Marie was questioning Boris's lineage, or it could have been something about a piece of property," Grace said. "I'm not sure. They were talking so fast, I couldn't tell. Then my aunt closed the door, and I couldn't hear anything else."

"Whatever it was, I guess they resolved their differences," Bernie remarked.

"Why do you say that?" Grace asked.

"Because she's here," Bernie answered.

Grace snorted at Bernie's naïveté. "Quite the opposite." She scratched her chin with a ragged fingernail. "All these ladies are here because they have a beef with my aunt." And she filled Libby and Bernie in on the details. "Charlene Eberhart tried to enact a law limiting cats to three to a household and making it a fineable offense to have them go outside, while Allison Hardy works for an organization that wants to liberate all companion animals." Grace used air quotes around *companion animals*. "That's why they're here."

"I still don't get it," Libby said.

Grace indicated the tent with a wave of her hand. "This is my aunt's demonstration of power," she said. "She gets off on making people do things they don't want to do."

"But they could have said no," Bernie observed.

"And, theoretically, I could have said no to the dress," Grace told her. "But I didn't."

"So, why didn't you?" Libby asked.

Grace laughed bitterly. "And risk the wrath of the great Susie Katz? No. I don't think so."

"Why not?" Bernie inquired. "What could she do to you?"

"Aside from fire you," Libby added.

"Yes," Bernie said. "Aside from that."

Grace shook her head slowly. "You obviously don't know her very well, do you?"

"I don't know her at all."

"Exactly. Because if you did, you would never say what you just did."

Grace's statement stayed with Bernie. She knew Susie Katz was rich, but really? What could she do? Lop off everyone's heads? Consign them to the outer reaches of hell? As she thought about the possibilities, she watched Mrs. Gertrude Van Trumpet, the high priestess of cat weddings, slowly mount the dais. Bernie looked at her watch. It was almost three. The wedding was about to begin.

Chapter 4

When Bernie first caught sight of Mrs. Van Trumpet, she couldn't help thinking that she was a very short woman to have such a long name. Gertrude Van Trumpet cleared four feet ten at the most. But to be fair, Mrs. Van Trumpet's hair added another foot to her height. At least. It was piled into a beehive and lacquered in place sixties-style. If a zombie apocalypse occurred, Mrs. Van Trumpet might not survive, but her hairdo would remain intact.

She was dressed in white. Obviously, Bernie thought, the rule about not wearing white to a wedding if you weren't the bride didn't apply to cat weddings. Bernie was fairly certain that Mrs. Van Trumpet's silk suit, her white silk blouse with a bow tie around her neck, and her matching white silk pumps had all been made to order. She had a small white shoulder bag slung over her left shoulder and was carrying a red briefcase decorated with pictures of cats in her right hand. Once Mrs. Van Trumpet had settled herself behind the dais, she took a large white binder out of her briefcase, opened it, and began going over what Bernie assumed were her notes.

Grace pointed to Mrs. Van Trumpet. "If truth be told, I don't think she's such a big fan of Susie's, either."

"Why do you say that?" Bernie asked.

Grace shrugged. "Just a feeling I get." She looked at her watch. "Gotta go and get the little darlings ready." She frowned. "Cross your fingers that nothing bad happens."

"It won't," Libby declared, trying to be positive.

Grace looked at Libby as if she was insane. "With eight cats? Are you nuts?"

"So, what if it does?" Libby asked.

"Then there'll be trouble," Grace told her.

"Okay," Libby said. "But surely, she won't be able to blame you for the shenanigans of—"

"Of course she will," Grace snapped, interrupting Libby. "She blames me for everything. Well, me and Ralph. We're her whipping boys."

"What happens if something does happen?" Bernie asked.

"Good question," Grace answered. She looked at her watch again and said, "I have to go. The ceremony is about to start."

Libby turned to Bernie after Grace left, and said, "I wonder why she stays. I wouldn't."

"Me, either, but she must need this job."

"Or she really, really likes cats," Libby suggested.

"She'd have to in order to do what she does," Bernie noted, after which she changed the subject to the question of when she and Libby should get the ice swans.

Five minutes later, the song "Memory" from *Cats* came on, signaling the start of the event. Marie, Allison, and Charlene turned to look at the wedding procession, while Mrs. Van Trumpet put down her notes, folded her hands on the dais, and waited for Boris and Natasha to march down the aisle. Metaphorically speaking, of course. Since cats don't march. Ever. For anything.

Susie's nephew Ralph entered from the far aisle with the groom's best cats, while Grace entered from the nearer aisle with the bridal party. Like Grace, Ralph was dressed in head-to-toe pink, and while his outfit wasn't quite as outrageously awful as Grace's, it was bad enough. Susie had dressed her nephew as a footman. No wonder he looked so unhappy, Bernie reflected. What male wanted to be seen in pink tights and a waistcoat? The only thing lacking was a wig. Instead, Ralph was wearing a bright pink fedora, which somehow made everything even worse.

Libby and Bernie watched as Susie's niece and nephew pushed two small white coaches down their respective aisles. The coaches had been decorated with pink and white streamers, leopard flowers, pink leopards, and red roses and covered with white netting to keep the cats from jumping out and taking off. Inside each coach sat three pissed-off Russian blues. Ivan, Vladimir, and Serge had bow ties affixed around their necks, while Anya, Olga, and Katya were wearing white lace collars.

A panoply of noises issuing from the coaches ranged from mews to yowls to hisses and growls, although given the netting, it was hard to tell who was doing what. Bernie was thinking that Susie should have given the cats something a little bit stronger than catnip as she watched the procession wend its way slowly down the aisles.

"I guess Grace and Ralph aren't the only unhappy beings here," Libby whispered to Bernie.

"I know I wouldn't be happy if I were them," Bernie replied as she watched the procession advance.

"Are you talking about the niece and nephew or the cats?" Libby asked.

"Both," Bernie said. "I'm talking about both." *And the guests*, she added silently.

Once they reached the altar, Ralph and Grace turned and faced the entrance to the tent. The music was playing louder now, successfully drowning out the cats. A moment later, Susie Katz, wearing a gold sequined caftan that swooshed as she moved, entered the tent and walked down the center aisle. Or tried to, because Boris and Natasha were not cooperating.

Natasha was wearing a white veil that fastened behind her ears, while Boris had on a black tux. Both wore sapphire-studded leather collars. The attached leashes echoed the theme. A line of sapphires ran down the leashes' length. Susie had planned to have Boris and Natasha trot down the aisle beside her.

But the best-laid plans of men and all that. First, Natasha refused to move, and when she did, Boris sat down and attacked his leash. Then Natasha attacked Boris's leash. Boris retaliated and attacked Natasha. Susie stopped and separated them, putting one cat on one side of her and one on the other.

A couple of yards later, the same thing happened. Susie untangled the leashes again. They went another foot when the cats resumed their fighting. Finally, Susie conceded defeat, picked each Russian blue up, and carried them the rest of the way. Once they reached the altar, Susie put them down, and they proceeded to attack each other, leading Susie to pick them up again.

"Doesn't look like the start of a good marriage to me," Bernie leaned over and whispered to Libby. "I wonder if we'll get to cater the divorce."

Mrs. Van Trumpet glared at Bernie and loudly cleared her throat. Bernie took the hint and stopped talking.

"That's better," Mrs. Van Trumpet said. She took a pair of reading glasses out of her briefcase and rested them on the bridge of her nose, signaling that the ceremony was about to begin.

The music stopped. The service started.

Mrs. Van Trumpet looked around the tent, cleared her

throat again, pushed her glasses up on her nose with her index finger, and began. "Boris and Natasha, we are here to join you in the sacred ceremony of catamony," she said in a voice that could wake the dead.

Libby leaned over to Bernie and whispered, "For a little person, she's awfully loud."

"Ahem," Mrs. Van Trumpet said, favoring Libby with a stern look.

Libby stopped talking.

"May I proceed?" Mrs. Van Trumpet asked.

Libby pointed at herself. "Are you asking me?"

"You were the one talking, weren't you?"

Libby blushed. "By all means, continue," she mumbled.

Mrs. Van Trumpet smiled a triumphant smile and looked back down at her binder. "Now, where was I?" she asked for dramatic effect. She turned a few pages, frowning as she did. "Ah, here we are," she said a minute later. She looked up from her binder and cleared her throat for the third time. "We are here to join Boris Spectorski, son of Peter and Anastasya, grandson of Alexi and Dima, great-grandson of Serge and Olga, and Natasha Abramova, daughter of Polina and Igor, granddaughter of Vladimir and Svetlana, and great-granddaughter of Elena and Misha, in the bonds of holy catamony."

Mrs. Van Trumpet gazed out at her audience. One member of the bridal party began licking herself. Mrs. Van Trumpet ignored her and continued reading. "Do you, Boris, promise to take Natasha in flea, tick, and lice infestations, through litters and weaning, through litter box problems, cat tree disagreements, and hair balls for your wedded wife? And do you promise to be true to Natasha, and to groom her the way she likes to be groomed, and not to go tomcatting around, even when she has grown old and feeble and can no longer clean herself adequately?"

Boris meowed.

"He does," Susie said, answering for him.

Mrs. Van Trumpet turned to Natasha, who was now perched on the top of Susie Katz's head, kneading her scalp and sucking on her hair. Bernie thought she saw little trickles of blood in Susie's updo, but she couldn't be sure.

Mrs. Van Trumpet cleared her throat for the fourth time, took a sip of water from the silver goblet Susie had thoughtfully provided for her, and continued with the ceremony. "And do you, Natasha," and she repeated Natasha's pedigree, "promise to stay with Boris," here she repeated Boris's pedigree, "through fleas and ticks and lice and whatever other infestations occur? Do you promise to share your Tender Vittles and poached salmon with him and make room for him on the cat bridge, on the bathroom shelf, in the linen closet, as well as in your cat bed? And do you promise to share any mice, rats, moles, or voles that you may capture with him?"

Natasha didn't answer. Instead, she continued sucking Susie's hair. Susie reached up and pulled Natasha's tail, which was dangling in front of her face. Natasha let out a resounding growl and jumped onto the ground. Boris joined her a moment later.

Mrs. Van Trumpet looked up from her binder and readjusted her glasses. "I'll take that as a yes." Then she picked up a large stick of incense that had been lying on the podium and lit it with a gold lighter. The smell of patchouli wafted through the tent. She waved the incense stick from side to side, then up and down.

"In the name of the Egyptian cat goddesses Mut, Wadjust, Bastet, Menhit, Sekhmet, Mafdet, Pekhet, and Tefnut and the Egyptian cat gods Merui, Mihos, and Shut," she intoned, "I join you, Boris, and you, Natasha, in the bonds of sacred connubial bliss. May you be fruitful and multiply, and may your kittens do likewise, and so on and so forth down to eternity, until they populate the earth."

Then Mrs. Van Trumpet came down from the dais and walked over to where Boris and Natasha were standing and stopped. She waved the stick of incense in front of Boris and Natasha. They both sneezed. "By the powers invested in me by Orinnik and Hecate and by the gods of this universe and the next, as well as all the tigers and lions and leopards of this world, I pronounce you, Boris, and you, Natasha, married, and may the great cat goddess Bastet and her kittens watch over you and yours and grant you long and happy lives." Then she turned and walked back to the dais, closed her binder, and put it in her briefcase.

There was a polite sprinkling of applause from the audience.

Mrs. Van Trumpet smiled, looked up, and said, "Let the festivities commence."

Which was when things got interesting, depending, of course, on how you defined the word *interesting*.

Chapter 5

Libby and Bernie didn't know who suggested opening the presents before the meal instead of after it, because they'd been getting the caviar and the ice swans out of Susie Katz's fridge. When they'd left the tent, everyone had been heading toward the banquet tables, and when they came back, everyone, both felines and Homo sapiens, was congregating around the small round table that had been set up to receive the presents.

"Great," Libby said, surveying the scene. "So much for scripted. How long do you think the present opening is going to take?"

Bernie shrugged. "At a guess, allowing for the oohing and aahing factor, forty minutes. Hopefully." There were only six presents. How much time could that take?

By common consent, she and Bernie plunked the cooler they were carrying on the ground between the two tables earmarked for the meal.

Libby sighed. "The swans should be good for an hour at least, before they start to melt."

Bernie flicked a speck of dirt off her shirt. "And the caviar?"

"It should be fine," Libby replied. It had been messengered to them at the store this morning. "I hope it's fine." She didn't have any experience with this kind of product, so she didn't really know.

"I wonder if it was really flown in from Russia?" Bernie said.

"Instead of repackaged in California?" Libby asked.

Bernie nodded. There was a lot of scamming that went on in the fish business, because it was difficult to ascertain sources. "I hope Susie can taste the difference, because I can't." Bernie and Libby had both had a taste. They hadn't been able to resist.

"Me either." Libby brushed a lock of hair off her forehead with the back of her hand. She was trying to let her bangs grow out, and they had gotten to that annoying length at which they were too short to pin back but long enough to get into her eyes. "I don't really like the stuff," she confessed.

"Ditto that," Bernie agreed. "But given the price she's paying, I certainly hope Susie does," Bernie told Libby as she studied the rest of the guests. Marie was wearing a tight black dress, a big picture hat, and light beige stilettos, Allison looked as if she was going to a garden party in the English countryside, while Charlene was wearing a navy suit that would have been at home in the boardroom. By now five minutes had gone by—okay, maybe three—and no one had made a move to open the gifts yet.

"We'd better ask Susie when she wants us to put the caviar out," Libby suggested. The last thing that she wanted was to be responsible for it going bad. Given what she knew about Susie, she'd probably sue them for a million dollars, claiming emotional distress.

Bernie nodded. "And the swans." She pictured their beaks melting as she watched Susie. Their client had clasped her hands together and was beaming as the sisters walked toward her.

"You shouldn't have," she was gushing to her guests while Boris and Natasha played with the edges of the white lace tablecloth covering the table. A moment later, Natasha caught one of her nails in the lace and pulled. The tablecloth began a slow slide to the ground. So did the presents.

"The tablecloth," Bernie cried, pointing.

Susie looked. "Oh my God," she said, catching the tablecloth with her right hand before everything fell. "Don't just stand there gawking," she snapped at Grace while Susie scooped Natasha up with her left hand and pulled the tablecloth back with her right. "Do something."

"Coming," Grace said as she ran over, bent down, and began untangling the hissing cat from the tablecloth. It was not an easy task, since Natasha had managed to get her nail caught in three of the loops.

"Hurry up," Susie ordered.

Grace briefly glanced up. Bernie could see a spot of blood on her forehead where one of Natasha's nails had connected with Grace's skin.

"I'm doing the best that I can," she replied.

"Well, do better," Susie told her.

A moment later, the cat was free.

"You should have been paying better attention," Susie chastised Grace as she pressed Natasha to her chest. "She could have torn a nail."

"A tragedy," Grace whispered under her breath as she took a tissue out of her dress pocket and dabbed at the blood, which was now slowly dribbling down the bridge of her nose.

"What did you say?" Susie demanded, looking, Libby reflected, as if she could kill.

"Nothing," Grace muttered. "I didn't say anything."

"That's better," Susie said, and she went back to concentrating her attention on the cat. "There, there, my precious," she murmured, stroking Natasha's fur. "Mumsy won't let anything happen to you."

After a minute, the cat calmed down and Susie put her on the table with the gifts. She did the same with Boris. Then she turned to Grace and Ralph. "Really," Susie said. "I expected better from both of you."

"Sorry," Ralph said.

Grace didn't say anything.

"Grace?" Susie prompted.

Grace continued blotting.

"Don't you have something to tell me?" Susie asked. "Well?" Susie said after a minute had gone by. She was tapping her foot. "I'm waiting."

Ralph gave Grace a nudge. She ignored him. He gave her another nudge. This time she looked at him. He gave her a tiny nod, and after a moment she nodded back.

"I'm sorry," Grace told her in a grudging tone.

"And?" Susie prompted.

"And it won't happen again," Grace answered, looking as if she was going to explode.

"No, it won't," Susie said. "The least you can do after everything I've done for you is do your job," she continued. "God only knows, it's not that difficult. All you have to do is pay attention."

Ralph flushed and looked down at the ground.

Susie pointed at him. "And that applies to you, too, Ralphie."

Ralph took a deep breath and let it out. "You're right," he muttered after a minute had gone by. "We should have been more careful. It won't happen again."

"Let me put it this way," Susie said. "If it does, there are some changes that will be made, big changes. Understood?" she asked, turning to Grace.

"Understood," Grace muttered. "We won't let them out of our sight."

"Good." Susie smiled. The storm was over. She clapped her hands. "Now let's get Ivan, Vladimir, Serge, Anya, Olga, and Katya up on the table. That way they'll be able to see Boris and Natasha's presents. You'd like that, wouldn't you?" she asked, bending over the cats. Then she turned to Grace and Ralph. "Well, lift them up. What are you waiting for?" she demanded.

Neither Grace nor Ralph answered. Instead, they picked up the six cats and put them on the table. Now there were eight altogether. Too many kitties for the space, in Bernie's humble opinion.

Susie lowered her face until it was even with the cats. "Are we excited?" she cooed at them.

Boris meowed, while Serge swatted at the table decorations and Vladimir tried to tear the wedding veil off of Natasha, who reciprocated by going for his bow tie.

"No, no, no, Natasha," Susie said, separating the two cats. "Let Vladimir see. He's just jealous."

Bernie watched as Charlene Eberhart sighed loudly and looked at her watch.

Susie shot Charlene a look. "Do you have a problem?" she asked Charlene in a sickly sweet voice.

"What makes you say that?" Charlene replied.

"You keep looking at your watch. Is there somewhere else you have to be?"

"Well . . ."

"Are we boring you?" Susie said.

"As long as you're asking," Charlene replied, in spite of the warning tone in Susie's voice. Libby groaned as she listened to Charlene say, "Well, even you have to admit this is ridiculously . . ."

"Ridiculously what?" Susie asked, her voice rising.

"Ridiculously . . . wonderful," Charlene said, thinking better of what she was about to say.

"How nice of you to say that," Susie replied, looking inordinately pleased with herself, as Libby cleared her throat and tapped Susie on the shoulder.

Susie whirled around. "What do you want?"

"Sorry to bother you," Libby said, "but my sister and I have a question."

"Can't it wait?" Susie demanded. "We're in the middle of something important here."

Bernie stepped forward. "Actually, it can't." And she explained about the caviar and the swans.

Susie dismissed her concerns with a wave of her hand. "My God! Do I have to take care of everything?"

"We're just—" Libby began, but that was all she managed to get out before Susie said, "Just incompetent. If you knew anything, you'd know that the caviar will be fine. Which, obviously, you don't." She shook her head. "I don't know what I'm paying you two for. For all the help you've been, I could have done everything myself."

Bernie felt herself flush. "We're also concerned about the swans melting. I need to know if we should put them back in the freezer or not," she said, forcing herself to continue. This was one person she was never going to work for again, she decided. Ever. Despite what Libby had said, the money just wasn't worth the aggravation. No amount of money was. She wondered how Ralph and Grace did it.

Susie frowned. "Fine. We'll do half the presents now and half later. Now please. Don't interrupt again. Haven't you heard that caterers should be seen and not heard?"

"I'll bear that in mind," Libby said.

Susie waved her arms in the air. "It was a joke! Can't you tell a joke when you hear one?" Then she turned back to the kitties before Libby could answer. "Right, my sweet-ums?"

At which point Allison Hardy rolled her eyes. Libby thought she heard her mutter, "They're not people, you know. They don't deserve to be decked out in ridiculous clothes for your entertainment." But she couldn't be sure, because she and Bernie were in the middle of walking back to the cooler.

"I thought she was in jail," Bernie said, indicating Allison with a shrug of her shoulder, once they'd gotten there. She fought the urge to open the cooler's cover and check on the four swans, because that would only let the warm air in. On the one hand, she wanted the swans to melt out of pure bloody-mindedness, but on the other hand, she didn't want to have to deal with the repercussions.

"She was in for just a couple of months," Libby replied as Boris launched himself at Olga, who in turn side-stepped, leaving Boris to overshoot his mark and land on the ground. He was furiously grooming himself in a fit of embarrassment when Grace picked him up and put him back on the table.

Susie reached for a present and showed it to Boris and Natasha. "Let's open this one first," she suggested. She held it out, and Natasha swatted at the silver wrapping paper. "Clever girl," Susie cooed as she took over the rest of the job. She tore off the remainder of the wrapping paper, which Boris immediately started batting around. "It's from Tiffany," Susie announced. She read the card. "Humbleness is a gift no one wants but everyone needs. Best, Marie."

"A fortune cookie quote," Susie exclaimed. "How sweet." Then she took the top off the box and looked inside. A small silver toothpick sat nestled among layers of pale blue tissue paper. "Oh, Marie," Susie cried as she lifted the toothpick out. "A little knickknack. How . . . unusual. Where did you ever get this? You really"—Susie emphasized the word *really*—"shouldn't have."

Marie smiled frostily. Bernie thought she had all the warmth of an anaconda.

"I wanted you to have something to remember this day," she replied as Natasha climbed into the box and peed in it.

"Bad girl, bad girl," Susie cried. She looked up. "Ralph. Grace. Fetch me some towels immediately."

Bernie looked at her watch again. Five minutes had passed. She was just about to make a snotty comment to Libby when she felt a tap on her shoulder. She jumped and spun around. A teenage boy was standing behind her. He was dressed in jeans, a green T-shirt with a picture of the Brooklyn Bridge on it, a lightweight beige jacket, and sneakers. A baseball cap and sunglasses completed his outfit.

"Sorry I scared you," he said.

Bernie waved her hand in a gesture of dismissal. "No problem. Don't worry about it."

"Is this Boris and Natasha's wedding?" he asked.

Bernie nodded.

The boy's phone buzzed. He ignored it. "Are you Susie Katz?"

Bernie pointed to the table in the tent that everyone was clustered around. "The lady in the gold caftan is. Why?"

"I have a package for her."

"I'll take it," Bernie told him. Then she asked him where it was, because he wasn't holding anything.

The boy gestured down the hill, toward a beat-up Honda Civic that looked as if its next stop was going to be the junkyard. "It's in there. I'll go get it."

He was back a couple of minutes later with it. "Here

you go," he said, holding out a shoe box–sized package wrapped in gold paper with a big blue bow on top of it. Then he drew it back. "Maybe, *I* should give it to Susie Katz," he said, having a sudden change of heart.

"It'll be fine," Bernie assured him. "Honestly." She held out her hands. "Give the package to me."

"Are you sure?" the boy asked.

"Positive," Bernie replied, thinking of Susie's reaction to the last interruption.

"Because I was told to put it in her hands," the boy continued.

"Believe me when I say that you don't want to do that," Bernie told him.

The boy cocked his head.

"I'm doing you a favor here," Bernie added. "She is not in a good mood, and the farther away you stay from her, the happier you're going to be."

The boy shrugged, handed Bernie the package, and left.

Lucky you, Bernie thought as she watched him walk to his car. She checked the time on her phone. One hour and fifty minutes to go before they could get out of there.

Chapter 6

"What's this?" Susie asked, looking at the package in Bernie's hands. She'd spotted the Honda driving away and charged over to see what was going on.

Bernie explained.

"Who's it from?" Susie demanded.

"He left before I could ask. I assume there's a card in the box."

"I'm not paying you to assume things," Susie snapped. "I'm paying you to find out."

Libby deflected. "It's probably from an admirer," she suggested, although she couldn't imagine Susie Katz having one of those.

The idea pleased Susie, and she smiled. "You're right. It probably is," she agreed after a moment had gone by. "Of course it is. My cats have lots of admirers, you know."

"I'm not surprised," Bernie said. A lie. "They're quite pretty." Which was the truth.

"Pretty?" Susie yelped indignantly. "They're more than pretty. They're magnificent."

Magnificent was a word Bernie reserved for things like the Sistine Chapel or Michelangelo's *David*, but she didn't say that. Why make things even worse than they already were? Instead, she apologized for her word choice. "You're right," she said while she repeated in her head, *The customer is always right*.

Susie snorted. "Of course I'm right. That's how I got where I am today." Susie pointed to the eight Russian blues, which kept on jumping off the table as soon as Grace and Ralph put them back on. "You're looking at the new champions of North America. A new lineage is born today," Susie announced triumphantly.

If you say so, Bernie thought. Then she wondered if she'd actually said that out loud, because Susie was glaring at her. Bernie prepared herself for another nasty comment, but Susie didn't say anything.

Instead, she took the package out of Bernie's hands, walked back to the table, and set it down. It was as if someone had pulled a switch. In a matter of seconds, the cats became transfixed. They weren't trying to scatter any more. They were clustered around the package. Their ears were pricked forward; their eyes focused; their tails waving back and forth. They were all on high alert.

Something is in there that the cats really like, Bernie thought. Later, in retrospect, she realized that she should have been a bit more suspicious of the package's contents, but at the time she thought it contained something like catnip or raw tuna or maybe even chicken livers. And in her defense, evidently, Susie thought the same, because she rushed to open it.

"Since everyone seems so excited, we'll open this present first," Susie announced to her guests in the high singsong voice she used when speaking to her cats. Then she turned to Boris. His whiskers were quivering in anticipation. "I wonder what it could be?" she asked him.

Boris let out a noise between a meow and a growl.

"I bet I know," Susie exclaimed. She cocked her head and batted her eyelashes. "I bet it's a catnip plant." She wagged a finger at Boris. "You lucky, lucky boy. I hope you're not going to be too naughty, now. You have to share with your bride and your guests."

At which point, Natasha extended a paw and swatted at the package. Boris hissed at her. "Don't be rude," Susie chided him before turning back to Natasha. "That goes for you, too," Susie told her. "I love surprises, too, don't you?" Susie chirped.

Natasha's tail went faster. Back and forth. Back and forth. Swish. Swish. Swish. It reminded Libby of a windshield wiper on a rainy day.

"Let's see if I'm right," Susie trilled.

As Bernie watched the cats, she had a premonition of disaster. Something wasn't right here. "Don't open it," she blurted out as Susie ripped the paper off the box.

Susie stopped what she was doing, her hands hovering above the box, and glared at Bernie. "Why don't you do what you're supposed to be doing and not concern yourself with things that are none of your business?" she snapped. Then she turned back to the cats, all Little Miss Sunshine again, her anger reminding Bernie of a thunderstorm that came and went on a summer's day.

"I have a bad feeling about the box," Bernie whispered to Libby.

"Don't be silly," Libby whispered back.

Bernie leaned closer to her sister. "I'm not."

"So now you're gifted with ESP."

Bernie put her hands on her hips. "Maybe I am."

"Yeah? In that case, tell me what's going to happen."

"I don't know," Bernie confessed. "But something."

Libby snorted. "You need to get a grip."

"Bet you a dollar I'm right."

"You're on," Libby told her as she watched Susie tear the last of the wrapping paper off the box and toss it on the ground.

The box had had four layers of paper, and half a roll of tape had secured the paper. Libby could understand this if the wrapping paper was tissue paper, but it wasn't. It looked like expensive paper. Which made Libby wonder why the box had needed four layers of wrapping paper to begin with. Maybe Bernie was right, after all. Maybe this wasn't going to be good.

"This is so exciting. Now, what do you think this could be?" Susie asked her guests while Libby ran through the possibilities in her head. No one answered Susie. Instead, Charlene bit her lip, Allison studied one of the tent poles, and Mrs. Van Trumpet and Marie examined their hands. Susie ignored them and concentrated on the cats. "Let's find out, shall we?" she said to Boris.

Boris mewed.

"I'll take that as a yes," Susie sang as she peeled off the tape that was securing the lid to the box and then removed the lid.

And that was when all hell broke loose.

Chapter 7

First, Bernie and Libby saw two rounded ears, two large eyes, and a long, pink nose adorned with whiskers peeping over the edge of the box; then they saw two little paws.

"It's a mouse," Bernie cried.

"Two mice," Libby said as two more rounded ears, two more eyes, and another nose made their appearance.

"It's a mischief of mice," Bernie noted, spotting a third mouse.

The cats didn't say anything. They just stared, too stunned to move. They couldn't believe what they were seeing. But the three mice certainly did. They jumped out of the box, onto the table, and then onto the ground, landing with soft plops.

A fourth mouse jumped down to the ground, followed by a fifth and a sixth. They kept on coming, just like circus clowns packed into a clown car, Libby noted. She wondered how whoever had done this had managed to cram so many mice into the box as Susie screamed and pushed the box away from her. This was a mistake, because it fell onto the ground. Still more mice ran out. By now the cats had gotten over their shock, jumped off the table, and were in hot pursuit, while the guests had started yelling and running this way and that. The word *overreacting* occurred to Bernie as she watched the spectacle unfold. Meanwhile, Susie, looking to get away, bumped against the table with the presents on it, and it and the rest of the presents crashed to the ground.

"My vase," Allison cried. "My vase is broken."

"Oh, do shut up. You probably got it at Target," Charlene told her right before a mouse started running up her leg. Charlene screamed, jumped up and down, grabbed the mouse, threw it onto the ground, and ran outside the tent. Allison ran after her.

By now most of the mice, some of the cats, and two of the humans had vacated the tent by one means or another and were outside on the lawn.

"Do something. Do something," Susie screamed as she watched her cats running this way and that. "Boris, Natasha, come back. You'll get lost."

"Somebody has a sense of humor," Bernie observed from the tent entranceway as she watched Boris tear off his bow tie and Natasha get rid of her little lace veil.

"Somehow, I don't think Susie is going to see it that way, Bernie," Libby replied.

"Neither do I, Libby, neither do I," Bernie said as she watched one of the Russian blues streak past Charlene, in hot pursuit of a mouse, noting that as she did, Charlene made no attempt to intercept the cat, a fact Bernie found interesting. She held out her hand. "I'll take that dollar now," she told her sister.

Libby fished in her pocket, came up with a crumpled one-dollar bill, and slapped it in Bernie's palm.

"Thanks," Bernie said, stuffing it into her pocket. "I

have to say this isn't the most successful event we've ever catered," she noted as she watched the show unfolding.

"An understatement if there ever was one," Libby replied.

"So, no more animal-themed events for us," Bernie said.

"I think you can take that to the bank. Unless maybe someone wants to give a party for their goldfish. We could do that."

"No, we couldn't, Libby."

"Fish aren't animals."

"They're close enough," Bernie was saying when Susie ran up to her. She was panting, and her face was red.

"They're heading to the woods," Susie cried, pointing to Boris and Natasha. The woods abutted a meadow, which in turn flowed into the lawn. "You have to get them before they get lost." Susie shuddered. "A coyote could eat them."

Bernie nodded. "We'll try."

"Don't try. Do it," Susie yelled. Then she was off and running. "Grace, Ralph, where are you?" she screamed as she exited the tent and ran across the lawn.

"Good question," Libby said. She looked around. Susie's niece and nephew were nowhere to be found. Maybe they'd gone back to the house, although Libby couldn't think of why they would have done that. Unless, of course . . .

Bernie turned to Libby. "Do you think one of them did this?"

Libby thought about Bernie's question. She didn't have to think very long. "It wouldn't surprise me. At all," she said after a moment. "From what I can see, their aunt . . ."

"Is quite the bitch," Bernie said, finishing her sister's sentence for her.

"I was going to say an unpleasant human being, but your word works just as well," Libby replied as she and her sister stepped outside.

Susie Katz was standing twenty feet away. The sisters watched as she took a step, stopped, and began swaying from side to side. Then she slowly slid down in a heap. Bernie and Libby rushed over to her.

"Are you all right?" Libby cried when she reached her side, noting with alarm that Susie's face was still red and that she was breathing heavily.

"I'm fine," Susie said, although she obviously wasn't. She started to get up.

"Don't," Bernie said, gently pushing her back. "I'll call nine-one-one."

"I'm okay. Honestly," Susie said, removing Bernie's helping hand. "It was just a bout of dizziness. I'll be okay in a minute."

"I think you need to rest," suggested Bernie. Even though Susie's color looked better, Susie was still breathing heavily. Bernie wondered if she was having a heart attack.

"I can't," Susie cried, her face getting red again. "I need to find my babies before they get lost." Her eyes began to fill with tears. "I just can't think. . . ." She stopped, unable to go on.

Libby and Bernie looked at each other.

"We'll find them," Bernie reassured her. "You go lie down. We'll bring them to you."

Susie reached up and grabbed Bernie's hand. "You promise?"

"Absolutely," Bernie and Libby said together.

Susie smiled. "Thank you. Thank you so much. My babies are all I have. And I'm sorry for the way I acted. I tend to get a little . . . overbearing from time to time."

"I hadn't noticed," Bernie said, disregarding her father's adage about sarcasm being the refuge of the weak-minded.

Susie's lower lip started to quiver. "Who would do this?"

The sisters shook their heads.

"I don't know," Bernie replied, even though what she wanted to say was, "Anyone here."

"Their collars are worth a lot," Susie said, outrage lending strength to her voice. "Sapphires are expensive." And she named the figure. "You don't think this was a robbery, do you?"

Libby shook her head. "No." If it was, it was the strangest one she'd ever seen.

Susie reached up and grabbed Bernie's hand. "I want you to find my babies, and then I want you to find out who did this. Promise that you will," Susie said, squeezing Bernie's hand. "Please. I'm begging you."

"Don't worry," Bernie said as she gently disengaged her hand from Susie's. She couldn't bring herself to say no.

"Everything is going to be fine," Libby reassured Susie. "Go inside and lie down."

Susie nodded and held out her hands. "Now please help me up."

The sisters did. Then they watched as Susie slowly made her way to her house, a large, oddly diminished figure swathed in gold lamé moving slowly and painfully down the hill.

Libby sighed. "I actually feel sorry for her," she said.

"Me too," Bernie replied. "It *really* was a mean thing to do."

"It was, wasn't it?" Libby replied, thinking of the expression on Susie's face and the way her shoulders slumped. "It's not funny."

"Well, it was a little funny," Bernie said.

"Yeah. Okay, it was a lot funny," Libby conceded. "But it was still a mean thing to do. I thought Susie was going to have a heart attack."

"Maybe that was the idea," Bernie said.

"There are easier ways to accomplish that goal," Libby noted as she gazed out at the lawn. By now all the cats were outside chasing the mice. She sighed. "I guess we should collect them."

"The mice?"

"Ha. Ha," Libby said. "Do you think this really is about getting those collars?" she asked her sister.

"No. Do you?"

Libby shook her head as she tried to locate the kitties and the people. It didn't help that they'd all gone off in all directions. Boris seemed to be heading for the woods, while Natasha was scurrying up a birch tree. Ivan was under a bush, while Serge and Vladimir had gotten distracted and were attacking a garden hose. From what Libby could see, everyone still had their collars on.

"Where are the other three Russian blues?" Libby asked. She could see the little white collars Anya, Olga, and Katya had been wearing in the grass, but not the cats who had been wearing them.

"I see Anya over there," Bernie said, pointing to a shadow moving along the side of a large, oblong igneous rock outcropping.

Libby squinted. It took her a moment, but she finally spotted her. Her grayish blue coat blended in with the rock, making her difficult to see.

Bernie pointed again. "And Olga and Katya are over there."

Libby nodded. She could see them now. Olga was sitting on a low-hanging branch of a black locust, while Katya was standing next to the trunk of a Chinese elm. Libby was surprised at how well their coats blended in with their surrounding environment, and if it wasn't for the collars they were wearing, she might not have seen them at all.

The people, on the other hand, were a lot easier to spot.

Charlene was heading toward the far side of the house; Mrs. Van Trumpet was leaning against one of the tent posts, fanning herself with the edge of her hand; Allison was trotting toward her car; and Marie was standing in the middle of the grass, looking for something in her tote.

"No one seems particularly concerned about Susie or the cats," Libby noted.

"No, they certainly don't," Bernie replied. "I guess we should go get the kitties before something else does."

Libby sighed. This was not how she'd planned the day.

Chapter 8

It took Bernie and Libby three hours to capture all eight of the Russian blues. It was a long three hours. By the end of it, the cats were tired and raggedy and ready to go home, and so were Libby and Bernie.

In the first hour and a half, they'd gotten five. As they'd caught each one, they put it in one of the small coaches Ralph and Grace had pushed down the aisles, and fastened the netting so the kitties couldn't get out. Not that they had seemed to want to. In fact, they had seemed happy to be back in captivity. The bits of caviar Libby had fed them didn't hurt, either.

"What?" Libby had said to Bernie when she caught the expression on her sister's face. "I'm not doing anything Susie wouldn't want me to."

"I suppose," Bernie replied. She knew what Libby was saying was true; it was just that she was having trouble feeding the cats something that cost over a thousand dollars an ounce.

"Some help wouldn't hurt, either," Libby observed as she watched Olga start cleaning herself.

Bernie looked up from examining a scratch on her arm

she'd gotten from a pricker bush. "It's amazing how everyone has vanished. Where are they?"

"Not doing this," Libby said as she counted the cats they'd managed to round up so far. *Three more to go,* she thought. She shook her head and frowned. They'd never make it back to A Little Taste of Heaven in time. Thank God they didn't have any other events on their calendar today. She called the shop to tell Amber and Googie that they were going to be late.

"What did they say?" Bernie asked when Libby put her cell back in her pocket.

Libby took a drink from her water bottle. "They can cover for us."

"Excellent," Bernie remarked as she prepared herself to get the cats who were still at large.

It took another hour and a half. They had to climb trees, crawl through the undergrowth, and battle pricker bushes, but they did it. Then they pulled the coaches back to Susie's house and walked through the door, which was unlocked.

"We're here," Libby called as she and Bernie wheeled the cat coaches into the hallway. They undid the netting, and the cats tumbled out and scattered. "Susie." All Libby wanted to do was go home, take a bath, and have a bite to eat, but they had to talk to Susie first and see what she wanted them to do with the rest of the food.

Susie didn't answer.

"Maybe she's taking a nap," Libby suggested.

Bernie shook her head. "Doubtful. Not with her precious babies missing."

"She could be in the bathroom and not have heard us," Libby said.

"Maybe," Bernie conceded as they began walking through Susie's house. The other cats, the ones not invited to the wedding, plus Ivan, Anya, and Serge followed them, winding around their feet and generally being a pain in the butt.

"Susie," Bernie kept calling, but there was no response.

"I hope she didn't have a heart attack and die," Libby said.

"Don't say that," Bernie told her, picturing Susie's red face. "We should have called nine-one-one."

"Yes, we should have," Libby said, picking up her pace.

A few minutes later, the sisters stepped into the study. Boris and Natasha had run on ahead of them and were perched on Susie's desk, while Susie sat in the chair she'd been in when Bernie and Libby had first talked to her.

"There you are," Libby said.

Susie remained silent. Her back was to them.

"Are you feeling better?" Libby asked Susie.

Susie didn't answer. Bernie and Libby exchanged glances. They were getting another bad feeling on a day replete with them. Meanwhile, the cats had jumped onto Susie's lap. The motion caused the chair Susie was sitting in to slowly swing around so that she faced Bernie and Libby.

They gasped.

Bernie put her hand to her mouth. "Oh, my God," she said.

Susie, on the other hand, said nothing at all.

"Well, I guess we know why Susie didn't answer us," Bernie observed after a moment. "After all, it's hard to talk with a letter opener stuck in the middle of your throat."

Libby stepped closer to the desk to get a better look. Susie's eyes seemed to follow her as Boris butted his head against one of her hands and meowed. "Not that anyone would have heard her, anyway, even if she had yelled for help."

"Except for her killer."

"Yes. Except for him. Or her."

Bernie pointed to Susie's face. "Look at her expression and the way she's sitting. I think it's safe to say that she knew whoever did this."

"Not necessarily. Whoever did it could have approached her from behind," Libby objected.

"Maybe," Bernie conceded as one of the Russian blues jumped down from a bookshelf and sauntered out of the room. "But it would be difficult to stab her in the throat from that position."

"Difficult, but not impossible," Libby said.

"True." Bernie clicked her tongue against the roof of her mouth while she thought. "What about the cats?"

"What about them?" Libby asked.

"They would have given her a warning."

"They're not like dogs. They don't bark," Libby countered.

"But they would have moved around," Bernie argued. "Which Susie would have noticed."

Libby started nibbling on one of her cuticles, realized what she was doing, and stopped. "So, what's your point?"

"My point," Bernie repeated, "is that she knew whoever did this, and it's probably someone right here in River City."

Libby wrinkled her nose. "River City?"

"From *The Music Man*," Bernie said impatiently. She'd recently started watching old musicals.

"How could I not know that?" Libby said as she dug around in her pants pocket and came out with a couple of squares of dark Venezuelan chocolate. She handed one to her sister, unwrapped the remaining square, and plopped it into her mouth. No matter what anyone said, chocolate helped her think. "At least," she said, changing the subject, "we have a time line. We know this happened in the past three hours." Then she pointed to the letter opener. "That's Susie's."

Bernie nodded. "It certainly is." She remembered seeing it on her desk. The letter opener had a silver blade and an engraved teak handle that ended with an extremely realistic image of a cat with ruby eyes. "I mean, who uses a letter opener these days? Who has letters to open?"

"Evidently, Susie has." Libby corrected herself. "Had." Libby started to reach into her pocket for another square of chocolate, then remembered she didn't have any more. "Meaning this was probably a crime of opportunity. The person who killed her used what was at hand—so to speak."

"Agreed," Bernie said. "So, we can posit that words were exchanged." She looked around the room. Nothing seemed to be in disarray. "But nothing more."

Libby was about to say, "Unless somebody straightened up after themselves," when she heard a noise behind her. She stiffened and whirled around. So did Bernie. A moment later another cat sauntered out from behind the sofa, jumped up on one of the cushions, and began cleaning its hind leg. Libby and Bernie laughed out of relief. But then they heard another noise coming from behind the sofa.

"Probably another cat," Bernie said.

"Probably," Libby agreed.

But this time the cat didn't come out.

"Here, kitty, kitty," Libby cooed, trying to get the cat out.

Meanwhile, Bernie began looking around for something she could use as a weapon. Just in case it wasn't a cat back there, after all. She spied a paperweight on Susie's desk and picked it up. It wasn't ideal. But it would have to do. She was weighing it in her hand when she heard a muffled sneeze.

"That doesn't sound like a cat sneeze to me," Libby said.

"Meow, meow."

"And that doesn't sound like a cat," Libby said. "Come out and show yourself."

Two more meows followed. They weren't any better than the first two.

"That's pathetic," Libby said to the sofa. "You should be embarrassed. You're not even close."

"Listen," Bernie added. "I've got a gun. If you don't come out now, I'll shoot."

"No you don't," the person behind the sofa said. "You're lying."

"No I'm not," Bernie said.

Libby wrinkled her forehead. "Ralph? Is that you?"

"Yeah," he said, sighing. "Unfortunately." A moment later, there was a rustle behind the sofa and Ralph stood up.

"See? I knew you were lying," he told Bernie when he saw the paperweight. "You know, that's really expensive Baccarat," he informed her. "You should put it down before you drop it."

"Somehow, I don't think Susie is going to care," Bernie told him as she pointed to Ralph's shirt, pants, and leggings. They were no longer just pink and white. Now they were splattered with red. "You want to explain the blood?"

Ralph took a step back. "I know what you're thinking, but I didn't do it," he said. He raised his hand. "I swear I didn't." He pointed to Susie. "I found my aunt like that."

Libby folded her arms over her chest. "Right. And I suppose her blood just jumped onto your clothes?"

Ralph bit his lip. His Adam's apple bobbed up and down. "I was trying to see if she was alive or not. She wasn't," he said, looking down at the floor.

Bernie rolled her eyes. "No kidding."

"Hey, I've never seen a dead body before," Ralph explained. "So forgive me if I wanted to make sure."

"Why didn't you call nine-one-one?" Bernie asked.

"I was going to, but then I heard the front door open, and I heard you guys come in," Ralph explained, looking from Bernie to Libby and back again.

"So," Bernie said, "you decided to hide behind the sofa instead of coming to get us. That makes no sense at all."

"I was scared," Ralph explained.

Bernie pointed to herself and Libby. "Of us? You were scared of us?"

"I thought you might be my aunt's murderer, coming back to look for something, and that if you saw me, you would kill me, too," Ralph stammered out.

Bernie snorted. "Ralph, I'm disappointed by your lack of creativity. At least if you're going to make up a story, make up a good one."

"It's the truth," Ralph exclaimed. He held his hand up again. "I swear."

"And you didn't recognize our voices?" Bernie asked, shaking her head. "We've been calling for Susie for the past five minutes."

"I told you. I thought you might be Susie's killer," Ralph told her, repeating his previous statement. "In fact," he said, rallying, "how do I know you're not?"

"Seriously?" Libby asked. She was beyond incredulous. "And why would you think that? What possible motive would we have?"

Ralph moved his head from side to side. Libby thought he looked even more miserable than usual. "I don't know." He readjusted his glasses and studied the carpet he was standing on. After a minute, he looked back up. "Okay," he confessed. "I guess you could say I panicked."

Libby echoed his words. "You guess, Ralph?"

"Okay, I panicked."

"Because you'd just killed your aunt? That would certainly make me panic," Libby observed in a kindly voice.

"No." Ralph's face flushed. He stamped his foot on the floor, like a child having a tantrum. "I didn't say that."

"Then what did you say?" Bernie asked, a look of concern on her face. She leaned in closer. "Tell me. I really want to know."

Ralph waved his hands in the air. "I am telling you."

Bernie gave him her best "You can trust me" smile. "Tell me again, Ralph, because I'm not getting what you're saying."

"What I'm saying," Ralph said, his voice cracking in frustration, "is that I've never seen a dead person before, let alone one that's been . . ."

"Murdered," Bernie said, finishing Ralph's sentence for him.

Ralph balled and unballed his hands. "I didn't do this," he cried, his tone alternating between fury and helplessness. "You've got to believe me. I'm telling the truth."

Strangely enough, Libby thought he was, although if you had asked her why, she couldn't have told you. "It's not me you're going to have to convince," she told him.

"Or me," Bernie added. "It's the police, and I gotta tell you, it ain't gonna be easy."

Ralph took a step closer to Bernie and Libby. "That's why you have to help me. You have to find out who did this. Otherwise, I'm a boiled duck."

"Cooked goose," Bernie said, absentmindedly correcting him.

Ralph put his hands out. "What are you talking about?"

Bernie explained. "The expression is 'cooked goose.' Otherwise, I'll be a cooked goose."

"I don't care if I'm going to be a roasted squirrel," Ralph cried.

Bernie was about to say she'd eaten squirrel several years ago, and she wouldn't recommend it roasted or otherwise, when she thought she heard something. "Shush," she said.

"Why?" Libby asked.

Bernie held up a finger. "Listen," she said. "Don't you hear it?"

Libby cocked her head. "Hear what?"

"The creak, Libby."

Ralph nodded. "I do. It's the front door opening. My aunt has been after me to oil it for weeks."

Then they heard voices, followed by the thud of the front door closing and the sound of cats meowing.

Chapter 9

Libby, Bernie, and Ralph stood there listening while Boris rubbed up against their legs.

Someone called, "Susie, are you here?"

"It's Allison," Libby whispered as she picked up Boris and rubbed his ears. He began to purr.

Bernie nodded. "I know."

"She's probably in the study," someone else suggested.

"And that's Charlene," Libby mouthed.

"Let's look in the den first," a third person said. "Sometimes Susie likes to stay in there."

"Grace," Ralph noted as Boris's purring grew louder.

"She could be taking a nap," a fourth person suggested.

"That's Marie," Bernie and Libby said together as they heard a couple of meows coming from outside the study and the scribble scrabble of claws on the hardwood floor.

"She never sleeps in the daytime," Grace responded.

Bernie put a finger under her nose to stop herself from sneezing. "Looks like the gang's all here," she observed. "Except for Mrs. Van Trumpet."

"Which is interesting on several different levels," Libby said as Boris turned around and tried to bite her. "Not fast enough," she told him as she put him down on the floor.

He waved his tail from side to side, jumped up on Susie's desk, and began to groom himself.

"Is it interesting that Mrs. Van Trumpet isn't here or that the others are?" Bernie asked her sister.

"Both," Libby replied.

Ralph pointed to the hallway. "Shouldn't we go out there and tell them what's happened?" he asked.

"And call nine-one-one," Libby added.

"I want to see their reactions first," Bernie said.

Ralph chimed in with, "Seems like a good idea to me."

Bernie pointed to a partially hidden alcove on the other side of the hallway. "We can hide in there."

Libby shrugged her shoulders. "Fine." She was too tired to argue. So Bernie, Libby, and Ralph stepped inside and settled down to listen. Charlene was the first to speak.

"Susie," she called out a couple of moments later. "Why isn't she answering?" she demanded when there was no answer. Libby decided her voice had a peevish quality to it.

"Maybe she has her headphones on and she can't hear us," Grace suggested.

"Some wedding this has turned out to be, not that one should dignify that word with this travesty," Allison groused. "Speciesism at its worst. And after forcing us to attend this misbegotten thing, the least she could do is conduct herself like a proper hostess. Just because someone has money doesn't make them less of a bozo."

"She doesn't talk to people. She talks to cats. Or have you forgotten?" Charlene shot back.

"Works for me," Marie said. "The less I have to do with Her Majesty, the better."

"I don't think she means any harm," Grace said.

"What do you mean? She filed an official complaint against me with the CFA, or have you forgotten?" Marie demanded of Grace.

"Yes, but you did it first," Grace replied. "She told me so."

Marie stood up straighter. "I may have brought up a few questions about your aunt's cats' lineage, but I certainly never made an official complaint."

"That's not what she said," Grace told her.

Marie snorted. "Well, she was lying. First, she came to me and asked me to withdraw my Svetlana. She said she was giving me the chance out of the goodness of her heart!" Her voice quivered with outrage. "And then, when I said no, she went to the CFA. At which point I started doing research on Boris and Natasha."

"Even if what you're saying is true—and I'm not saying it's not—I think it's better to try to forgive, don't you?" Grace told her.

Allison snorted. "You always were a mealymouthed hypocrite," she told Grace, "and you always will be."

"That is so unfair," Grace squawked.

"Come talk to me after you've spent two months in jail," Allison said. "Then talk to me about forgiving."

"But you had to know Susie was going to retaliate when you tried to free her cats."

"Yeah, but I didn't know old Judge Munson was in her pocket."

For a moment there was silence, followed by the yowl of a cat, a muttered curse from Marie, and the sound of something breaking.

"Are you all right?" Charlene asked.

"Fine," Marie muttered.

"Susie's not going to like that," noted Grace.

"Ask me if I care," Marie retorted.

Libby was wondering what had broken when the quartet came into view.

"So where have you guys been?" she asked.

"Looking for the cats," Charlene said. "Of course."

"Of course," Bernie echoed. "Together?"

Charlene laughed. "No. Of course not. We just happened to all get the same idea at the same time."

Marie nodded. "I just figured that since I didn't see you guys or Susie, you must have found the cats."

Grace, Charlene, and Allison nodded.

"So, did you?" Grace asked.

"What?" Bernie asked.

"Find the cats," Allison said.

"Yes, we did," Bernie told her. "They're all safe and sound."

Grace clasped her hands together and looked heavenward. "Thank God for that."

The expression "Butter would melt in her mouth" popped into Bernie's head.

As Libby watched the women, she wondered where they'd been. Certainly, none of them looked as if they'd been crawling through the undergrowth or shimmying up trees. What had they been doing for the past three hours? Aside from killing Susie. Libby clicked her tongue against the roof of her mouth as she tried to decide.

"Is Susie in there?" Charlene asked Libby as Charlene headed towards the study door.

"In a manner of speaking," Libby replied, which was more or less true.

Charlene snorted. "Listen, either she is or she isn't. I am not in the mood. It's been a tiring afternoon, and I have a few things, a few very important things, I have to discuss with her."

"Don't we all?" Libby replied, stirring the pot.

"At least all the babies are back," Grace noted. "Thank God for that. I can't imagine what would have happened if you didn't find all the kitties." She wrinkled her brow. "You did find them, didn't you?"

Libby nodded. "My sister just said we did."

Charlene snorted. "Remember, we saw them, Grace."

"I'm just making sure, Charlene," Grace replied as Allison brushed by Libby and went inside the study. Everyone else followed.

Ralph started to say something to her, but Bernie squeezed his arm and shook her head. Ralph swallowed his words and instinctively stepped behind Libby. Bernie glanced down at her watch, wondering how long it would take for the first scream. She figured a couple of minutes. She was wrong. It took less.

Chapter 10

Bernie watched Allison as she walked over to Susie. "Hey," Allison said. Then she took one look at Susie and started to scream. The sound filled the room.

"What's the matter?" Marie asked, running over to Allison. "Oh, my God, Susie's dead," she gasped out when she saw what Allison was looking at.

"Yup," Bernie couldn't resist saying. "She certainly is."

"I don't believe it," Charlene said, while Grace moaned, "Oh no. It can't be."

Libby, on the other hand, didn't say anything. She just stood by the door, folded her arms across her chest, and watched everyone's reactions. Given the situation, everyone appeared to be appropriately shocked, but then again, Libby reflected, what had she expected? The murderer would have had time to prepare him- or herself.

The thing she found the most interesting was that Grace and Charlene had stayed far away from Susie, while Marie and Allison had run over to her. Maybe that meant nothing. Maybe it was as simple as Grace and Charlene were more squeamish. Or maybe it meant that one of them was guilty and didn't want to get near the person they had killed. Or maybe Marie and Allison had run over to make sure they hadn't left any incriminating evidence behind. Libby sighed and uncrossed her arms. Or maybe, and this was probably it, she was just trying to read things into the scene that weren't there.

"Oh, my God," Charlene said after a minute had gone by. Then she repeated herself about not believing it as her eyes darted this way and that. "I really can't."

"Me either," Allison said, and she started to cry, big gut-wrenching sobs that filled the room and, given what she'd just said about Susie, struck Bernie and Libby as genuine as a three-dollar bill.

"Oh, do be quiet," Charlene said to Allison after another minute had gone by. "You're giving me a headache."

"How can you be so heartless?" Allison demanded between sobs.

"Seriously, knock it off," Charlene replied. "You hated her."

"It's true we had our differences, but I didn't hate her."

Charlene snorted and rolled her eyes. "Tell me another one."

"And even if I did, which I didn't," Allison replied, "Susie was a human being. She didn't deserve to die this way. No one does. Have some decency, for heaven's sake."

Charlene rolled her eyes again. "Will you please shut up!"

"There's no need to speak to me like that," Allison shot back. By now she'd stopped crying.

"Sorry," Charlene replied, although judging from the expression on her face, she clearly wasn't.

Allison sniffed bravely, took a tissue out of her bag, and dabbed at her eyes. "There," she said. "Are you happy now?"

"Yes, I am," Charlene told her, taking care to avert her gaze from Susie.

Allison placed her hand over her heart. "Don't you care?" she asked Charlene, all quivery sincerity. "Don't you care at all?"

"Of course I care," Charlene responded. "Which is more than I can say for you."

Allison drew herself up, outrage written across her face. "How can you say something like that?"

"Simple," Charlene told her. "I just did. You called her white trash not more than five minutes ago. Or at least words to that effect."

"But I didn't mean it."

"Then you shouldn't have said it," Charlene said.

"Like you never say anything bad about her," Marie told Charlene.

Allison pointed to Susie's body. "I knew this would happen. I knew it," she said, changing the subject. "I told her that bad blood breeds bad blood. I told her about karma, but she wouldn't listen."

Then Allison turned to Ralph, who'd been standing with his back against the wall, looking as if he'd rather be anyplace but there, and pointed an accusing finger at him.

"He's the one you should be blaming, Charlene," Allison intoned. "My God, look at him. He's covered in Susie's blood."

Ralph began to explain, but Allison cut him off before he said five words.

"Why did you do it?" she demanded, shaking a finger in his direction. "I know your aunt was a hard person to get along with, but still. Murder? You could always have left your job and gotten another one. There's never any need for violence."

Ralph's head snapped up. He took a step toward her. "Don't you try to palm this one off on me," he said, Allison's accusation seemingly energizing him.

"You're covered in her blood," Allison repeated. She shivered. "How do you explain that?"

Ralph gulped. Two red spots appeared on his cheeks. "I was trying to see if my aunt was alive." He pointed to Libby and Bernie. "Ask them."

"That's ridiculous. How could she be alive with a letter opener stuck in her throat?" Marie demanded, joining in with Allison. "Tell me that."

"Don't answer that, Ralph," Grace directed before turning to Marie and Allison. "You leave my brother alone," she told them. "I'm damned if you're going to pin this thing on him."

Allison put her hands on her hips. "So, *what* are you saying?"

Grace leaned forward. "You figure it out."

Allison pointed to herself. "Are you saying, I did it?"

"If the shoe fits and all that," Grace shot back.

"What about the blood on your brother's shirt?" Allison asked, waving a hand in Ralph's direction. "How do you explain that?"

"You heard what he said," Grace responded. "He doesn't have to repeat it. In fact, he doesn't have to tell you anything."

"You probably helped him," Charlene said to Grace, jumping into the fray.

"What an awful thing to say," Grace cried. "I did no such thing."

"It makes sense to me," Marie said. "After all, Susie made your life a living hell, too."

"What about you?" Ralph said, pointing at Marie. Then he gestured at Charlene and Allison. "You all hated her. Don't think we don't know that. She told us. The only reason you're here is that she threatened you. She said, 'Jump,' and you asked, 'How high?'"

"No. That's you, not us," Marie spit out.

"Not true," Grace said.

"Oh yeah?" Marie retorted. "Then why are you two wearing those ridiculous outfits?"

"Ha," Marie said when Grace didn't answer. "You have nothing to say, do you?" she demanded as she waved her hand in the air, as if she were batting at an irritating insect.

Ralph leaned forward. "Then, Miss High-and-Mighty, tell us where you were for the past three hours?" he asked.

"We were looking for the cats," Marie told him.

"I didn't see you," Grace said. She gestured at the three women. "Any of you."

"Maybe that's because you and your brother weren't there," Allison retorted.

"Yeah we were. You didn't look hard enough," Grace told her.

"Yeah. I did," Allison said. "And you guys weren't there. You guys just disappeared."

"Are you calling me a liar?" Grace demanded of Allison.

"Well, she's not calling you the queen of the Nile," Marie snapped.

Which was when, Bernie told her dad later, things went south.

Neither Libby nor Bernie saw the inciting incident—as the police were calling it—because they'd been watching Charlene, who was looking at something on Susie's desk. So they didn't see whether Grace tripped and extended her hands to keep her balance and shoved Allison by accident, which was what Grace said, or whether Grace did it on purpose, which was what Allison said.

But there was no doubt about what happened next. Allison pushed back. Hard. Grace flew backward and slammed into Marie. This caused Marie to fall against a side table. The table overturned, and the vase sitting on it shattered, and some of the shards flew up and hit Marie in the leg.

Marie screamed. "I've been wounded. I'm bleeding," she cried as a line of red dots appeared on her calf. "Call an ambulance." But it couldn't hurt that much, Libby decided, because Marie didn't pause before starting toward Grace. She pointed to her leg. "Look at what you've done."

"No, you look at what you've done," Grace said, indicating her aunt. "You have no shame. None at all."

"That's funny coming from you," Marie retorted as she clenched her fist and drew her right arm back.

Grace put her hands on her hips and jutted her torso forward. "What are you going to do? Punch me?" she challenged.

"Both of you stop it," Bernie cried as she got between the two women, which, Libby later remembered thinking, was a bad idea. "Behave yourselves. You're both acting as if you're five."

They didn't listen. Marie took a swing at Grace, Grace ducked, and Marie caught Bernie with a glancing blow to the jaw instead. Bernie hadn't been expecting that. Caught off balance, she took three steps back and plowed into Ralph. He in turn was propelled backward and collided with Grace with a resounding thud.

This is like dominoes falling, Bernie thought as Grace, caught off guard, took several steps back, her arms windmilling to keep herself upright. Meanwhile, Libby, who had been running over to help her sister, got smacked in the nose by Grace's right arm. Libby gasped and put her hand up to her face. Blood spurted out her nose and started to run down between her fingers.

"Jeez," she said, tipping her head up and feeling around for something to staunch the flow.

Meanwhile, Boris, who had been watching the drama

unfold, decided he had had enough of human foolish-
ness—they were interrupting his sleep—so he jumped
down from the desk and started trotting out the door. Unfortunately, Libby took a step forward at the same time
and tripped over the cat, who yowled indignantly and
scooted out of the room as fast as he could. Libby tried to
right herself, but to no avail. Despite her best efforts, she
fell against the chair Susie was sitting in. The chair tipped
over, and Susie landed on the floor, on her side. The im-
pact had the effect of dislodging the letter opener in Susie's
throat. Then, to make matters worse, Libby fell on top of
her, which provoked a fresh round of bleeding from
Libby's nose.

The room went silent. Everyone stopped doing what they
were doing.

"You were right, Libby," Bernie said as she helped her
up. "We should have called nine-one-one, after all." The
police, she knew, would not be happy.

Which was putting it mildly.

As Libby had feared, Lucy, officially known as Lucas
Broadbent, chief of the Longely police force, was apoplec-
tic. In fact, Libby thought that in all the years she'd known
him, she'd never seen him achieve this level of fury. And
that was saying a lot. His jowls were quivering with rage,
and she honestly thought he was going to have a stroke.
She wanted to tell him to calm down, but under the circumstances, silence seemed like the best alternative.

"Do you know what you just did?" he asked Libby,
pointing at the place on the floor where Susie lay. "Do you
know? Do you know?" he repeated, his voice rising with
each repetition.

She didn't answer, since he'd already asked the same
question at least fifty times.

"I'll tell you what you two did," he screamed. "You compromised the crime scene."

Bernie tried to intervene. "We didn't expect—"

"I don't care what you expected," Lucy yelled, his voice getting even louder, a feat that Bernie didn't think possible. "I don't care what you thought. All I know is that I now have an impossible mess to deal with." He shook a finger in Bernie's and Libby's faces. "I should arrest you two. I should march you off to jail right now."

"On what gr . . . ," began Bernie, but as she watched Lucy literally turning purple—she'd never seen a person do that before—she decided silence would be more prudent.

"Do you know who this lady is?" Lucy screamed. "Do you know what she's worth? Do you know how bad I'm going to look if I can't solve this thing?"

Now it was Libby's turn. "That's why—"

"That's why I'm giving you a week to get me some answers." Lucy stuck his face in Libby's. His breath was most unpleasant. "One week. And if you don't, I'm throwing you and your sister in jail."

"Can he do that?" Libby asked Bernie once Lucy had stalked out of the study.

"Yeah, Libby," Bernie replied. "I'm afraid he can."

Chapter 11

Day one . . .

Six hours had elapsed since the wedding fiasco, and Bernie, Libby, and their father, Sean, were sitting in the living room of their flat, having a snack. Usually, the noises from A Little Taste of Heaven percolated upstairs, but it was quiet now, since the store had closed for the night half an hour ago, and the staff had finally departed.

As Sean listened to his daughters' recitation of their day's events, he sat back in his armchair, stroked Cindy the cat, who was, as per usual, sitting on his lap, fed her bits of salmon and caviar, and watched his neighbor across the street dash into his house with a newspaper over his head in a fruitless effort to keep the rain off him.

"Well," he observed when Bernie stopped to take a breath, "you've certainly had quite the day." Given what he was hearing, he couldn't decide whether to commend his daughters for their actions or remonstrate them for their foolhardiness. Caught in indecision, he stopped petting Cindy, leaned forward, buttered a square of home-made pumpernickel, and carefully laid a piece of smoked salmon on it.

"That's one way of putting it," Libby replied as she bit into a slice of chocolate mousse cake with hazelnut frosting and poured herself another glass of milk. Ordinarily, she would be eating the salmon, too, but she needed the chocolate. For her nerves. Also, at the moment she couldn't deal with anything that reminded her of the afternoon.

"Who would have thought a cat wedding would lead to mayhem?" Sean mused. "I guess it turned into a real cat-fight," he said, chuckling at his own joke.

"Not funny, Dad," Libby said after she'd swallowed.

"I rather thought it was," he replied as he took a bite of the open-faced sandwich he'd just made himself. "This is really quite good," he noted after he'd tasted it.

"It should be, given what the stuff cost," Bernie observed as she poured herself a cup of mocha java from the French press sitting on the coffee table and added a goodly amount of cream and one lump of demerara sugar to it.

Next, she made herself a sandwich like her dad's, sprinkled some capers and a little bit of chopped tomato on top of the salmon, and ate it. She sighed with pleasure. Scotch smoked salmon really was excellent, she decided. And afterward she was going to have the two hazelnut French macaroons that hadn't sold for dessert. This was, she thought, the perfect mid-evening snack. Or late dinner. Because, what with everything that had happened, she and Libby hadn't had time to eat.

Libby and Bernie's dad pointed to the platter sitting on the coffee table. "Is this the salmon you bought for Susie?" he asked.

Bernie nodded and took another bite of her sandwich.

"So what are you doing with the rest of the food from the wedding?" Sean asked before he started asking the more important questions.

Bernie answered. "Salmon croquettes, salmon Floren-
tine, salmon BLT sandwiches. You get the idea."

"And the caviar?" he asked.

"We have just enough left for us. The other two tins
were gone by the time we got back to the tent," Bernie
told him.

"You think one of the guests snatched them?" Sean
asked.

"Well, I don't think it was a strolling chipmunk," Libby
answered after she licked a spot of icing off her fork.

Sean took another bite of his sandwich. "Did you report
the theft?"

Bernie shook her head. Given everything that had happened, the theft of two tins of caviar seemed minor.

"You should have called nine-one-one," Sean said, taking a dab of caviar, putting it on the tip of his finger, and
holding it out for Cindy. Personally, he'd never been a big
fan of the stuff.

"About the caviar?" Bernie asked, knowing full well
that wasn't what her father was referring to, but wanting
to postpone, if only for a minute, the conversation she
knew was about to ensue.

Sean gave his younger daughter his patented look, the
look that had been known to elicit full confessions from
hardened criminals when he was the Longely chief of police. "Really?" he said.

"I know, Dad," Bernie said, capitulating. After all, given
what had happened, there wasn't much she could say to
defend herself. "What we did wasn't too bright."

Sean snorted. "That's one way of putting it."

"I get it, Dad," Bernie told him. "Trust me, I get it."

"So, why didn't you?" he asked.

"Honestly?" Bernie asked.

Sean nodded. "Yes, honestly."

"I don't know," Bernie told him. "I guess it was one of those 'seemed like a good idea at the time' kind of things."

"I bet Lucy didn't think so," Sean observed.

"That's the understatement of the year," Bernie remarked gloomily.

"I'd be pretty pissed, too, if I were him," Sean reflected of his archenemy. "I might even have carted you both off to jail for obstruction of justice and anything else I could think of. You're lucky he didn't."

"I thought he was going to have a heart attack," Libby recalled. "I've never seen anyone turn that color before. Thank God he didn't drop dead."

Sean shook his head. "What a mess," he observed as Cindy got up, circled around, mewed, and sat back down on Sean's lap.

"We know, Dad. We know," Bernie said. "The question is, how can we fix it?"

"How indeed?" Sean replied. Then he stopped speaking, as he had spotted a car parking in front of the store. "Ah," he said. "He's here."

"Who's here?" Libby asked.

"Clyde," Sean replied. "I figured he might be able to shed some light on what's going on over in Lucyville."

Bernie and Libby bounded up and gave their dad a hug.

"No need," said Sean, waving his daughters away, although he couldn't hide the grin on his face.

Clyde was Sean's oldest friend and had remained with the Longely Police after Sean had been forced to retire as chief of police. Everyone listened as the downstairs door opened and closed and Clyde walked up the stairs.

"I'm here," he called as he came through the door, his

face glistening with rain. He pointed to the coffee table. "Is that caviar I see sitting there?"

Libby nodded. "Left over from the wedding."

"And Lucy didn't confiscate it?" Clyde asked.

"Lucy didn't see it," Bernie told him. "The tin was in the cooler out in the tent."

"We weren't going to leave it," Libby said.

"Why would you have?" Clyde rubbed his hands together. "Well, I, for one, am glad you didn't."

"Shall I get you a plate?" Libby asked him.

"And some tea—Russian tea, if you have it—would be nice," he responded.

Bernie got up. "And I'll get you a towel."

"That would be much appreciated," Clyde told her as he settled himself on the sofa. He was a big man, six feet four and 250 pounds, and the sofa springs groaned under his weight. "You and your sister have certainly gotten yourselves into a pickle," Clyde remarked when Bernie came back from the bathroom. She handed him a towel and watched him dry his face and hair with it.

"We certainly did," Bernie agreed, sitting back down.

"Even worse than you usually do," Clyde said as he folded the towel and laid it on the edge of the coffee table. Then he added, "This time Lucy is definitely out for blood," not that Bernie didn't know this already.

"So, Lucy hasn't arrested anyone yet?" Sean asked Clyde.

"Nope."

"Not even Ralph?"

Clyde smiled apologetically. "Not even Ralph. For the moment, Lucy is buying Ralph's story."

Sean frowned. "Lucy have any favorites in the race?"

"If Lucy has any, he isn't sharing them with me," Clyde told his friend.

"That's what I was afraid of," Sean replied as he watched big, fat drops of rain splatter on the windowpanes.

"We're really screwed, aren't we?" Bernie asked Clyde.

"Well, let's just say you have a lot of work ahead of you," Clyde responded, trying to be as diplomatic as possible.

Chapter 12

Five minutes later, Libby came up the stairs, bearing a tray laden with the tea, cups, lemon slices, sugar, and cream. "It's Russian," Libby told Clyde, indicating the teapot with her chin.

"Excellent," Clyde said, rubbing his hands together. Then he took a piece of the pumpernickel and spooned a large amount of caviar onto it with the mother-of-pearl spoon Libby had provided. "Wonderful," he pronounced after the first bite. "It reminds me of the time I worked on a cruise ship as a steward. We used to steal little bites before the plates went out."

"You never told me you worked on a ship," Sean said.

"You never asked," Clyde told him.

"Because I didn't know," Sean retorted.

Clyde took another bite. "It's all about knowing the right questions to ask, isn't it?"

"I suppose it is," Sean said, thinking back to his investigating days. You had to know enough to ask the right questions or else be very, very lucky.

"I guess we have to do some research," Libby said, jumping into the conversation.

"What has Lucy come up with?" Sean asked Clyde. After all, that was why Clyde was here.

"Not much," Clyde answered. He leaned over, poured himself some tea, and added two sugar cubes and a touch of cream before continuing. "He's just done the basics. Record-wise, everyone is clean. More or less. Marie has three unpaid parking tickets, Charlene is behind on her taxes, and so is Allison, who served two months in jail for disrupting a cat show and refusing to leave the premises. Susie brought the charges."

"That's what Allison said," Bernie commented. "When was that?"

"Last year," Clyde told her.

"Because it wasn't in the local paper," Bernie noted.

Sean leaned forward. "And Grace and Ralph?" he asked.

"Nothing," Clyde answered. "They started working for their aunt after she came up here. They both graduated from Tompkins Cortland Community College. Grace has a boyfriend, and Ralph seems to be overspending on his credit cards. But that's about it."

"Nothing else?" Bernie asked.

"Well, Ralph got five parking tickets, and Grace got two," Clyde said. "But they both paid them. Does that count?"

"Not really," Bernie told him.

Libby sighed. *Too bad*, she thought. "Has Lucy looked into Susie Katz?" Libby asked.

"You mean other than the obvious sources?"

Libby nodded.

Clyde shook his head and took a sip of tea. "His Highness is not happy," he said. Then he explained. "If Susie Katz was your average nobody, Lucy wouldn't care. But she's not. She's high profile, and the media is on his back already."

"How did they find out?" Sean asked.

Clyde shrugged. "Don't know, and it doesn't really matter. What matters is that Lucy needs to come up with answers, and he needs to come up with them fast. If he doesn't, he'll need someone to blame, and those someones"—he gestured to Libby and Bernie—"are you two. Unfortunately. This time you really went too far."

"It's not as if Libby meant to trip on Boris and knock Susie off her chair," Bernie objected. "Who knew everyone was going to get into a fight? Things just got out of hand. Really out of hand."

"Evidently. I know you didn't mean for any of this to happen, but that doesn't change the situation." Clyde took another bite of caviar. "This is the real deal," he said appreciatively, changing the subject. "It must have cost a fortune."

"As much as a small country," Libby said. "Well, almost."

Clyde whistled when he heard the price. "So, I guess money can buy happiness, after all."

"If you like caviar," Sean noted. "For myself, I'd rather have KFC."

Clyde snorted. "I always knew you were a boor." Then he added a little chopped egg to the roe and took another bite.

"So, you were saying about Lucy . . . ," Bernie prodded after Clyde had swallowed.

"What I was saying about Lucy is that he's not going to change his mind," Clyde remarked. "He doesn't have a clue—"

"He never has . . . ," Sean said, interrupting.

Clyde glanced at Sean. "Unfortunately, that's neither here nor there." He looked at Bernie and Libby. "You should have called nine-one-one."

"We know, we know," Libby said.

"I already told them that," Sean told Clyde.

"Multiple times," Bernie added. "Not that you and my dad always followed the rules."

"It's true, we didn't," Clyde admitted. "But at least your dad and I knew enough not to contaminate the crime scene beyond redemption."

Bernie opened her mouth and closed it again. She couldn't think of anything she could say on her or her sister's behalf.

Sean finished his sandwich and made himself another one. "Maybe," he said when he was done, "we should skip the blame game and focus on what to do now."

Libby ate the last of her piece of cake and put her fork down on her plate. "Obviously, we have to find out who killed Susie."

"Obviously." Sean fed another caviar pearl to Cindy. "And how do you propose to do that?"

Bernie and Libby looked at each other. They didn't have a clue.

"It'll be fine," Libby said.

Sean gave her the look.

"Okay. So, we do have a small problem," Libby admitted.

Sean raised an eyebrow. "Small?"

"All right. It's not so small," Libby allowed. "We can't account for anyone's whereabouts."

Clyde leaned forward. "How so?" he asked.

Libby replied. "Once the mice were let out of the box, the cats and people scattered. We were so intent on catching the cats, we weren't paying attention to where everyone was," she explained. She picked up her fork and started playing with it. "I didn't really see anyone around me."

"That goes for me, as well," Bernie added.

"And you guys"—Clyde pointed at Libby and Bernie—"captured all the cats?"

The sisters nodded.

"Didn't you think it was a little odd at the time that everyone apparently vanished?" Clyde asked.

"It occurred to me," Bernie admitted. "But then, the whole day was odd."

"And, frankly, we were too involved with what we were doing to give it much thought," Libby added.

"So, you have no idea where anyone was?" Clyde asked. "Am I correct in that assumption?"

"Yes," Libby and Bernie said together.

"But I do remember thinking that everyone showing up at the house at the same time was strange," Bernie said. "An unlikely coincidence."

"Meaning that you think that everyone had a hand in what happened?" Sean asked.

"I don't know," Bernie said. "It was just an observation."

"Not true," Libby said to her sister. "Everyone showed up except for Mrs. Van Trumpet."

Bernie nodded. "Libby's right."

"So, what happened to Van Trumpet?" Clyde asked.

"As far as I know, she left," Bernie said. "The last I saw her, she was leaning against a tent pole. I assume she just got in her car and drove off. She didn't strike me as someone who did chaos very well."

"You should talk to her," Clyde suggested. "Make sure. She could have doubled back and gone into the house."

Libby agreed. "Especially since the door wasn't locked."

"I don't think she liked Susie very much," Bernie reflected.

"No big surprise," Libby said. "I don't think anyone did."

"Except Susie's cats. Susie's cats liked her just fine," Bernie said.

"What makes you say that Mrs. Van Trumpet didn't like Susie?" Libby and Bernie's dad asked.

Bernie shrugged her shoulders. "Nothing, really. Just the way she acted around her."

"Do you think she disliked her enough to kill her, Bernie?" Sean inquired.

Libby answered instead. "I don't think so. As far as I know, Susie hired her for the wedding. I don't think they knew each other before."

"You should find out," Clyde said. "And sooner would be better than later."

"I'd say," Bernie replied as she watched Cindy jump off her father's lap and go over and start drinking out of her bowl of water. When she was done, she leaped on top of the sofa and settled herself near Bernie. Bernie nodded in her direction. "Too bad she can't talk to Boris and Natasha and tell us what happened."

Libby laughed at the idea. "I wish."

"How about the mice?" Clyde asked, sitting back and stretching his legs out.

"What about them?" Libby asked.

"Well, you told Lucy you had no idea who the delivery boy was."

"We don't," Libby said.

"Can you at least describe his vehicle?"

Bernie answered. "It was an old, rusted-out green Civic."

Libby contradicted her. "It was gray."

"No, Libby. It was definitely green, sage green. Which has gray undertones."

"There were no undertones. The car was gray—"

"This is not helpful," Clyde said, interrupting the sisters.

Libby and Bernie stopped.

"I don't suppose you got the license plate number of the vehicle?" Clyde asked.

"No," Bernie answered. "We were too busy."

"Do either of you think you could identify the driver if you saw him again?" Clyde asked.

"He was cute," Bernie said.

"Great," Clyde said. "Wonderful. I'll put that out as an APB."

"Sorry," Bernie said, hunching her shoulders up.

"Is there anything you can tell me?" Clyde asked, begged really. "Anything at all?"

"Nope," Libby replied. She'd been trying, without success, to picture the driver ever since the police had arrived on the scene. There had been nothing notable about him. He was just a big blur. "Maybe the mice were a practical joke," Libby said, which was what she'd first thought when she'd seen them. "Maybe they didn't have anything to do with Susie's murder."

"Do you really believe that?" Sean asked.

"Well, it's possible," Libby said, defending herself from the disbelief in her father's voice.

"Anything is possible," Sean shot back. "But is it likely?"

"It might be," Libby said. "Think about it. There's no way the person who sent them could have predicted what was going to happen. For all that person knew, the cats could have killed all the mice immediately or the mice could have been captured, and the wedding would have continued as planned."

"Libby's right," Bernie said. She got up from the sofa and started pacing back and forth. "I think whoever killed Susie took advantage of the situation. It's a big leap to go from disrupting the wedding to killing Susie."

"Unless the mice were sent as a distraction, allowing the murderer to slip into the house," Sean said.

"The time frame is wrong," Bernie said.

"Not if the murderer was someone other than the people you saw there."

Clyde shook his head. "Now you're making things more complicated than they already are, Sean. Let's just stick to the people who we know were present."

"Possibly," Sean said, unwilling to let go of the idea he was hatching.

Libby interrupted them. "This thing, that is, the murder, could have started out as a joke and gotten out of hand. Let's suppose our unsub sent the mice to Susie as a practical joke and then saw Susie collapse. He or she got concerned and went to speak with her because she or he felt guilty and wanted to see if Susie was all right. And then let's suppose that this person found Susie sitting at her desk and, for whatever reason, told Susie what she or he had done.

"So, Susie flips out and says whatever she says. Maybe she threatens the person, or maybe Susie says something unforgivable. In any case, our murderer flips out, picks up Susie's letter opener, and stabs her with it. Then our murderer runs out the front door—leaving it unlocked—and goes . . . somewhere."

Bernie stopped pacing. "At which point, Ralph comes in and finds his aunt."

"Exactly," Libby said.

"That would work," Sean admitted.

"It seems the most likely scenario," Bernie commented as she sat back down on the sofa.

"It's plausible," Sean reluctantly agreed.

"I think it's more than plausible," Bernie argued. She went on. "After all, if the murder had been premeditated, whoever did it would have brought their own weapon to the wedding. But they didn't. They used the letter opener on Susie's desk instead. To me, that suggests a lack of intent."

"I'm not arguing with you," Sean told Bernie. Then he smiled at his daughters as Clyde topped off his tea. He had no doubt that they would get to the bottom of this. It was just the time frame that worried him.

"Let's recap, shall we?" Clyde said as he added another cube of sugar to his cup. "If I am correct, we have no idea where anyone was at the time of our victim's death, we have no clear motive for her death, and we don't have any forensic evidence. Does that about sum it up?"

Bernie and Libby both nodded.

Clyde continued. "The only thing we do have is the time frame, plus the strong possibility that this crime was not premeditated and that it was committed by someone who was present at the time." Clyde looked from Bernie to Libby and back again. "Am I correct again?"

"You are," Libby said.

"So," Clyde went on, "given what we know, do you have an idea of how you and Bernie are going to proceed?"

Bernie smiled. She'd been thinking about it. "We do."

"Would you care to enlighten us?" Sean asked when his younger daughter didn't say anything else, although he had a pretty good idea what her answer was going to be.

"Certainly," Bernie replied. "Libby and I are going to get a drink."

"At RJ's?" Sean asked.

"Is there anyplace else?" Bernie replied.

The answer to that was no.

Chapter 13

There was nothing special about RJ's. It didn't have fancy drinks, offer obscure microbrews, great food, or an amazing decor. But people came. They came to have a quick beer and a burger at lunch, or to relax and have a beer on their way home from work, or to play a round of darts or shoot a game of pool, or just to hang out with their friends. They came because they felt comfortable there, and they came when they needed to find something out.

RJ's was Longely's gossip central, which was the reason Bernie and Libby were going there now. Of course, the fact that Bernie's boyfriend, Brandon, was a bartender on the evening shift also helped, since bartenders, like hairdressers, were people who knew everything worth knowing about everyone.

By the time Bernie pulled into RJ's parking lot, the rain had tapered off to a drizzle. The droplets reflected off the pavements, surrounded the street lamps with a soft glow, and added an aura to the blinking neon beer signs in RJ's window, signs that had been there for as long as Bernie remembered.

"Not a busy night in Bean Town," Bernie commented

about the quarter-filled lot as she parked Mathilda off to the left, away from a large water-filled pothole. Then she turned Mathilda off, pocketed the keys, and hurried inside, with Libby following close behind her.

As Libby shut the door, Bernie smiled as she smelled RJ's familiar mixture of hops, hamburgers, and floor wax. Looking around, she estimated there were thirty people in all. Not a lot. She saw six guys in the back, shooting pool, a man and a woman playing darts, and another couple hunkered down in a booth, having an earnest discussion, while the rest of RJ's customers were sitting either at the bar or at the tall tables near the far wall.

Tonight, unusually, she didn't know anyone here except Brandon, who was drawing a Guinness for a customer, and Marvin, Libby's boyfriend, who had his head down and was looking at his cell phone as he sat alone at the bar. Normally, she knew half a dozen people from their shop— at least.

"I thought you said Marvin couldn't come," Bernie remarked to Libby as Brandon nodded to Bernie and she nodded back.

Libby corrected her sister. "No. I said he wasn't sure." She studied Marvin for a minute. *He's getting bald*, she thought affectionately as she noticed the thinning patch of hair in the middle of his head. He also looked tired. Libby decided she wasn't the only one who had had a rough day as she headed toward him. By the time she and Bernie reached him, their shoes crunching over the peanut shells scattered over the floor, Brandon had come over and was putting a couple of Irish whiskeys down in front of Libby and Bernie and a pint of Guinness in front of Marvin.

"I figure you're going to need these, considering the day you guys had," Brandon said.

"I see good news travels fast," Bernie replied as she grabbed a handful of sweet potato chips out of the bowl in front of her and started eating. She wasn't hungry, but she wanted—no, she needed—something in her mouth, something that crunched.

"Always," Brandon said as he took the towel he had slung over his shoulder and mopped up a small spot of water he'd somehow managed to overlook on the bar. "Especially here. We don't need social media. We have the Longely big mouth network." Then he spotted a customer waving to him from the other end of the bar and raised his hand to show he'd seen him. "Be back as soon as I can," Brandon told Bernie as he headed toward the guy.

Bernie watched him go, a big, burly, red-headed guy with a bad haircut, wearing an old, worn flannel shirt and baggy jeans, and was amazed again by the fact that she'd fallen in love with him. He was rough around the edges, not her type at all, but then her last forays into romance hadn't worked out so well, so maybe he was her type, after all. In any event, she wasn't here for that right now—although she was always happy to see Brandon. No. She was there to find out what, if anything, Brandon knew about the players in their afternoon drama, Brandon being the gossip king of gossip central.

Bernie was still thinking about Brandon when Marvin slid the bowl of salted peanuts sitting in front of him over to Libby. "Here," he said to her. "Have one."

"Don't mind if I do," Libby said, smiling at him. "Thanks for coming out."

He nodded. "You have but to call, my lady."

Libby grinned. Marvin always made her do that. If you had told her three years ago she'd be going out with a guy who was a funeral director, she would have told you you were crazy, but it only went to prove you just never knew.

Look at Bernie and Brandon, she thought. Who could have predicted that? And although she hated to admit it, she and Marvin were alike in certain ways. They were both a little chubby, a little schleppy, a little on the clumsy side. Maybe she felt so comfortable with him because she could relax and be herself instead of Miss Perfect.

"Is it true?" Marvin asked, interrupting Libby's thoughts.

"Is what true?" Libby inquired.

"That Lucy's going to arrest you?"

Libby took a sip of her whiskey. "Only if we don't figure out who killed Susie Katz, aka Susie Abrams, by next week."

"Not a problem," Marvin said.

Libby made a pock-pock sound with her mouth. "Hopefully."

"Definitely," Marvin told her. "Does he mean it, do you think?"

"Oh, he means it, all right," Bernie told him. "Of that I have no doubt. He'd be more than happy to toss us to the lions. It would definitely make his day."

"Lucy really hates your dad, doesn't he?" Marvin said.

"He does, indeed." Bernie ate another chip. "So, moving along, what's happening to Susie Katz?"

"I take it you mean her corporal entity?" Marvin asked.

"Considering you don't have the scoop about what happens on the other side, yes," Bernie replied.

"She's at the medical examiner's now. They're doing an autopsy."

"I figured," Bernie said. "Not that there's any doubt about how she died." She paused for a moment as she pictured Susie Katz with the letter opener jammed in her throat. "Are you getting her body when they're done?"

"As a matter of fact, we are." Marvin took a sip of his Guinness and wiped a bit of foam off his upper lip.

"When?" Libby asked.

"When the tox screens come back."

"They're doing tox screens?" Bernie asked. "Why?"

Marvin shrugged. "Protocol, I assume."

Libby took another sip of her Jameson. She could feel the crick in her neck start to uncrick. "And then what?"

"And then the usual," Marvin said. "We bury her."

"In Longely?" For some reason, Bernie had expected Susie Katz to be buried in New York City.

"Yup. Right here," Marvin said. "Right in our little old town."

"Who's claiming the body?" Libby asked.

Marvin took another sip of his beer. "The niece and the nephew."

Bernie raised both eyebrows.

"Why are you surprised?" Marvin asked.

"Grace and Ralph seem awfully young."

"I don't think she has any other family," Marvin replied. "Or if she does, they haven't come forth and contacted us."

"Maybe they will," Libby said.

"They could, not that it will make any difference. We have a notarized letter from Ms. Katz authorizing her niece and nephew to take care of the burial arrangements," Marvin explained. "Of course," he added, "I suppose the letter could always be challenged in court if anyone wanted to. Anything can be."

"Interesting." Bernie took a gulp of her Jameson and sighed in pleasure as the liquor warmed her insides. "So, what kind of service do Ralph and Grace want?" She was curious given what she'd seen of their relationships.

Marvin took a handful of peanuts out of the bowl in front of Libby and began to shell them, dropping the shells onto the floor and popping the peanuts into his mouth. "They don't want one," he answered when he was done.

This time it was Libby's turn to raise both eyebrows.

"They want a burial and that's it," Marvin clarified. "No service, no obit, no nothing. In fact, they chose the next to cheapest casket available," he added.

"At least it wasn't *the* cheapest," Libby said.

Marvin frowned. "It comes pretty darn close, I can tell you that. Her niece and nephew probably would have her cremated and would shove the ashes in the back of a closet somewhere and be done with it if their aunt hadn't specified that she was to be buried."

Bernie made a face. "That's kinda sad."

"There's no kinda about it," Marvin retorted as he ate another peanut and took another sip of beer. "I guess they didn't like her very much."

"You could say that, but then, not many people did," Libby replied. "Except for her cats. Her cats loved her."

"I'm surprised she didn't insist they attend the funeral," Bernie said, thinking about the wedding.

Marvin shuddered. "I can't even imagine."

"I can," Libby said, picturing this afternoon's events.

"At least she didn't want them killed and buried with her like the pharaohs did," Bernie said. "You know, so they could accompany her into the afterlife."

"People don't do that kind of thing now," Libby pointed out as she shifted her weight on the bar stool.

Bernie tossed her head impatiently. "I was kidding, Libby."

Marvin corrected her. "Sometimes people do," he said. "Not that we would ever honor a request like that," he hastily added in response to the aghast expression on Libby's face.

"Susie would have a fit if she were here," Libby mused

as she thought about the cat wedding and all the glitz and attention to detail that it had entailed. "I mean, Susie was nothing if not flamboyant," she observed after she'd finished off the rest of her Jameson. "This is just zeroing her out."

"That's probably the point of the exercise," Bernie said. "The niece and the nephew are finally getting their revenge."

"I wonder if there's going to be a fight over the body," Libby said, contemplating whether someone would step forward and try and wrestle control of Susie's burial away from Ralph and Grace. She was thinking of a recent court case involving a famous DJ that had been plastered all over the news.

"More to the point, I wonder if there's going to be a fight over her estate." Bernie ran her forefinger around the edge of her glass and raised her voice so she could be heard over the shouts of the guys playing pool. "Because it's certainly worth fighting about."

"We don't know that," Libby objected. Then she posed the opposite point of view. "Susie could be in debt."

"Possibly, but not probably," Bernie replied. "Look what she spent on the wedding."

"Sometimes the people who spend the most have the least," Libby countered.

"True," Bernie concurred. She sighed. Running A Little Taste of Heaven had taught her that, if nothing else.

Marvin took another sip of his beer and said that he'd be surprised if there wasn't a fight over the estate. "In my experience," he continued, "tenth and eleventh cousins from Outer Mongolia come crawling out of the woodwork when you have an estate worth five thousand dollars, let alone an estate like this. You wait and see." He paused. "The lawyers are going to have a field day with this one. There won't be anything left by the time they're done."

Bernie reached for another handful of chips. "So, Marvin, do you know who does get the bulk of her money?"

Brandon answered the question instead of Marvin. "That's easy," he said.

Bernie jumped, her hand almost knocking over her shot glass. She looked up. Brandon was standing in front of her. "How come I never hear you coming?" she complained.

Brandon did a karate chop. "Because I'm stealthy like a ninja."

"Yeah, a two-hundred-and-fifty-pound ninja," Bernie cracked.

Brandon drew himself up. "Please. A two-hundred-and-twenty-five-pound ninja." Then he turned, grabbed the bottle of Jameson, and poured another shot for Bernie and topped off Libby's glass.

"Okay, big guy, so who does get the money?" Marvin asked. He was fairly certain that Susie's nephew and niece were getting something—after all, why else would they be tasked with Susie's burial?—but they weren't getting everything. Otherwise, they'd have been more generous. In his humble opinion.

Instead of answering, Brandon nodded at Marvin's nearly empty glass. Marvin shook his head and covered it with his hand. He had a strict one-beer limit, especially when it came to Guinness. There was a reason the advertisements for it used to call a pint of the stuff a sandwich in a bottle.

Brandon nodded, returned the bottle of Jameson to the shelf, turned back around, and answered Marvin's question. "From what I hear, the bulk of Susie's estate is going to a variety of organizations having to do with cats."

"Why am I not surprised?" Bernie said.

"I've also heard that she was buying up a lot of real estate," Brandon added, "so there's less in the estate than one would imagine. A lot less."

"Was she buying it down in New York?" Libby asked.

"One would think so," Brandon replied. "But no. She was buying stuff up around here."

Bernie sat up a little straighter. "I wonder why."

"Not a clue," Brandon told her. "Maybe a big company is coming in. Although," he reflected, "I haven't heard anything like that, and I would have."

Bernie frowned. "Neither have I." That fact probably didn't have anything to do with Susie's death, but at this point any information was welcome. "Interesting. Was she buying commercial or private?"

"Both," Brandon said. "At least that's what Evan Molina told me."

"He made us an offer on our building a couple of years ago," Libby reflected.

"It probably wouldn't hurt to go talk to him," Bernie allowed.

Brandon pointed to a man walking out of the bar. "It also wouldn't hurt to talk to him."

Bernie raised an eyebrow. "Andy Dupont?"

"Why should we?" Libby asked.

"Why do you think?" Brandon asked back.

"If I knew, I wouldn't be asking," Libby responded.

Brandon grabbed a bottle of water from under the counter, opened it, and took a sip before replying. "I hear Susie's nephew owes him big-time."

"From whom did you hear this?" Bernie asked.

"Leonard French was saying something to that guy Caster, the one that's a TV sports announcer. But that's all I heard, because they stopped talking when I put their beers down." Brandon beckoned Bernie closer. "But I can find out the rest if you want. For a price. Of course." And he twisted the ends of an imaginary mustache and leered.

Bernie giggled. "Are you suggesting what I think you are?"

But before Brandon could answer, Libby cut into the conversation. "Why do you think it's true?" she asked.

"Why would they lie?" Brandon countered. "Besides, I've seen Ralph and Andy in here together a fair bit."

"Maybe Andy was selling Ralph a car," Libby said, hypothesizing.

Brandon put the cap back on the bottle of water before replying. "Naw. I don't think so."

Libby waited for Brandon to explain. Fifteen minutes later, when he was done taking care of customers, he did.

Chapter 14

Brandon took another sip of water, checked the bar to make sure no one needed anything, and began where he'd left off. "So, as I was saying, over the past year or so Ralph starts coming in here once or twice a week, always looking for Andy, and when he finds him, the two of them go outside, in front of the tanning salon, which means they aren't discussing cars."

"Why not?" Libby asked, confused by the logical jump Brandon had just made.

"Seriously?" Brandon said.

Marvin intervened. "I don't get it, either."

Brandon shook his head. "I get why you don't get it, Marvin, but Libby's supposed to have the pulse of Longely."

"Only Longely's culinary pulse," Libby shot back. She nodded at her sister. "I bet Bernie doesn't know, either."

"Of course, I know," Bernie said.

"How do you know and I don't?" Libby demanded.

"You'd know, too, if you got out more," Bernie told her. Then she explained before Libby could say something about someone needing to mind the store. "Tommy," Bernie said, referring to RJ's owner, "told Andy that he didn't mind him meeting people in the bar, but he couldn't do business here. That way, the cops can't bust RJ's for gambling."

Libby turned to Brandon. "That's it?" she asked. "Because what you're saying seems pretty flimsy to me. Maybe Andy deals. Maybe Andy is Ralph's supplier."

"Andy doesn't do drugs," Brandon said.

"How do you know?" Libby asked.

"Because I do." Brandon put his water bottle down to punctuate his sentence. "Drugs would attract Lucy's attention, but he's willing to give gambling a pass. Even if Ralph was doing drugs, he was getting them from a different seller, but even if you're correct and he was getting them from Andy, the result would be the same."

"Which is?" Libby asked.

"That he owes Andy money," Brandon answered. "And before you get started," he went on, "a couple of weeks ago, I saw the two of them over at Andy's dad's car lot, and Andy did not look happy. He looked really pissed, and Ralph looked . . ." Brandon paused for a moment to find the right word. "Ralph looked scared. Put everything together and it seems as if what I heard was right. Ralph is into Andy for some big bucks."

"If that's true, it would certainly make me anxious," Libby observed.

"Especially since rumor hath it that Andy Dupont has ties to the mob," Bernie said, not that you'd ever think that by looking at him. With his horn-rimmed glasses, Brooks Brothers shirts and suits, he looked like a Wall Street banker from the fifties.

"What do you think?" Libby asked.

Bernie snorted. "I think Andy spread those rumors himself. He's Longely born and raised. Where would he get those ties?"

"How about from Leon Caputti, the guy that lives up

on Willow Hill? I heard he served five to ten for loan-sharking. Maybe Andy is tied up with him," Libby suggested.

"Or maybe Andy's off on his own," Bernie countered. "Dad says that Caputti always has been careful about keeping things out of his backyard—metaphorically speaking."

Libby frowned. "So, you're saying that Andy had that kid kneecapped last year all on his own?"

"That's exactly what I'm saying," Bernie said.

"What kid?" Marvin asked.

"Angie. The one who sold us our espresso machines," Libby replied. "Googie told me he owed some serious money to Andy. And then there was the deli over on Grant that went up in flames. Googie said that Ron Tyson owed Andy big-time, too."

"But you know what?" Marvin said.

"What?" Libby asked.

"It doesn't matter whether Andy Dupont is or isn't mobbed up." Marvin jabbed a finger in the air for emphasis. "What matters is if Ralph thinks he is."

"You may have a point there," Libby said after a moment's consideration. "If Ralph owes Andy money and he doesn't know that Andy is having him on . . . if he is . . ." She stopped and spread her hands out. "Well, then, Andy having mob ties becomes the real deal, even if it isn't."

Marvin drained his glass. "Which would give Ralph a motive for killing his aunt. You know, hastening his inheritance along."

"If he inherits," Libby said.

"He inherits something," Marvin replied.

"The question is, how much?" Bernie said. "Is it enough?"

Marvin ate another peanut. "I don't think it matters." Libby gave him a skeptical look, and he explained. "If you owe someone ten thousand dollars and you're getting only eight, you'll still go after the eight, figuring you'll get the other two somewhere else."

"Or," Bernie said, another thought having occurred to her, "maybe Ralph was stealing from Susie, and she found out and was going to have him arrested."

"Lots of possibilities." Libby finished off the last bit of her Jameson. "But getting back to the original topic, who did Susie's will?"

"That would be Bison," Marvin said.

Bernie sighed. "Of all the lawyers in all the offices in Longely, he has to be the one. . . ." Bernie's voice trailed off as she gave up trying to imitate a line from *Casablanca*.

"He's definitely not a big fan of yours," Brandon noted.

"No kidding," Bernie replied. Bison didn't like Bernie and Libby and their "shenanigans," as he put it, and had made no secret of his feelings over the years, telling them that to their faces on several occasions. They had about as much chance of finding out something from him as they had of tunneling into Fort Knox. "Actually, I'm surprised Susie Katz used him," Bernie went on. "I would have thought she'd have used some big-shot estate lawyer down in New York City instead of a local nobody."

"It doesn't matter," Libby said. "Whoever she picked wouldn't talk to us, anyway." She flicked a peanut shell onto the floor. "But maybe Andy will."

Bernie made a rude noise. "Why should he?" she asked, and then she answered her own question. "He won't. There's no reason why he should."

"He might if there's something in it for him," Brandon suggested.

"Like what?" Libby asked.

"Like money," Brandon said.

"Fear would work better," Marvin noted.

"Yes, it would," Libby agreed. "But not for us." They weren't exactly imposing figures.

"How much do you think it would take to make it worth his while?" Bernie asked Brandon.

Brandon made sure no one needed him before he answered. "At least a couple of thou."

"Ha. Ha," Bernie said. "Seriously."

"I am being serious," Brandon said, although he had no idea if what he was saying was true or not.

"A couple of thou?" Libby squawked. "What happened to a twenty?" she cried.

Brandon laughed. "Economy of scale. The price of everything is going up these days. Food, rent, information."

"Ridiculous," Libby huffed.

"He's joking, Libby," Bernie said to her sister.

"Mostly," Brandon replied.

"I think I'll ask him," Bernie said, sliding off her seat. "See what he says."

"Be my guest," Libby told her.

But Andy wasn't in the parking lot. He'd already left. As Bernie went back in the bar and sat down she realized that was fine with her. On her way to speak to Andy, the day had caught up with her, and she needed to go home and go to bed.

"We'll talk to him tomorrow," Bernie told Libby as she finished the last of her drink. "After all, it's not as if we don't know where he lives, so to speak."

Chapter 15

Day two . . .

The Dupont car lot was situated on the outskirts of Longely. Jammed with rust-spotted vehicles that no amount of detailing work could turn into things of beauty, it was always getting code violations. It was a shady operation that specialized in cheap used cars and usurious financing, the kind of place that preyed on the poor and the uninformed.

When Bernie and Libby walked into the trailer that Andy's father, Big Al, called an office, Andy was sitting with his chair tipped back, his feet up on the desk, and his cell phone glued to his ear. As Bernie looked around, she saw that nothing had changed since she'd bought her first car there fifteen years ago, a car she'd saved up her pennies to buy, a car that had burst into flames two months later—not that she held a grudge or anything.

The same three calendars featuring girls with big boobies in skimpy swimsuits were still tacked up on white walls that had only gotten dirtier with time. The venetian blinds on the windows were still sagging. The two desks on either side of the room were still piled high with papers, old coffee cups, and car magazines.

"Nice to see you've improved the place," Bernie said as Libby closed the door behind them.

"One minute," Andy mouthed to Bernie, holding up his hand before turning back to his phone. "Listen," he said to the person he'd been speaking to, "gotta go. I'll call you back in a few." Then he put his feet on the floor, sat up, straightened his shirt collar, and smiled his salesman's smile.

"Come to get rid of that piece of junk you call a van?" he asked. "I have to say, it's about time. I can make you a pretty good deal on a couple of 2016s. They're in mint condition. Absolutely perfect. Less than ten thousand miles. Owned—"

"By a little old lady from Pasadena who drove it only on Saturday," Bernie said, interrupting Andy's spiel.

Andy's smile grew a little less bright. "I was going to say, 'Driven by a guy who ran a food delivery service for a month before he gave it up.'"

"Why did he do that?" Libby asked, not that she would believe what Andy was going to say. She just wanted to hear the story he was going to spin.

"He found out he didn't like driving," Andy answered. He got up. "Let me show you the vehicle. Maybe we can even give you a little something on a trade-in."

"We're not here for that," Bernie said.

Andy stopped. He looked confused. "Then what are you here for?"

"To talk about Ralph."

Andy squinched his eyes together. His smile had vanished to wherever his smiles went. "Who's Ralph?"

"Ralph Abrams," Bernie replied.

Andy mimed trying to remember. "Did I sell him a car?"

Libby shook her head.

Andy looked apologetic. "I'm sorry, but I don't know who you mean."

"Really?" Bernie told him.

"Yes, really," Andy said. He glanced at his watch. "Listen, if you're not interested in buying anything, I have work I have to get back to."

Bernie leaned on the edge of the desk. "Let me refresh your memory. Ralph is a tall, skinny redhead. He lives, or did live, with his aunt on the old Connor estate. He and his sister take care of her cats."

"Oh." Andy snapped his fingers. "That Ralph, the one that lives with the lady who just got herself killed. I saw it on the evening news."

"That's him, all right," Libby replied.

Andy shook his head. "Terrible, terrible thing. Such a shame. Poor guy. But I don't know him."

"We hear differently," Bernie said.

Andy frowned and pushed his glasses back up the bridge of his nose with his forefinger. "Then you hear wrong."

"I don't think so," Libby said. "Ralph owes you money."

Andy contrived to look puzzled. "Does he owe you money, too? Is that why you're here?"

"Yeah," Bernie said. "He owes us for the cinnamon rolls he ordered and didn't pick up. The interest compounds daily."

Andy snickered. "Must be tough collecting five dollars."

"The stakes are a little lower than when people owe you money," Bernie conceded.

"That's true," Andy said. "We can always repossess their car. I don't think you'd want to repossess the cinnamon rolls. It would be an . . . unpleasant process."

"We understand your processes can be pretty unpleasant, too," Libby said.

"Sometimes the collection agencies do overstep their bounds," Andy allowed.

"My sister's talking about the methods you use in your other enterprise," Bernie explained.

Andy snorted. "That ridiculous story again."

"Not from what we heard," Libby said.

Andy contrived to look bored.

"So, you're not denying it?" Bernie asked when he didn't reply as she absentmindedly began glancing through the papers on the desk. They seemed to be mostly receipts for auto supplies.

"Do you mind?" Andy said.

"Is there something here you don't want me to see?" Bernie asked.

Instead of answering, Andy sighed, flicked a dark speck off the front of his pale blue shirt, and shook his head in a gesture more of sorrow than anger. "I know that's what people say about me, but it's a lie. I don't do that kind of thing." He scratched behind his ear. "That's the trouble with living in a small town," he observed. "The gossip. People should mind their own business. If they did, we would all be better off."

"Andy, my sister and I don't care if you do or don't run a bookie operation," Bernie replied.

Andy put his hand to his chest. "Phew. That's a relief. I was worried for a minute there. Not. Because I don't."

Libby stepped in. "Andy, we just want to know how much Ralph is into you for."

Andy glanced at his phone for a minute and texted something before answering Libby. "You need to work on your listening skills," he told her. "How can he be into me for anything when I already said I don't run that kind of operation?"

"Did you threaten him?" Bernie asked.

"Jeez." Andy threw his hands in the air. "Give me a break. Are you deaf or what?"

"We need the answer," Bernie persisted.

"To the secret of life?" Andy retorted. "Don't we all."

Andy watched as Libby took two hundred dollars out of her wallet and showed it to him.

"What the hell is that for?" Andy asked.

"To help you remember," Libby told him.

Andy rolled his eyes. "You're kidding me, right?"

Bernie did her chagrined look. "Put it away, Libby." She turned to Andy. "I told my sister not to embarrass herself. I told her you wouldn't endanger your operation for chump change."

Libby put her hands on her hips. "Since when is two hundred bucks chump change?" she demanded.

Andy snorted. "Obviously, you're running in the wrong circles."

Bernie cocked her head. "I told her you'd help us because it's the right thing to do."

Andy pantomimed pressing a button. "Bzzt. Wrong answer, Bernie."

Bernie gave it another try. "And because you want to help us solve Susie Katz's murder."

Andy pretended to push the button again. "And it's another wrong answer, folks," Andy said, playing a game-show host. "One more wrong answer and our contestants will be eliminated."

"Just say yes or no," Bernie urged. "How hard can that be?"

Andy pressed the imaginary button for the third time. "And it's good-bye to the Simmons sisters. Better luck next time," he told them.

"That wasn't a question," Bernie protested.

"It was in my book," Andy said.

"Book. Ha-ha. Very funny," Bernie said.

"I'm glad you think so," Andy said. He pointed at the door. "I believe our time is at an end. It pains me to say this, but it's time for you and your sister to leave."

"You know, we already know that Ralph owes you money," Bernie said, trying one last tactic.

"Good for you," Andy replied. "Now, are you going to leave, or am I going to have to have you escorted out?"

"By whom?" Bernie asked. "Because I don't see anybody here except you."

Andy smirked. "There will be."

"Is that whom you were texting?" Bernie demanded.

Andy's smirk grew bigger. "Why don't you wait and see?"

Bernie folded her arms across her chest. "Thanks. I think we will."

Libby tugged at Bernie's sleeve. "Come on," she urged. "Let's go."

Bernie planted her feet on the floor. "I think I'd rather stay."

"We don't have time for this," Libby told her.

A fact Bernie regretfully knew to be true. "Fine," she relented after a minute had gone by as she allowed her sister to drag her away.

"Drop by anytime you want to trade in your van," Andy told Bernie and Libby on their way out the door. "My offer still stands."

Chapter 16

"Andy doesn't give up, does he?" Libby said as she closed the door behind her.

Bernie was about to say, "That's why he's a good salesman," but she was distracted by the sight of two large, shaven-headed, hard-bodied guys, decked out in sweats, wifebeaters, and Ray-Bans, getting out of a rusty pickup truck and walking toward them.

"Looky, looky," Bernie said as the men got closer. "I think Andy's cavalry has arrived."

"Impressive," Libby said, taking in the view.

"Indeed, they are," Bernie agreed.

"The guy on the left looks familiar," Libby noted.

"That's because he worked as a bouncer at the Metro before he got fired for breaking John Gleason's arm in two places and stomping on his head."

"That's Nino?" Libby said, remembering. For three years, he'd come into the shop twice a week to get three cheese Danish and a large French roast, black, and then he'd stopped coming. "He used to be skinny, and he had a ponytail. He hasn't been around for a while," Libby added.

"That's because he's been in jail," Bernie told her. "I thought he got four years." She stopped to calculate. "Evidently, I was wrong. It's been less than six months since he went in."

"Well, that explains the bulking up." Libby scratched her nose. "Who's the other one?"

"I think that's Nino's cousin."

Now that she looked, Libby could see a family resemblance. "What's his story?"

"I heard he got himself in trouble with the wrong people down in Staten Island and decided a change of scene might be beneficial to his general health."

Libby sneezed, then sneezed two more times. This was turning out to be a bad allergy year. "I wonder if those guys are the guys Andy was texting," she said once she'd stopped.

"Could be," Bernie replied. "Although summoning them for us does seem like overkill," she added. "I mean, we're not exactly scary. Annoying, yes. Scary, no."

"I'm glad he did, though," Libby suggested.

Bernie turned toward her. "How so?"

Libby rubbed her arms. She felt a chill. She wondered why, and then she realized that the temperature had dropped and she was wearing a T-shirt and jeans. "Well, if these are the guys who paid Ralph a visit . . ."

"Which we don't know," Bernie pointed out.

"I said *if*," Libby replied, underlining the last word with her voice.

"Okay. If they did, they would have scared the bejesus out of Ralph," Bernie observed, going along with Libby's hypothesis.

Libby nodded. "I mean, we're not talking about two librarians here. These guys look like members of the brute squad."

"Indeed, they do." Bernie clicked her tongue against the roof of her mouth. "Although Nino looks scarier than he is."

"I wouldn't say breaking someone's arm in two places indicates a placid character," Libby noted.

"Placid," Bernie repeated, rolling the word around on her tongue. "I like it. Good word choice."

Libby nodded. "Although," she added in the interest of fairness, "Nino has always been nice to me."

"Me too," Bernie said. "He's okay until he starts drinking. Then he gets irritable."

"Nice to know," Libby said.

Bernie scratched her chin. "Yeah, I could see where a visit from Nino or his cousin could make Ralph do something rash."

"It would make me want to get out of town," Libby said as she studied the sky. Gray clouds were coming in, blocking out the sun. "Or get a gun."

"Or ask my aunt for money," Bernie reflected. By now the two men were closer. "Let's ask them, shall we?" Bernie said to Libby as she started walking toward them.

"If they threatened Ralph?" Libby inquired.

"Well, I'm not asking them out to the prom," Bernie retorted.

"Ah. And they're so cute, too."

"Yes. Adorable in a WWE kind of way."

"Sure. Why not?" Libby replied. "Bring on the drama." After all, what was the worst that could happen? Aside from pissing off people you didn't want to piss off, that is. She sighed. Usually, this was the time she'd be walking away, but that wasn't an option with Lucy on their backs.

"Hi," Bernie said when she reached Nino and his cousin.

Nino and his cousin scowled.

"Nice to see you again," Libby said to Nino. "I didn't

recognize you at first. I like the new you, though," she told him, appealing to his vanity. "Very Vin Diesel."

The corners of Nino's mouth twitched. He smiled despite himself. "You really think so?" he asked her. "You like the whole Mr. Clean look?"

Libby nodded. "But I liked the ponytail, too," she told him.

"Because this whole shaving the head thing is a lot of work," Nino confided.

"I would imagine," Bernie commented. "Not to mention the sunburn factor."

"I hadn't thought of that," Nino admitted.

"So, when are you coming back to see us again?" Libby asked him.

"Soon," Nino replied.

"Good," Libby told him. "Because while we still have the cheese Danish, you might also like our new chocolate croissants. I'll give you a couple of free samples." She nodded at Nino's cousin. "Bring your friend along, too."

"Cousin," the cousin said. "I'm his first cousin. And I'm gluten intolerant."

"We have some gluten-free blueberry and carrot muffins that are quite excellent," Libby told him. She was about to tell Nino's cousin about their other options when Bernie started talking.

"So, do you have a name?" Bernie asked the cousin.

Nino and his cousin exchanged a look.

"You can call me Al," Nino's cousin said.

"You don't look like an Al," Bernie observed.

Nino's cousin's smile was as friendly as that of a rattler looking at its prey. "Well, I am," Al said.

Bernie nodded. "Okay then, Al. My sister and I were wondering how much you and Nino would charge?"

"For what?" Nino said, clearly looking puzzled.

"For collecting some money for us," Bernie said. "We

can pay you guys in free coffee and Danish." Bernie flashed a particularly charming smile.

"Funny lady," Nino said.

"I'm serious," Bernie told him. "We'd really like to hire you. My sister and I understand you were quite ferocious with Ralph Abrams."

"Who told you that?" Al asked Bernie, and Bernie noted he'd said, "Who told you that?" instead of "Who is Ralph Abrams?"

Bernie nodded in the direction of the trailer. "Andy. He was quite glowing in his recommendation."

"He was, was he?" Nino growled, sliding into his tough guy persona.

"Definitely," Bernie replied. "Actually, I was thinking," she added, "that you could handle our business on the side. You know, when you're not busy doing stuff for Andy and his crew. We're losing a fortune in unpaid cinnamon rolls." She was met by silence. "So, what do you say?" Bernie asked after a minute had gone by.

Nino and Al looked at each other.

"I told you," Al said to Nino.

"Told him what?" Bernie asked.

"None of your business," Nino snapped.

Bernie shrugged. "Jeez. Calm down. I'm sorry for asking."

"Look," Nino said to Bernie, "I don't know what you're trying to do, but you should stop doing it."

"I'm trying to offer you a job," Bernie told him. "No need to get your tighty-whities in an uproar."

"I don't wear those," Nino told Bernie. "I wear boxers. Better air flow."

"More information than I need," Bernie told him.

Libby jumped into the conversation. "I'm going to level with you."

"Wow." Nino folded his arms across his chest and stared at Libby. "The suspense is killing me."

"Yeah. I can see you're all agog," Bernie said.

Nino widened his eyes. "Agog? Somebody buy you the *Word of the Day Calendar*?"

"Yeah, they did," Bernie responded. "I can get you one for your birthday if you'd like."

Nino snorted and readjusted his sunglasses. "Tell you what. Let's skip the foreplay, stop wasting time, and get right down to it."

"Let's," Libby agreed. "We want to know if you asked Ralph Abrams for the money he owes Andy Dupont," she explained.

Nino scratched his chin with his thumbnail. "And why would I do that?" he asked.

"Because Andy hired you to do it," Bernie said.

"And you know this how?" Nino asked her.

"Like I said," Bernie replied, "Andy told me."

Al turned to Nino. "Can you believe her?" he asked Nino, gesturing to Bernie with his thumb. "Making up this kind of stuff. How dumb does she think we are?" Then he answered his own question. "Pretty dumb, I'd say."

Nino held up a hand to indicate that his cousin should stop talking. Then he looked down at Bernie and adjusted his sunglasses for the second time in as many minutes. "Look," he said. "I like you. I like your sister. I like your cheese Danish, and I think your coffee is great. I enjoy going into your shop. You've always been nice to me, so I'm going to give you a word of advice, because I don't want to hurt you. Stay away from me, and stay away from Andy. He's not a nice person. Things happen to people he doesn't like, and he doesn't like people who poke around in his business." And then, before Libby and Bernie could say anything else, Nino nodded to his cousin and they both started walking to the trailer.

"Interesting," Bernie said as she watched the two men enter the trailer.

"You think?" Libby asked.

"Yeah. I do."

"I don't know," Libby replied as they walked back to their van.

"What's to know, Libby?" Bernie rummaged around her tote for the keys to the van. "Nino practically told us he and his cousin worked for Andy."

Libby sneezed again. Her eyes were starting to water. She needed to take an allergy pill. "I know what he said. There's nothing wrong with my hearing. But the whole scenario just seems too neat. We show up at Andy's and ask him about Ralph, and he throws us out but happens to summon the very people that scared Ralph."

"I see your point, Libby."

Libby gestured to herself and her sister. "I mean, look at us. Do we pose a threat? Not likely. All Andy had to do was not say anything, and we'd be on our way. Why bother bringing in the heavy guns?"

"I don't know." Bernie shrugged. "Maybe Andy's a nervous kind of guy. Or maybe you're right."

Libby clapped her hands. "Be still, my heart. I never thought I'd hear those words coming out of your mouth."

Bernie ignored her sister, opened the van's door, and climbed in. "Personally, I think you're complicating things, but I guess we'll see what Ralph has to say."

Ralph was next on their agenda. Then, if they had time, they'd pay a visit to Evan Molina, the real estate agent, as well.

Chapter 17

As it turned out, Libby and Bernie didn't get to talk to Ralph that day. There was no one home when they drove up to what they both kept thinking of as the old Connor estate. As they passed by the neon cats, Libby couldn't help thinking they seemed dimmer, more forlorn, as if they were mourning their mistress's death.

Gravel crunched under the van's tires as Bernie parked in front of the house's main entrance. Then she and Libby got out. The sun had vanished, suddenly covered by black storm clouds, and Bernie thought she felt a few raindrops on her arms. The groundskeeper, who had been trimming the hedges when they'd driven up, put down his shears and came up to them as Libby was about to ring the doorbell.

He was a good-looking guy, on the taller side, and his long hair was tied back in a ponytail. He smiled at them, his face crinkling into an infectious grin. "No one's home," he informed the sisters, tipping his baseball cap up and scratching under it. Despite the dip in the temperature, Libby could see that the back of his paint-stained T-shirt was damp with sweat. Then he hiked up his cargo pants and told the sisters that Ralph and Grace had gone out to run some errands.

"You want to leave a message?" he asked.

Bernie shook her head. "Thanks. No need. We'll come back later."

"Are you sure?" he asked as he nudged a rock off the porch step with the toe of his combat boot and watched it drop.

"Positive. Do you know what time they're supposed to be home?" Libby asked.

"Sorry. They didn't tell me. By the way, my name is Travis, Travis Deeds. I'd shake your hand, but"—he nodded down to them—"mine are a little dirty right now."

"No problem," Bernie said, taking a liking to him. "Do you take care of all of this yourself?" she asked, waving an arm in front of her in a gesture meant to encompass the entire estate.

"A lot of it," the groundskeeper said.

"But you can't do all of it," Libby said, thinking of how much it would take to keep a place like this running.

Travis laughed. "Mrs. Katz used to hire people on."

"I wonder how Grace and Ralph are going to manage," Bernie mused. "This really is a lot to take care of."

"It'll be fine as long as the cats are here," Travis observed. Then he repeated what Marvin had said, which was that according to the scuttlebutt, Grace and Ralph had got the house and an annuity to stay and take care of the cats.

"What will happen when the last of the cats die?" Libby wondered aloud.

Travis shook his head. "Won't happen. Gracie and Ralph will make sure there are always kittens around." Then he changed the subject. "Glad I wasn't here for the wedding."

"I wish I hadn't been," Bernie said.

"I feel kinda guilty." Travis grimaced. "Here I was seeing *Wonder Woman* when all hell was breaking loose."

"I don't think it would have mattered. There wasn't anything anyone could have done," Bernie told him. The leaves on the trees were dancing, showing their undersides, as the wind picked up. It wouldn't be long before the rain came. "You sound as if you liked her," Bernie observed.

"I didn't dislike her," Travis replied. "I know everyone did, but she was always okay with me. Maybe because I did my job and kept out of her way." Travis continued. "I'll tell you one thing, though. She sure did like her kitties. She liked them better than anything else. She certainly liked them better than people, that's for damn sure. If it didn't have fur, she didn't want to know from it." He pointed up to the sky. "I better get back to work while I can." Then he walked back to the hedge he'd been clipping, picked up his shears, and started where he'd left off.

Bernie sighed and looked around. Everything looked the way it had when they'd left. The tent and the area around it were still festooned with yellow crime-scene tape, the tape standing out like a beacon against the darkening sky. For some reason, the yellow reminded her of forsythia.

Then Bernie pointed to the tent. It was flapping in and out in rhythm with the gusts of wind. Under the gray sky, the tent had turned from marshmallow to dirty-water white. A couple of overturned chairs lay next to the tent wall, while a hodgepodge of pieces of wrapping paper, little lace collars, bow ties, and dying tiger lilies littered the grass.

Most weddings were happy events. But not this one. Susie Katz had never intended her cats' nuptials to be a celebration, Bernie reflected. She had intended it to be an exercise of power, a way to say, "Screw you," to her best enemies. There was no doubt about that. The question was, which one of the people there had hated her enough to kill her? At this point, she and Libby had a ways to go before they could answer that.

A moment later it began to pour. Bernie and Libby ran for the van. When they got inside, Bernie got out her cell and called Evan Molina.

"See him," her dad had urged this morning. "You'd be surprised what he knows."

Chapter 18

Spring and summer were house-selling season, Evan Molina's busiest times of the year, so Bernie was surprised when she got him on the phone, let alone that he had time to see them.

"We're on," she told Libby as she tucked her cell back in her tote. "He's at Breugger's."

"Big surprise," Libby replied. Breugger's was Evan Molina's unofficial office.

"And," Bernie continued, "he can give us an hour before his next appointment if we come now."

"He's going to nag us to sell," Libby predicted.

"It's the price of admission," Bernie noted as she fastened her seat belt. "Anyway, he can nag all he wants to. We're staying put."

In the past few years, tempted by high offers, four stores on the block A Little Taste of Heaven was on had shut their doors. Good-bye to the Golden Word, Bob's Pharmacy, the Ace hardware store, and Minnie's Paws for Pets, and hello to two high-end clothing boutiques, a store that sold salt, and another one that sold men's shaving supplies. The character of Longely was changing, and Libby didn't like it. She didn't like it one bit.

The drive over to see Evan Molina took longer than expected due to roadwork on Ash and Wadley. The rain didn't help, either. At one point, it came down so thick and fast that there were a couple of times when Libby had to pull over to the side of the road because she couldn't see out the windshield. Fortunately, the downpour was brief, and by the time the sisters reached Breugger's, the rain had dialed itself back to a drizzle.

Evan Molina was sitting in one of the booths by the window, drinking a coffee, nibbling on a toasted, buttered sesame bagel, and reading the local newspaper, when Libby and Bernie walked in. He looked up, waved, and folded the paper up.

Libby noted he was wearing his usual outfit: a rumpled white shirt, a dark blue knit tie, a tweed jacket with patches at the elbows, and khaki pants. His wire-rimmed glasses had slid halfway down the bridge of his nose, and Libby could see a spot on his chin where he'd nicked himself shaving.

Evan had always reminded Libby of one of her English college professors. Not only did he look like Professor Frantz, but he also had the same slow speech, the same habit of always pausing to think before he spoke. Which wasn't a bad thing, Libby reflected.

"You know, I could be holding my meetings at A Little Taste of Heaven instead of here," Evan told Libby as she slid into the booth across from him, having just ordered and gotten her coffee. "Think about it. It would be good for you, good for me."

"And our coffee is better," Libby said, having just taken a sip of hers.

Evan laughed. "It certainly is." Then he gestured around Breugger's. It was midafternoon, and the shop was almost empty. In the morning there were lines out the door, but now he and two other people were the only customers in there. "You need a bigger place, a place you can grow into, a place you can put booths in. You know what they say. You either grow or you die. Nothing in life is static."

Bernie slid into the booth next to her sister. "Always the salesman." She took a sip of her coffee and wrinkled her nose. It tasted as if someone had run a few coffee beans through some hot water.

Evan laughed. "You gotta try, right?"

"Right," Bernie said. "But we're not interested in moving."

"I've got the perfect place for you," Evan said.

Libby gave Bernie an "I told you so" look before turning back to Evan. "You are persistent, I will give you that."

"What would it hurt to look?" Evan countered.

"We're really *not* interested," Libby said.

"Okay. I get it. But times change. Places change. Sometimes for the better, sometimes for the worse."

"So we noticed," Libby said.

"Longely's a hot commodity now. In ten years, who knows?" Evan lifted his hands, palms up, in the air. "All I'm asking you to do is drive by this place. If you like it, great. You'll call me. And if you don't, you'll just continue on."

"Fine." Bernie leaned back in the booth. "You win. We'll look." At least it would shut Evan up.

Libby glared at Bernie. "We will?"

Bernie made a "Leave it alone" gesture with her hands to Libby.

"That's all I'm asking. And if, perchance, you want to move," Evan said, ignoring Libby's glower, "I have someone in mind who would really like your property and would be willing to pay quite a bit for it." He paused. "Think about it," he said to Libby.

"I don't have to," she snapped.

"Main Street is changing," Evan said. "Retail is changing."

"We know," Bernie said. "It's fairly obvious."

"It's my job to foresee the trends," Evan told her. He absentmindedly ran his hand over the top of his head.

"That's what has made you the best Realtor in this area fifteen years in a row," Bernie replied.

Evan blushed. "No. What makes me the best in the business is a lot of hard work."

"That too," Bernie said.

"If we change our mind," Libby assured him, having decided to rein herself back in, "you'll be the person we come to."

"Good to know," Evan said. "But seriously, look at the property. It won't cost you anything. Five minutes, at the most."

"Where would we live?" Libby countered.

"It has two units upstairs," Evan told her. "That's one of the beauties of the place. You could live in one and rent out the other, or you could combine them." He held up a finger and delivered his kicker. "And there's an elevator, so your father wouldn't have to deal with the stairs."

Libby raised her hands in surrender. "I give up. You've worn me down. We'll go see it."

Evan smiled.

Libby leaned forward. "Now about . . ."

"Susie Katz?" Evan asked.

"Yes," Bernie said.

"Speaking of Longely changing," Evan commented, "I can tell you a lot of people were not happy when Susie bought the old Connor estate to begin with . . . and then, when she put those neon cats all over the place. Well . . . you can imagine."

"I heard some of the neighbors tried to have the town remove them," Libby said.

"Charlene Eberhart, to be specific. But Susie Katz

promised to enlarge the library, and surprise, surprise, somehow the cats weren't such an eyesore, after all." Evan shook his head. "In retrospect, I'm sorry I sold her the property, although there really wasn't any way I could have not sold it to her. It was for sale, and she had the money to acquire it. End of discussion."

Evan sighed. Then he got up, walked over to the island where the milk and sugar were kept, picked up three packets of sugar, and returned to his seat, where he ripped the packets open and stirred them into his coffee. "My wife doesn't allow sugar in the house," he explained. "She calls it the new drug, God help me."

"That seems rather extreme," Libby ventured.

Evan grimaced. "Tell me about it. No more ice cream. No more cookies. No doughnuts. Oh well. I lived through the fat-free phase. I guess I can live through this one, as well."

"Susie Katz," Bernie prompted. "You were starting to tell us about Susie Katz."

"Ah, yes." Evan rested the stirrer on his napkin. "Susie Katz. Now, there was a character."

"Nice way of putting it," Bernie said.

"She didn't bring out the best in people," Evan observed.

"No, she did not," Libby agreed.

Evan smiled again. Smiling was what he did. It was his default expression. Sometimes, Libby wondered if he was like that at home or if he had a set number of smiles per day and used them up during business hours.

"She even got to me a couple of times," Evan admitted, interrupting Libby's thoughts. He took another bite of his bagel.

Bernie snorted. "Why should you be different?"

Instead of answering the question, Evan said, "I have to

say, your call was not unexpected given the circumstances."
He took a sip of his coffee to wash down the bagel. "Ah,
better. Word has it that our fearless chief of police is not
happy with you."

"You could say that," Libby agreed.

"I heard he threatened to arrest you," Evan continued.

"He's a big kidder," Libby lied.

"I hope you're right," Evan told her as he straightened
his tie, patting it into place. "Susie will not be missed,"
Evan said. "I know that's a terrible thing to say, but it's
true. She was . . ." He stopped for a minute, trying to find
a polite way to say what he wanted to. Finally, he settled
on something and added, "A very difficult human being."

"She was tough to work with," Libby agreed.

"She was a bitch," Bernie said.

"She was that and then some," Evan said. "Don't repeat
that," he said hurriedly.

"We won't," Bernie assured him.

"But it was more than that." Evan paused for another
minute, searching for the correct words. "Some people
play to win. She played to hurt."

Bernie cocked her head. "Explain please."

Evan spread his hands apart, palms down. "She was
aware that what she was doing was going to be hurtful,
was going to cause people angst, and that knowledge
seemed to heighten her pleasure. She actively enjoyed
hurting people—in a psychological sense."

"In other words, she was a sadist," Bernie said.

Evan nodded. "Exactly."

Libby leaned forward. "Can you be more specific?"

Evan didn't reply immediately. Instead, he washed
down the last of his bagel with a couple more sips of coffee. "You know," he said when he was done, "people tell
me things, they trust me to go into their houses, go into

their closets, and they trust me to fix things. I'm kind of like a doctor or a psychiatrist in that regard."

Bernie raised an eyebrow. If Evan saw it, he ignored it.

"If I were a blabbermouth," he continued, "I don't think they'd do that, which would mean I wouldn't get their business."

"I understand," Libby said, although she really didn't. She thought Evan did the business he did because he knew how to price things correctly, but what did she know? "Don't you think these circumstances transcend that in this case?" she asked.

Instead of answering, Evan reached for his paper cup, then realized he'd drunk the last of his coffee, and withdrew his hand.

"We're just looking for background information about Susie Katz. That's all," Libby assured him.

"Specifically, her real estate transactions," Bernie explained. "We hear she was buying up a lot of real estate and that you were handling it for her."

"Yes, I was," Evan said. "And you are correct. She was in the process of buying up a fair amount of business property. That's true. The strip mall down near Diane Street and the abandoned typewriter factory over by Ridley were two of her recent purchases. She was going to turn them into mixed-use facilities." Evan picked up a crumb from his bagel and deposited it in his coffee cup. "Those are a matter of public record."

"Meaning that there are other purchases that aren't?" Bernie asked.

Evan nodded. Bernie studied his face.

"And those are the interesting ones, aren't they?" she said, guessing. "The ones we should pay attention to."

Evan nodded. "Two, to be exact."

Libby looked at her watch. Their time was growing

shorter. Soon Evan would be off to his next appointment. "So, are you going to tell us or not?"

"I'd love to tell you," Evan replied, "but there are some rocks one shouldn't turn over."

Bernie frowned and leaned forward. "Exactly what does that mean?"

"I don't know," Evan confessed. He laughed. "It's sounds good, though, doesn't it?"

"I suppose," Bernie said slowly. She wasn't quite sure how she should respond.

"I've always wanted to say that. It's a line from a TV show," Evan explained when he saw the blank expressions on their faces. "One of those detective shows," he clarified.

"Right." Bernie sighed and started to get up. Evan wasn't the only one who had a schedule to keep. This was turning out to be a waste of time, and they still had to pick up peanut butter, onions, and potatoes, as well as napkins, paper plates and cups, at Sam's Club. "Okay, then. Thanks, anyway."

Evan held up his hand. "Wait."

"I'm sorry," Bernie said. "This has been very interesting, and you know Libby and I always like talking to you, but this isn't shedding a lot of light on the present situation, and we have a slew of stuff we have to get done, so if you're not . . ."

"Oh, but I am," Evan replied. "I'm just trying to explain to you why I can't give you specifics."

Libby took another sip of her coffee and made a face. "Then what can you give us?"

Evan leaned back, folded his hands, and rested them on the table. "I can give you the lay of the land."

Bernie sat back down. "I guess we'll take what we can get," she said.

"I can definitely point you in the right direction. Once

you hear what I have to say, I'm sure you and your sister are smart enough to figure out the rest," Evan told her. He cleared his throat and began. "There are some people Susie Katz really didn't like. . . ."

"No kidding," Libby said.

Bernie elbowed her sister in the ribs. "Let the man finish talking."

Libby rubbed her side. "I get it. Go on," she told Evan.

Evan nodded. "As I was saying, when Susie didn't like someone, she went out of her way to make their lives as unpleasant as possible."

"This is not a news flash," Libby couldn't help blurting out.

"I realize that." Evan raised his hand. "Just have a little patience." He paused for a moment before continuing. "Which, I think, is why she expanded her horizons and began to dabble in private real estate. Now, there are people in this community, as there are in every community, to whom the economy has not been kind, who appear to be doing better than they are. That's not a news flash, either, I know." He paused again, and Bernie and Libby waited.

"They owe money on their houses and their cars." Evan paused for a third time. "More than they can pay. In the past number of years, a variety of companies have grown up to answer this need. The one I'm thinking of operates on a strictly confidential basis. No ads. Strictly word of mouth. All very hush-hush. 'We will give you money to keep going in exchange for the deeds to your property,' they say. 'You can buy the deeds back at any time,' they promise. 'No risk to you, and no one has to know,' they state."

"And this is legal?" Bernie asked.

"Let's just say this company operates in the gray area." Evan raised a finger in the air to emphasize what he was going to say next. "But what this company doesn't tell you is that they frequently bundle the deeds together and sell them to another company for pennies on the dollar, and then these companies do what they want with the debt, usually foreclosing on the property that is in their possession." Evan stopped, patted his tie again, and gave Bernie and Libby a meaningful look.

Libby got it first. "So," she said, "Susie Katz bought the debt."

Evan corrected her. "One of her shell companies did."

"And she had a lot of those?" Bernie asked.

"I don't know about that, but I know that she definitely had one."

Libby clarified. "And this house . . ."

Evan held up two fingers.

Libby corrected herself. "Right. You said two houses." Then she guessed the names of their owners.

Evan nodded again. "That is correct."

"And being Susie, she probably didn't do that as a charitable act," Libby postulated. "Like, she wasn't giving their houses back to them."

"Not quite," Evan agreed. "But they thought she was, because she told them she was helping them out."

"That sucks," Libby observed. "To think someone is helping you and then to find out they're kicking you in the teeth. That could make you really, really mad."

"Homicidally so," Bernie noted. "When was Susie going to foreclose on their homes and kick them out?"

"Soon," Evan said.

"How soon?" Bernie asked.

"Very soon, according to my sources," Evan said.

"Who are your sources?" Libby asked.

"Sorry," Evan said. "I can't reveal those."

"Because you're FBI?" Libby asked.

"No," Evan snapped. "Because it would be bad for business."

Bernie decided it was time to run interference. "How accurate is their information?"

"I wouldn't take it to the bank," Evan replied, "but they've been right a bunch of times."

"Could you be a little more specific?" Bernie asked.

"The sales were supposed to be finalized around the time of the wedding."

"Interesting," Bernie said. She thought for a minute. "Suppose Susie was going to sign the final papers at the wedding, and suppose she'd told everyone that she was going to give their houses back to them, but she was really going to do the opposite, and suppose one or both women found that out ahead of time."

"That certainly would piss me off," Libby commented. Despite herself, she took another sip of coffee. It was even worse cold than it had been warm.

"Me too." Bernie brushed her hair off her face with the flat of her hand. "Evan, tell me something. What happens when the holder of the deeds to those properties dies before the foreclosures can be executed?"

Evan balled up his napkin and stuffed it and the coffee stirrer into his empty coffee cup. "Then the deal is null and void. The phrase 'No harm, no foul,' or whatever the saying is, seems to cover it."

"Well, that's certainly a motive," Libby observed.

"Indeed, it is," Bernie agreed.

"This is all speculation," Libby observed.

"But it is very suggestive," Bernie said. Then she asked Evan a question. "Do you know what Susie was planning to do with the houses?"

"I heard she was going to raze them," Evan promptly replied.

"Wow. That's like rubbing salt in the wound," Bernie said.

"And do what with the land?" Libby asked.

Evan readjusted his glasses. "Nothing. Just keep it."

Libby frowned. "But why would she do that? That's such a waste."

"Given what I know about Susie, I would say she was going to do it as an object lesson," Evan replied. "She was using the houses to show people what happens if you cross her." He stifled a cough. "From what I heard, the whole thing started with some sort of cat-related thing."

He looked at his watch. "Gotta go," he told them. "My client awaits." He put out his hand. Bernie and Libby shook it. "Happy hunting, and don't forget to look at the property I told you about." Then he left.

Bernie and Libby followed him out the door shortly afterward.

Chapter 19

"I didn't think Charlene and Marie were in that bad shape finance-wise," Libby said as she and Bernie walked back to the van. It had stopped raining, the sun had come out, and the air had the fresh grassy smell that spring rains brought.

"Me either," Bernie agreed. "I know Marie is still working at the library part-time."

"Yeah, but that wouldn't be enough to pay the bills." Libby thought some more. "Maybe whoever they invested their money with didn't do such a good job."

"Or maybe they're just living above their means," Bernie suggested. "Charlene did take that four-month cruise around the world, and Marie redid her kitchen and bathroom."

"Not small-ticket items." Libby started to bite one of her cuticles, realized what she was doing, and quit.

"Not at all," Bernie agreed.

"Well, if what Evan says is true, and Susie did that to me, I'd want to kill her, too. Your friend comes and says she's going to help you, and then she stabs you in the back instead. That's just plain bad."

"But the three of them weren't friends," Bernie objected. "Anything but. That's what I don't understand. Why would they believe her?"

Libby sidestepped a puddle. "Maybe they didn't."

Bernie took off her raincoat and slung it over her arm. It had gotten warmer while they were inside. "Maybe you're right. Maybe Marie and Charlene came there armed with a countermove."

"Like what?" Libby asked.

"I don't know," Bernie told her. She could see the scene, though. One of the women telling Susie what she was going to do, and Susie laughing at them, and Marie or Charlene grabbing the letter opener and stabbing Susie with it. She shook her head and changed the subject. "So, do you want to see Evan's place or not?"

"Sure. What the hell," Libby said. Despite herself, she had to agree with Evan about one thing. It would be nice to have more space for customers.

Counting the detour—Evan's place turned out to be fifteen, not five, minutes away—it took the sisters a little under two hours to finish their errands. They got back to the shop just before the predinner rush started. They had just finished unloading their supplies and had walked into the front of the store to check the register and see what needed to be done when Amber finished with her customer and came up to them.

"We're low on sugar, and we had a run on the chocolate gingersnaps. They're all gone," she announced.

Libby groaned. "All of them?" She'd baked five dozen this morning. "You're kidding."

"Nope," Amber replied. "I sold the last five, ten minutes before you walked through the door. Evidently, they're our new big hit," Amber told her. "Plus, Mrs. Small ordered five dozen for tomorrow afternoon for her mah-jongg club."

"Great," Libby said. She poured herself a cup of coffee, added cream and sugar, and took the last slice of spinach and mushroom quiche out of the display case. Dinner was a couple of hours away, and she was too hungry to wait.

Libby was pleased that the cookies had taken off—she'd played around with the recipe and added a bit more ginger, a dash more black pepper, and a lot more chocolate—but she'd been counting on their supply lasting for three days. Now she or Bernie would have to go back to the store and get more gingerroot, sugar, and candied ginger before tomorrow morning.

"Two more things," Amber added as Libby swallowed. "A lady came in looking for you."

"What did she want?" Bernie asked.

"She didn't say. She just said she'd be back. Also, you guys got a present."

"A present?" Libby repeated as she took in Amber's hair. She could have sworn Amber was wearing blond braids this morning. Now Amber's hair was black and short.

"It's a wig," Amber explained, noting the look of puzzlement on Libby's face. "I'm trying it out for a *Walking Dead* party I'm going to on Saturday. What do you think?"

"I like it," Libby said. "I like it a lot."

Libby remembered how Amber's constant shifts in appearance—she could go from Goth girl to Walt Disney's Belle overnight—had bothered her at first. It was like living with a shape-shifter. She never knew who was coming through the door. But the customers had liked it, and now she did, too. It added a note of excitement to the day, and, more importantly, it brought customers through the door because they wanted to see Amber's latest iteration.

"What present?" Bernie asked as she finished eating a banana and started restocking the napkin holders and the straw dispenser sitting on the side of the counter.

Amber shrugged. "I don't know. Some guy brought it in. Said it was for you."

"Did he say it was a present?" Bernie asked as she walked over to the coffee station and began tidying it up.

Amber shook her head. "No. But it's wrapped up like one. Shiny paper. It's such a waste." She tut-tutted her disapproval. "I can't believe trees have to die to make that kind of stuff. What's wrong with using newspaper?"

The sisters didn't answer. Instead, Bernie looked at Libby, and Libby looked at Bernie. They both had the same thought at the same time.

"Where's the present?" Libby asked, trying to keep her voice even.

"I put it in your office. Why? Is something wrong?"

"Maybe," Bernie said as she turned and headed toward the back. She hoped she was mistaken, but she had a bad feeling in her gut.

Libby told Amber to brew some decaf French roast—it was a big seller in the afternoon—and put some of the blond brownies where the gingersnaps had been, before joining her sister in the office.

The package Amber had mentioned was sitting on the desk, atop this month's bills. The box was a little larger than the one at the wedding had been, but it, too, was wrapped in several layers of gold paper and had a blue bow on top.

Libby frowned. "It looks like the present Susie got," she observed. "Same size, same type of wrapping paper."

"Same blue bow," Bernie said. "Definitely not from UPS or FedEx."

Libby picked the package up. She thought she could feel something moving inside.

Bernie put her ear closer to it. "I think I hear scratching."

"This is so not good," Libby noted.

"You're thinking what I'm thinking?" Bernie asked her sister after she'd lifted her head up.

"Is there anything else to think?" Libby asked.

Bernie was about to answer when their other counter person came in. Googie had been working for them for five years now and played in a band at night. He was the yang to Amber's yin, the rock to Amber's river. His pants and his shirts and T-shirts all looked the same. He always shaved. He never surprised. He never lost his cool.

"Hey," Googie said. "Aren't you going to open it and see what's in it?"

"No," Libby said. "We are most definitely not. At least not here."

Googie scratched his ear and scrunched down to get a closer look at the package. At six-four, he scrunched a lot. "Why? Is it, like, an explosive or something? Should we evacuate the building? You know, like, call the bomb squad."

"The exterminator would be more like it," Bernie said grimly. And she explained.

"That is so uncool," Googie said.

"I don't suppose you happened to see who delivered it as well, by any chance?" Libby asked, hoping that Googie could supply more details.

"Naw," Googie said. "Sorry. I was in the back getting the bread out of the oven. The guy was gone by the time I came back out."

"That's what Amber said," Libby noted.

Googie scratched his chest. "I mean we were getting slammed. It was nuts here."

Bernie sighed. That was the way things always went. They were either crazy busy or there was no one in the shop. Then she shuddered as she had a sudden vision of mice bursting out of the package and running all over their shop while their customers stampeded out the door. They'd have to close the place down and then reopen.

She shut her eyes as she thought about the publicity! What a nightmare that would be. With their luck, someone would probably post a video on Facebook, and it would go viral. There'd be no coming back from that. Maybe she was being paranoid, she told herself. Then she lifted the package up. She definitely felt something moving inside. Nope. She wasn't being paranoid at all. The only thing that would be worse was roaches. They had to get the package out of the store now, before the worst happened.

"What are you going to do with it?" Googie asked as Bernie started walking toward the door, package in hand.

"We're going to open the package by the river," Bernie said.

"And drown the mice?" Googie asked. "Because if you are—"

Libby put up a hand to stop him. "No. We're letting them go." She didn't like killing things if she didn't have to.

Googie smiled. "Good. Because otherwise I would have."

Chapter 20

"Why the river?" Libby asked once they were in the van. She'd carefully stowed the package in the back, wedging it in with a couple of cartons of recyclables so it wouldn't slip around.

"Because there are no houses down there," Bernie explained. She began to slowly back out of their driveway. "I hope we're wrong," she said as she waited for a car to pass.

"I hope so, too," Libby said. "But I don't think we are."

"Unfortunately, neither do I," Bernie replied as she leaned over and turned on the radio.

They didn't talk. Instead, they spent the rest of the ride thinking about the implications of what was in the box.

It took five minutes to get down to the park bordering the Hudson and fifteen minutes of circling to find a place for the van. The parking lots were full, now that it had stopped raining. It seemed as if everyone in town had driven down to the river to go for a run or a walk on the towpath. Libby finally found a spot in the farthest lot, parked, and got out.

Bernie climbed out and went around to the back of

Mathilda, took the box out of the van and, holding it as far away from her as she could, walked with Libby toward an outcropping of rocks that was well away from the jogging path. She didn't want anyone to see her and Libby releasing a box of mice into the grass. They might think the mice came from their shop. She cursed quietly as her heels sank into the soft dirt.

"Far enough?" Bernie asked when she had gotten near the rocks. They rose out of the grass in a pyramid shape, a reminder of the times when glaciers had moved across the area.

Libby looked around. No one was in sight. There were only the rocks, the grass, and the slope of the shoreline to the river. People's voices drifted in on the wind. "Perfect," she said.

Bernie set the box on the grass, crouched down, took off the blue bow, and tore the wrapping off the package. Libby watched the pieces of gold paper sparkle among the wet blades of grass. The top of the box was sealed with six pieces of Scotch tape.

"Considerate of whoever did this," Bernie noted as she peeled the pieces off with the tips of her fingernails, "not wanting to let them loose in A Little Taste of Heaven."

"So, this is a warning," Libby opined.

"I'd say. Because if the top wasn't taped down, the mice would have pushed it up and eaten through the paper in a couple of minutes," Bernie said. Then she remembered the three white mice she'd brought home for school vacation and the fate of the yellow raincoat she'd draped over their cage to keep them quiet at night. She'd woken up the next morning to perfect circles of yellow nylon in their nest. "But come to think of it, it wouldn't take too long for them to chew through the box, either."

By now there were squeaks coming from the inside of the box, not that they needed confirmation.

"Ready?" Bernie asked.

Libby nodded, and Bernie stood up and pulled off the top.

Suddenly there were mice everywhere. The sisters instinctively jumped back as the mice ran this way and that, looking for shelter.

"They're really kinda cute," Bernie said as she watched them scurry around. "I don't know why they scare people."

"All I know," Libby said as one ran over her shoe, "is they don't belong in our shop. Imagine what would happen if they were running around in there now?"

Bernie shuddered. It didn't bear thinking about. "How many mice do you think were in the package?" Bernie asked, changing the subject as she watched the mice disappear under rocks and behind tree roots and bushes.

"Too many," Libby said. "At least as many as were in the box at Susie's wedding. Maybe more."

"I wonder where whoever is doing this is getting them," Bernie mused, the question just occurring to her.

Libby looked at her. "The pet store?"

"No. They're field mice." Bernie pointed to a mouse over by the rocks that was sniffing around. "You don't buy them in pet stores."

"Someone is breeding them?"

"Possibly," Bernie said. "I guess that makes more sense than collecting them."

"Problem solved," Libby said. "Now all we have to do is find someone breeding field mice and we'll be all set."

"Absolutely," Bernie said absentmindedly, her attention now focused on the torn pieces of white paper lying in the grass, intermingled with the pieces of gold wrapping paper. She realized they hadn't been there before. Ergo, there must have been a note hidden in the layers of gold paper that she'd ripped up. *Damn.* She went over and picked up one of the larger pieces of white paper. It was damp from the rain on the grass. The word *greeting* printed on it had begun to run.

"What are you doing?" Libby asked as she watched her sister get down on her hands and knees and begin crawling around in the grass.

After Bernie explained, Libby joined her. Ten minutes later, they'd collected a handful of the white paper scraps. Libby and Bernie moved over to the rock outcroppings. They smoothed the pieces of paper out with the palms of their hands and began to put them together.

Five minutes later, they had the message. It read, *Next time you won't get a warning. Stop while you're ahead.* The message had been printed on a standard piece of white computer paper, in twelve-point type in the Times New Roman font, which was one of the most common fonts available.

"I wonder if there are fingerprints on the paper?" Libby asked.

"If there were, they're probably not there anymore," Bernie said.

Libby pinched her forehead with her thumb and forefinger. She could feel a headache coming on. "Wonderful."

"Actually, this is good news."

Libby put her hand down. "How do you figure that, Bernie?"

"Because we're ruffling feathers. If we weren't, we wouldn't be getting this reaction."

"And the bad news, Bernie, is that we don't know whose feathers we're ruffling."

"But we will," Bernie told her with more assurance than she felt.

"We'd better," Libby replied.

Chapter 21

Bernie pulled into their parking space next to A Little Taste of Heaven, saw that the line inside the shop was almost out the door, and cursed under her breath while Libby consulted her watch. She was surprised to find it was as late as it was.

"We better get in there," Bernie said.

"Well, it is that time," Libby noted. The hours between six and seven thirty accounted for a third of their business. Even more than their breakfast crowd, their dinner folks were tired and hungry and wanted to get their food and go home as quickly as possible.

As the sisters headed toward the door, the lady sitting on the bench in front of the shop got up and hurried toward them. She was wearing black leggings and an off-the-shoulder white T-shirt decorated with pictures of Russian blues in various poses. The outfit would have looked good on an eighteen-year-old but didn't do a chubby middle-aged woman any favors, Bernie decided. Neither did her makeup or hairstyle. The woman's platinum blond hair was swept up in a ponytail, and she had on enough electric-blue eye shadow to light up a small city.

But she looked familiar, Bernie reflected as the woman approached them. She just couldn't put a name to the face. "Do I know you?" Bernie asked as the woman stuck out her hand and Bernie shook it.

"'Fraid we haven't had the pleasure," the woman said. Then she introduced herself. "I'm Dana Ogden, head of the Longely Russian Blue Society."

Libby nodded. She recalled Googie saying something to her earlier about a woman wanting to speak to her and Bernie.

"I've been waiting for you," Dana said.

"Not too long, I hope," Bernie said as she studied the woman standing in front of her. Nothing came to mind. "Are you sure I don't know you?" she finally asked her.

"I'm positive." Dana clasped her hands in front of her. "We have to talk."

"Can it wait?" Bernie asked, gesturing at the mass of people inside A Little Taste of Heaven. "This is a really busy time for us."

"No, it can't," Dana Ogden exclaimed. "It's about Susie. . . ."

Libby leaned forward. "You have information about her death?"

"It's about me," Dana said. She took a deep breath and let it out. "My death. I'm in danger."

"Then you should go to the police," Libby suggested.

"I did," Dana Ogden cried. She balled her hands into fists. "They won't listen to me."

Bernie and Libby exchanged looks. Dana Ogden was definitely a little too tightly wrapped, but that didn't mean she didn't have something of interest to say.

"Why not?" Libby asked.

"Because I don't have any proof." Dana scrunched her face up.

"Proof of what?" Bernie asked.

Dana dropped her voice. "That someone's trying to kill me, just like they did Susie."

"And why would they do that?" Bernie asked.

Dana bit her lip. "I'm the head of the Russian Blue Society, you know."

"So you said," Libby replied, waiting for a further explanation. None came. When a minute went by and Dana still hadn't said anything, Libby said, "I don't understand." At which point Dana burst into tears.

"People are saying terrible things about the society and the show," she managed to get out between sobs. "They're saying that Susie bought last year's first-place ribbon."

"And that's why someone wants to kill you?" Bernie asked.

Dana nodded and burst into another bout of sobbing. After a minute, Dana's sobbing subsided to occasional sniffs. "I'm so . . . so . . . so . . . sorry," she said, apologizing, as she fished in her bag for a Kleenex. She found one and began to dab at her eyes with it. "It's just that I don't know where to turn, and people said that you could help me."

"Why don't you start at the beginning?" Bernie suggested. Dana Ogden's narrative wasn't making any sense. At least not to her.

Dana looked down at her hands and began to twist the Kleenex into a knot. Bernie noticed as she did that her hands were reddened from work, the knuckles enlarged. "I've devoted my whole life to the Russian blues," she exclaimed. "And to hear people saying that Boris's and Natasha's papers are fake, and I allowed them in the show, anyway, because I got paid off." Her face crumpled, and she broke into a fresh bout of sobbing. "It's horrible, simply horrible." Dana hiccupped twice, then went on with what she was saying. "Just the thought that people are talking that way makes me want to crawl up in a hole and die."

"So, what does this have to do with your being threatened?" Bernie asked.

"Think about it," Dana ordered.

Bernie did. Nothing came to mind.

"Don't you see?" Dana looked from one sister to the other. "That's why Susie was killed."

"Because she supposedly bribed her way into the title?" Libby asked.

"Yes. Exactly," Dana replied.

"I can think of lots of reasons to kill Susie, but this one would not be high on my list," Bernie said.

"That's because you're not a crazy cat person," Dana cried. "Susie was killed because she won first place, and now I'm in danger." Dana made a fist and struck her chest.

"I don't get the connection," Bernie replied.

"It's obvious. For revenge. Because I awarded Boris first prize, of course."

"Of course," Bernie said. Who knew that cat shows were blood sports?

Dana grabbed Bernie by the shoulders and shook her. "You've got to take this seriously. I could be the next victim."

"I'm trying," Bernie said. "It just seems . . . improbable."

"I've been threatened," Dana repeated.

"By who?" Libby asked.

Dana took a deep breath and let it out. "Marie."

"Then, as Libby said before, you should go to the police," Bernie advised. "Get a restraining order."

"She hasn't said anything, but the way she looks at me . . ." Dana shuddered. "I can feel it."

Bernie raised an eyebrow. "Because?"

"I told you. I awarded the ribbon to Boris instead of to Maximilian."

"That's Marie's cat's name?" Bernie asked.

Dana nodded. "She told me that she was going to pay me back." And Dana shuddered again.

"Did she say how?" Libby inquired.

"She didn't have to," Dana told her. "When I heard about Susie, I knew."

"So why now?" Bernie asked. She could see why Lucy had kicked Dana Ogden out of the police station. Her story didn't add up.

"What do you mean?" Dana stammered.

"I mean, why come to see us now? Why is this such an emergency all of a sudden?"

"Because I saw Marie," Dana replied after a moment of hesitation. She seemed more unsure of herself. "She was walking around my house. Casing it."

"Did you call the police?" Libby asked.

Dana didn't answer the question. Instead, she said, "She's going to kill me. I know it."

"So, this all goes back to the cat show?" Bernie asked.

Dana nodded quickly. "Yes. Yes, it does," she replied, looking relieved.

"Why not Allison, then?" Bernie asked.

"Allison?" Dana echoed. "I don't understand."

"You called the police when Allison let Susie's cats out at the show, didn't you?" Bernie asked.

"Susie made me," Dana said.

"But nevertheless, you were the one that did it, that started the ball rolling, so to speak," Bernie said in a pleasant tone of voice. "How come Allison isn't mad at you?"

"Because she understands," Dana cried.

"Unlike Marie?" Libby inquired.

Dana threw back her shoulders and stuck out her chin. "Marie is a very vengeful person."

"Is that why you're so eager to throw her under the

bus?" Libby asked. "Or is there something else you're not telling us?"

Bernie snapped her fingers. Yes, there was. She'd just remembered where she'd seen Dana before. "You're Dan Ogden's mom, aren't you?" she asked her.

Dana blinked twice. Bernie could see Dana was trying to decide what to do. Lie her way out of it or tell the truth. After a minute, she stuck out her chin and said, "So what if I am?"

"Didn't the police arrest Dan for going after Marie with a golf club?" Bernie asked.

"He broke the windshield of her car. So what?"

"The police thought it was a big 'So what?'" Bernie pointed out.

"It wasn't his fault. They should have picked her up," Dana shot back. "She was the one who caused everything with her lying and her cheating on my son with that guy."

Bernie crossed her arms across her chest. "Sounds like a country-western song to me."

Dana scowled. "I don't care what it sounds like to you. That doesn't change what I said about Marie," Dana insisted. "You don't know what she's like. She never forgets anything, ever."

"You're not exactly an unbiased observer," Bernie told her, thinking Marie sounded like Susie.

"Maybe not," Dana admitted, "but I'm telling the truth about this. My son lost his job because of her. No one will hire him now."

"That's too bad," Libby said before changing the subject. "So, is it true?" she asked quietly. "Did you take a bribe from Susie? Should Marie's cat have won?"

Dana's mouth twisted in outrage. "Of course not. That's a terrible thing to say."

"Is it?" Libby said. "I mean, if you did, then what you're

saying makes sense. I could see why Marie would be really upset."

Dana stared at her as she tried to decide what to say. Finally, she settled on, "I would never, ever do something like that." She put her right hand up. "I swear to the heavens."

Bernie crossed her arms over her chest. "Well, as long as you swear to heaven, then I guess we should believe you."

"Don't take my word for it. Ask Mrs. Van Trumpet," Dana spit out. Then Dana turned and marched toward the steel-gray Infiniti parked across the street.

"Nice ride," Bernie said to Libby. "It looks new."

"It does, doesn't it?"

"Hard to afford on Dana Ogden's salary."

"What does she do?" Libby asked.

"If memory serves, she teaches music two days a week at the Christian Brothers Academy."

"Yeah," Libby said. "I'd say she's not buying a car like that on her salary. Is she married?"

"Nope."

"A trust-fund baby?"

Bernie shook her head. "No. Her mom and dad worked out in the mills before they closed."

"Maybe she won the lottery."

"Maybe," Bernie agreed. "Or maybe Susie's money bought that car."

"That's a lot of money."

"Not if you have it, which Susie did, and you want something really badly, which Susie also did."

"True." Libby turned to her sister. "So, do you believe her about Marie?"

Bernie shook her head. "No. Do you?"

"Nope."

"So why do this?" Bernie said. "Why put on this production?"

"Simple. Because she hates Marie for what happened to her son, and she wants to see her in jail," Libby suggested.

"Family loyalty at work is a beautiful thing to see," Bernie said. "Plus, if she did take a bribe from Susie, she might have decided it's better to go on the offensive." Bernie pointed to the store. She could see the people standing around, waiting to be served, through the windows. "We'd better get in there."

"Indeed, we should," Libby said, noting the expressions on the faces of Amber and Googie. "We can speak to Mrs. Van Trumpet tomorrow."

"And Marie," Bernie added. "Don't forget about her. Maybe Dad would do it," she mused. "That would give us a little more time."

Libby nodded. The clock was ticking. They needed all the help they could get.

Chapter 22

Day three . . .

It was ten thirty the following morning and it was drizzling out as Sean Simmons walked out of the flat above A Little Taste of Heaven and got into Marvin's Kia. At least it wasn't a hearse, Sean reflected as he shut the door and put his seat belt on. At least these days Marvin was driving his own car. So that was a little better. And he hadn't brought his pet pig with him. So that was a lot better.

But really, even without the pig, the whole situation sucked. Marvin as chauffeur. Sean sighed the sigh of the put upon. Jeez, the guy had many virtues, but driving wasn't one of them. Even with GPS, he couldn't find his way out of a paper bag. Sean shook his head in wonder. If you'd told him twenty years ago that he wouldn't own a car, that someone would be driving him, he'd have told you, you were crazy.

But Libby had been correct. Unfortunately. His Chevy wasn't worth putting ten thou into. *Requiescat in pace.* Well, at least he still had his license. They could have that when he was in the ground. So, he could always rent a car if he needed to. He wasn't completely at other people's mercy.

"Ready?" Marvin asked Sean.

"As ready as I'll ever be," Sean replied. He rolled down the window as Marvin pulled away from the curb. When Marvin was out of line of sight of the shop, Sean instructed Marvin to go to the end of the street and take a right and then a quick left.

"But that's not what the GPS says," Marvin objected.

"That's because we're not going to talk to Marie. We're going to the old Connor estate," Sean told him as he took out a pack of cigarettes from his pants pocket, tapped the pack on the dashboard, and extracted a cigarette.

"But that's not where Libby wanted us to go," Marvin said nervously.

"That's where I want to go," Sean told him. He was an "It's better to ask forgiveness than permission" kind of guy. Always had been, always would be.

"But . . ." Marvin turned to look at him.

"Watch the road," Sean yelled when Marvin narrowly missed an SUV turning into the intersection.

"Sorry, Mr. Simmons," Marvin muttered. He was a good driver. He was. Except when he was with Libby's dad.

Sean checked to see that Marvin's eyes were on the road. When he was satisfied that they were, he resumed talking. "As I was saying," Sean said, "I want to look at the crime scene first."

"But . . ."

"I'll take care of Libby," Sean assured him. "After all, it doesn't do to get the father of your girlfriend angry at you, does it?" Sean asked.

"I guess not," Marvin said as Sean lit his cigarette. Which made him even more miserable.

Sean looked at the expression on Marvin's face, took pity on him, and said, "You know, she knows." He sat back and exhaled. "Both my daughters do."

"They know what? That we're going someplace else?" Marvin asked, this time careful to keep his eyes on the road.

"No. That I smoke," Sean said. "We just pretend that I don't. So, don't worry," Sean said to Marvin. He patted his arm. "It's not like you're keeping a big"—Sean made his voice go all dramatic—"dark secret from my daughter." He eyed Marvin. "Feel better?" he asked.

"A little," Marvin admitted.

"Good," Sean said. He took another puff of his cigarette and flicked the ashes out the window. "It's not as if I get to smoke one of these that often anymore," he observed. And then he spent the rest of the ride thinking about what he was going to do when he got to the old Connor estate.

It had stopped raining by the time Marvin drove through the gate. The place had definitely changed, Sean decided. He'd been there fifteen years ago, if he remembered correctly, for a domestic abuse complaint that had been phoned in by Mrs. Wellington and emphatically denied by Mr. Wellington, who had sworn that Mrs. Wellington's broken arm had occurred when she took a header down the stairs.

And despite Sean's best efforts, Mrs. Wellington had changed her mind and agreed with her husband when Sean had taken her statement. Sean shook his head. He recalled he'd felt bad leaving, but there'd been nothing he could do about that.

Then everything had been immaculate; then there hadn't been neon sculptures of cats on the lawn or pictures of cats painted on the shutters. He couldn't imagine what the neighbors had said when they appeared. That was not true. He did know what they'd said. They'd complained to the town board, which in turn had complained to Susie, who had spent enough money to make the problem go away.

That was what money did, Sean reflected. It fixed things. It made problems disappear. But not in this case. There hadn't been enough money to fix whatever it was that had sent Susie to her grave. And the way she'd died. Sean clicked his tongue against the roof of his mouth while he thought about that. Stabbing someone like that indicated rage. At least in Sean's experience, it did.

He stroked his chin as he pictured Old Lady Connor, with her white hair and her English country house clothes. She would be turning over in her grave if she could see her place now, between the cat statues and the dandelions and the speedwell that were taking over the grass, never mind that the grass needed mowing and weeds were beginning to pop up in the flower beds.

It was amazing how fast weeds grew, Sean reflected as he directed Marvin to the area where the tent had been.

"What about the crime-scene tape?" Marvin asked. It was still looped around small posts, adding a bright note of color to the landscape greens.

"What about it? Drive through it," Sean instructed.

Marvin looked at him. "I don't think we should."

"It'll be fine," Sean assured him. "The worst that can happen is that we'll be arrested."

"Arrested?" Marvin squeaked.

Sean told himself he had to stop teasing Marvin. The problem was it was so much fun. "I'm kidding, Marvin."

Marvin jammed on the brakes. "My father would kill me if I got arrested."

"You're not going to be." Sean raised his right hand. "I swear."

"Are you sure?"

"Of course I'm sure," Sean told him, trying—and failing—to keep from raising his voice. "Why would I lie to you?"

"I guess you wouldn't," Marvin conceded after thinking about the answer a minute too long for Sean's taste.

"You have to learn to relax," Sean said as Marvin started the car back up.

Marvin just grunted and kept driving.

When they got to within two feet of where the tent had been, Sean had Marvin stop the car, and he got out. He wished he could have seen the tent when it was up, as it would have given him a better sense of things, but the rental company had finally come and collected it and the chairs and the tables. The only reminder of what had happened was the crime-scene tape standing sentinel. *Oh well. I'll just have to make do with what I have*, Sean told himself. He took a couple of steps, halted, and studied the scene in front of him, re-creating the day of the wedding in his mind.

According to Libby, two of the tent's flaps had not been secured: the one in the back through which the wedding party had come in and the one behind the altar through which Mrs. Van Trumpet had entered. That flap had opened onto a large field that led down to a grove of trees. Unlike today, the grass would have been dry, but like today, everything would have been in full bloom and the air would have been thick with birdsong. He watched a hawk soaring on the thermals. Marvin joined him.

"What are we looking for?" Marvin asked.

Sean shook his head. He didn't know. "I just want to get a picture of the scene," he explained. "So," he went on, thinking aloud, "the cats were there"—he pointed to where the table that held the presents had been—"when Susie opened the package with the mice, and the cats scattered into the field and the forest. Then Susie collapsed and went back to the house, and in the time it took to round up the cats, someone went into the house and killed her."

Marvin nodded. "That's what Libby said."

"Here's my question."

Marvin waited.

"How did whoever released the mice know that they'd run outside the tent, that they'd go into the fields, once they set them free?"

"I don't know," Marvin allowed.

Sean lit another cigarette. "Think about it. There's no reason to think that the people at the wedding wouldn't have scooped up the cats and that the festivities wouldn't have continued."

"So, what are you saying?" Marvin asked.

"I'm saying that Susie's murderer didn't know chaos would ensue, didn't know that the wedding would be ruined and that Susie would go back to the house."

"Maybe they had a different plan and took advantage of the situation," Marvin said. "Maybe they improvised."

"Possible," Sean conceded. He took another puff of his cigarette and flicked the ashes onto the grass. "Well, I'll tell you one thing. Whoever killed Susie wasn't a professional, that's for sure," Sean said.

"Why do you say that?" Marvin asked.

"A number of reasons." And Sean proceeded to list them, ending with the package Libby and Bernie had received.

"I don't get the last one," Marvin said.

"It's simple," Sean explained. "The more you do, the more traces you leave, the more chance you'll be discovered." He pointed to the house. "Come on," he said. "Enough speculation. I want to look at the actual crime scene."

Chapter 23

Marvin turned his vehicle around, headed up to the house, and parked in the driveway.

"Here goes nothing," Sean said as he got out of the car.

Marvin watched Sean walk up the driveway, climb the three steps to the porch, and ring the doorbell. After a minute went by and no one answered the door, Sean rang the bell again. After another minute had passed, Sean used the knocker. It was a big brass thing shaped like a lion's head, and it made a loud thudding sound—as if someone was storming the castle—when he hit it against the door. Still no one came.

"Should we go?" Marvin called hopefully from his vehicle. "It doesn't seem as if anyone is here." *Please, God, let that be the case*, he said to himself.

"Give it a little more time," Sean answered as he started walking around to the back of the house. Someone was home. He knew that because there were two cars parked in the driveway.

"Hello," he cried as he followed the brick path around to the back of the house.

He'd gotten halfway around when the front door opened.

There was a slight creak. Sean heard it and turned around in time to see a woman who looked like Bernie's description of Grace step out onto the landing. She was wearing jeans and a T-shirt. Her red hair was pushed up in a bun on top of her head.

She wasn't wearing any makeup, and her eyelashes and eyebrows faded into her face. Sean decided she looked thirteen. He hoped she didn't know who he was. In fact, he was counting on it. Otherwise, what he was about to do wouldn't work. Of course, he could always come clean and tell her who he was, but he figured he might get more information this way.

"Yes?" she said, the expression on her face indicating she didn't know who he was.

Excellent, Sean thought as he smiled his most charming smile and retraced his steps. When he was standing in front of Grace, he said, "I hope you don't mind my coming around like this, but someone told me you had some Russian blue kittens for sale."

"How odd," Grace said, looking puzzled. "I don't know why they'd say that."

"You mean you don't, Miss . . ."

"Grace," Grace said quickly. "Grace Abrams."

"The person I was talking to said that you did." Sean looked embarrassed. "They told me that . . . you know . . . after your aunt's unfortunate demise, you were . . . downsizing."

Grace snorted and folded her hands over her chest. "Well, I don't know who you've been talking to, but they're wrong. There are other breeders," Grace told him. "Why don't you try those?"

"I hear yours are the best."

"My aunt certainly thought so," Grace said.

Sean looked bereft. "Can I at least come in and at least look at the kitties?" he asked, his voice wistful. "Just in case you change your mind at some point in the future."

"You can come in and look if you want, but we can't sell them. We'd be in trouble if we did," Grace told him. "We can stay here only as long as the cats do. When they go, so do we."

"Kind of like the apes and Gibraltar," Sean commented.

Grace looked puzzled. "Gibraltar?"

Sean explained. "There's a legend that when the apes leave Gibraltar, so do the English."

"Where's Gibraltar?" Grace asked. "Is that, like, down south?"

"Not quite," Sean said. Didn't they teach geography these days? he wondered as he bent down to pet a Russian blue that had snuck out the door and was weaving in and out of Sean's legs.

"No, no, Sasha," Grace told the cat as she scooped her up and began rubbing her ears. "They always want to get out," she explained.

"Who wouldn't?" Sean noted. "It's an exciting world out there."

Grace indicated the door with a nod of her head. "Are you coming in or not?"

"Coming in," Sean said. He lowered his voice. "This is embarrassing, but could I possibly use your facilities, as well?" He gave an apologetic shrug. "The indignities of getting old, but then, the other choice isn't much better, is it?"

"I suppose not," Grace said.

As he entered, Sean looked back at Marvin. He was sitting with his head in his hands. For a moment, Sean felt a twinge of remorse, but he conquered it and closed the door behind him.

"How many cats do you have?" he asked Grace, looking around. He spotted ten from the hallway.

"Enough," Grace said as she directed him to the bathroom. "More than enough."

"They're beautiful."

Grace smiled. "Yes, they are. Natasha and Boris are in the den. That's just down the hall. I think you'll want to see them. They're quite spectacular."

Sean nodded his thanks. Then he reached up and touched his throat. "Sorry to be such a pain, but could I trouble you for a glass of water?"

"Don't be silly," Grace said, as Sean knew she would. She put Sasha down, turned, and headed toward the kitchen.

This was his chance. Sean started down the hallway as quickly as he could manage. He figured he didn't have much time before Grace came looking for him. He cursed as he almost tripped over the Russian blue beneath his feet. "Sorry," he murmured as the cat scurried away and he regained his footing.

According to Bernie's description, the study was three rooms down, which put it one room before the bathroom. He passed the dining room and the media room. There were cats sitting on the dining room table and on the sofa in the media room. They all looked at him with glacial disdain as he went by. He got to Susie's study and went inside. Someone—he assumed it was Grace or Ralph or both—had put the furniture back where it was supposed to be and had wiped Susie Katz's blood off the floor and the desk chair, but there were still a few spots left.

Sean looked around. The computer was gone, taken, he assumed, by the police, but everything else seemed to be where Libby and Bernie had left it. The desk was the obvious place to look, so that was where Sean began. He opened the desk drawers in quick succession. The first one yielded paper clips, cough drops, several pictures of Russian blues, and a bag of Kit Kat bars, most of which had already been eaten.

The center drawer contained a ream of blank printer paper, several Magic Markers, a Rolodex, and a printed list of all the cat shows in the area for the coming year. A large box of Susie's business cards filled the third drawer. They read: AWARD-WINNING RUSSIAN BLUES FOR THE MOST DISCERNING. CALL THE TSARINA'S CATTERY. *Interesting*, Sean thought as he took two of the cards and slipped them in his pocket. She definitely had had plans.

Then he looked at the five yellow pads neatly stacked on top of the desk. There was one for each month, Susie having written the month's name on the first page in block letters. Sean picked up the pad for May and leafed through it. Caputti's name was listed on the second page, along with his phone number. *Interesting*, Sean thought, remembering Bernie's description of their meeting with Andy Dupont.

Sean went through a few more pages. He found Susie's to-do list for the wedding in the middle of the notepad, while the next pages contained her appointments for the week, the food she'd eaten, the cats' feeding schedules, things to be taken care of, and random doodles. On impulse, he tore several pages out, folded them up, and slipped them in his pocket. He had closed the drawer and had just decided to take a quick peek at the bookshelves, even though there didn't seem to be anything other than knickknacks on them, when he heard voices. They were heading his way.

"I don't have it now," a man was saying.

"But you can get it," the second man said.

Sean recognized the voice of the second man, but not that of the first. It was Andy Dupont. *Curious and curiouser.*

"No, I can't," the first man said.

Then both of them stepped in front of the study door.

"What the hell are you doing here?" Andy Dupont demanded when he saw Sean.

"Who are you?" Ralph asked Sean at the same time. "What the hell are you doing in my house?"

Sean was interested to hear Ralph say, "My house." At least he assumed it was Ralph, because he looked just like his sister.

Andy extended his right hand palm upward. "Ralph, meet our ex-police chief and the father of Bernie and Libby, the women who catered Boris and Natasha's wedding."

Sean nodded toward Andy. "Still in the game, I see." When Andy didn't answer, Sean turned to Ralph. "So how much are you into him for? It sounds like it's a lot."

"Seriously," Ralph said to Sean. "What are you doing here?"

"I let him in," Grace said. She was standing by the doorway, holding Sean's glass of water in her hand.

Everyone turned toward her.

Ralph frowned. He looked puzzled. "You let him in?"

"He was interested in the cats, and he had to use the restroom," Grace told her brother.

"Did you, now?" Andy said.

Sean smiled. "I might have exaggerated a bit on the last item," he confessed.

"So, I repeat, what are you doing here?" Ralph asked him for the third time.

"Honestly, looking at the crime scene," Sean explained. Which was true. "Sometimes I get nostalgic for old times. All that blood and gore. I just have to go out and satisfy my craving." He pointed at Andy. "Ralph, this man is not your friend. How much do you owe him?"

Andy took a step toward Sean. "That's none of your business."

"In this case, I think it is," Sean replied. "It gives Ralph a good motive to knock off his aunt."

"That's ridiculous," Ralph spluttered. "Are you accusing me of murder?"

"As my aunt used to say, 'If the shoe fits,'" Sean said.

Ralph took a step forward, but Andy put a restraining hand on his arm. "Ralph doesn't owe me anything," Andy told Sean.

Sean faced Ralph. "Is that true?"

"Yes," Ralph said, but he didn't sound convincing. "It is."

"You heard him. Now get out," Andy said.

"Then how do you explain what I just heard?" Sean asked.

"I don't have to explain anything to you," Andy said, taking a step toward him. "Get out, or I'm calling the police."

"Nice way to speak to a senior citizen," Sean told him.

Andy took another step toward him. "You used to be a big man around here, but you're not anymore," he sneered. "You're just a worthless, broken-down old man."

Sean turned to Ralph and pointed at Andy. "Are you going to let him order me around like that?" he demanded. "This is your house."

"Maybe you had better go," Ralph said apologetically.

"Can I at least use the bathroom?" Sean asked.

"Out," Andy yelled.

Sean raised his hands in a gesture of surrender. "I'm going. I'm going. No need to lose your temper."

Andy took a step toward him. "I'll do more than that, old man."

For a moment, Sean contemplated punching him out. Then common sense prevailed, and he left.

Chapter 24

"Mission accomplished," Sean told Marvin as he got back in Marvin's car. He dug through his pants pocket and came out with the papers he'd taken and glanced through them as Marvin stepped on the gas.

"Anything interesting?" Marvin asked as he drove down the long road to the gate.

Sean didn't look up. He was still contemplating his little dustup with Andy Dupont. "Could be," Sean said as he folded the papers up and put them back in his pocket. He'd changed his mind. He'd look at the papers later, when he could focus on them. "I'm not sure." For a minute, he thought about how the scene at the Connor estate would have gone when he was younger. When he had a badge. And a gun. And the ability to compel. There would have been none of that stupid charade, no backpedaling in the face of Andy Dupont. He would have just dragged him down to the station. Sometimes old age sucked.

"So, what did you find out?" Marvin asked, interrupting Sean's thoughts.

Sean told him. When he was finished, he said, "Take me to the Council Golf Club."

"Why? Who's there?" Marvin asked as he turned to look at Sean, realized what he was doing, and looked back at the road.

"Leon Caputti."

"I'm not sure that Libby . . . ," Marvin began. Then he stopped. He could feel Sean's glare, even though Sean wasn't looking at him. It was a psychic thing. Marvin backpedaled and searched for a more tactful way to say what he wanted to. He decided he'd be more successful if he appealed to Libby's dad's better nature.

He cleared his throat. "Mr. Simmons," he began, "I'm going to catch hell when your daughter finds out."

"That's ridiculous," Sean replied.

"But true," Marvin assured him, not sure whether what he was saying was in fact true or not. "She's very protective when it comes to you." Which was an accurate statement.

"Then don't tell her," Sean snapped. "She doesn't need to know everything."

So much for that plan, Marvin thought. He'd been about to chirp, "I see we're a little grumpy today," but his sense of self-preservation prevailed and the words died on his lips when he saw the expression on Sean's face. Instead, he focused on driving the car, while Sean opened the window, lit his third cigarette of the day, and thought about what he'd observed at the Connor estate and what it meant—if anything.

While Sean ruminated, Marvin thought about how much he wished Libby's dad still had his own car, but short of a miracle, that wasn't going to happen. He'd just have to get used to this. With that in mind, Marvin drove slowly, careful to keep his eyes on the road, hoping to avoid any more confrontations with Mr. Simmons.

Occasionally, he glanced at his watch. He had a casket

consultation at the funeral home in an hour and a half. Hopefully, he would be back there with time to spare. If not, one of his associates would have to take it. Not that his father would be happy about that. He always told Marvin that a good businessman was a man who tended his business instead of going gallivanting over the countryside. He didn't approve of his son driving Mr. Simmons around, nor did he approve of Marvin playing detective, as he put it. An opinion he expressed often and loudly.

The place Marvin was driving Sean to was ten minutes away. It was located on the outskirts of Longely, and despite its name, it didn't have a golf course or anything to do with Council Park, which was located five and a half miles farther down the road. For that matter, the place wasn't really a club, either, since no dues were paid or membership applications tendered.

The building had been thrown up in the fifties by one Albert Farnelli as a "screw you" to the Oaks Club, which had refused him membership. Farnelli had envisioned his club as the ultimate country club. It was to be constructed out of sandstone and marble and was to boast two swimming pools, a golf course, and a state-of-the art locker room with a sauna, a Jacuzzi, and a steam room. But fate had had something different in store. The only thing that remained from Farnelli's original plan was the kitchen. It wasn't a work of art, but at least it turned out a decent lunch.

The building was a ramshackle affair that looked as if it had been built with an Erector set. It was covered in cheap aluminum siding, and the walls meandered this way and that, finally ending at a concrete patio that overlooked a small pond, which housed a duck family grown fat on tossed bread. The golf course and the swimming pools had never materialized. By that time Farnelli had run out of money, but he'd been too cheap to change the sign hanging over the front door, so he had kept it the way it was.

Over the years, the CGC, as the place was referred to by its habitués, had become the default hangout for a group of guys who liked the fact that their wives didn't like to be there, that the kitchen served the kind of food their wives wouldn't let them eat at home, and that the bartender knew how to make a generous drink.

Leon Caputti was one of the founding members of the group and could be found there five days a week, between the hours of noon and 3:00 p.m. He called the club his office, which it was. The people in the club who knew what Caputti did didn't discuss it, and the ones who didn't know were smart enough not to ask.

"You want me to go in with you?" Marvin inquired when they pulled up in front of the club.

Sean shook his head. *God forbid.* "This could take a while," he said instead. "Go home."

"Are you sure?"

"I'm positive." Which he was. Sean needed privacy for the conversation he was about to have.

"But how will you get back?" Marvin asked, visions of an enraged Libby dancing in his head. He could hear her now. What did he mean, he'd left her father somewhere? There was no good answer for that.

"I'll Uber it," Sean assured him.

"Do you have the app?" Marvin asked.

"App," Sean blustered. Who knew that you needed an app? Not that he was going to admit that. Sean drew himself up. "Of course I have the app. And if they don't come, I can always call a cab. Or Michelle." Michelle was his fiancée.

"I'm—" Marvin began, but Sean cut him off before he completed his sentence.

"Marvin," Sean said. "I appreciate your concern, but I'm perfectly capable of doing this, and if you don't leave, I'm going to have to tell Libby you're cheating and eating Snickers in your car." Marvin had promised Libby he'd lose ten pounds. "I know," Sean told him, anticipating Marvin's next question, "because the wrappers are sticking out from underneath your seat."

Marvin groaned. This was the reward he got for being Mr. Nice Guy, he thought bitterly. "You don't play fair," Marvin complained, regretting the words the moment they were out of his mouth.

Sean smiled. "I never said I did. Really, Marvin, this is for your benefit. You want deniability."

Marvin thought about that for a moment. Mr. Simmons was right. His father wouldn't be happy if he found out he was anywhere around Caputti. "A funeral director must be a man of unblemished character," his dad was fond of saying, although when Marvin had asked him why that was the case, his dad had glared at him and walked away.

"Well, if you get stuck . . . ," Marvin began.

"I'll call," Sean assured him.

As Sean watched Marvin drive away, Sean reflected that the kid had a good heart. Probably better than his. He certainly wouldn't have been carting his girlfriend's dad around when he was Marvin's age. And then he put those thoughts away, pushed the door to the club open, and walked inside. Nothing had changed since Sean had been there last. Not that he expected it would. It was that kind of place.

Chapter 25

Sean passed the desk where you were supposed to sign in, a formality that had been dispensed with a long time ago, or at least that was what Sean supposed, since he'd never seen a sign-in log on the counter or a person behind it in all the times he had come here.

He walked by the lounge, where a television was going and three elderly men were dozing in their chairs, their snoring competing with the news announcer; then he went down the long hallway that led to the dining room. The walls were hung with dusty photos of groups of men that had been taken twenty years ago, and the tan carpet on the floor had a path worn down the center.

Sean could hear the sound of chatter rising and falling at the other end of the hallway. A moment later, he was in the dining room, a banquet hall that Farnelli had envisioned capable of serving two hundred, but fifty was the largest number it had ever achieved. The room itself was paneled in knotty pine, with crests mounted every ten feet or so. The effect was log cabin meets medieval castle.

"Hey," someone shouted.

Sean turned around and looked to see who was yelling.

It was Caputti motioning him over. As Sean moved in his direction, he thought that Caputti had aged well. Unlike himself. Caputti had always been a handsome man, and he still was. His silver hair was styled just so; his bright blue eyes were as sharp as ever; his face was a little plumper, which softened his features. The polo shirt he was wearing was blindingly white, and his tan set off the Rolex he was wearing on his left wrist.

"It's been a while," Caputti said as Sean took a seat across the way from him. "Still a Jameson man?" Caputti asked him as he put his hand up to attract a waiter's attention. Sean nodded as the waiter arrived, and Caputti ordered a bottle, two glasses, and two espressos.

"How's it going?" Sean asked Caputti.

Caputti shrugged. "I'm an old man now. I take it easy."

"Me too," Sean said.

Ten minutes later the waiter arrived with their order. The two men watched the waiter put down the coffees, cream, sugar, two shot glasses, and the bottle of Jameson and then leave.

"Too bad about Rose," Caputti said.

"And Stella," Sean replied. He'd always expected his wife would outlive him, and he suspected Caputti had thought the same.

Caputti nodded. "But the girls are good?"

"Very. And yours?"

"Excellent." Caputti poured each of them a shot. "We're lucky we have daughters."

"Indeed, we are," Sean said, and he lifted his glass. "A toast," he said.

"To our girls," Caputti said and drank. Sean followed suit. Caputti poured out two more shots, and Sean downed that one, as well. "I hear your girls are still pursuing their sideline," Caputti said as he put his glass down.

"Yes, they are," Sean replied.

"Rose would not be pleased," Caputti noted.

"No, she would not." Sean held out his palms. "She hated my business. But the girls are adults. They do what they want."

"Even worse," Caputti said, "now they tell us what to do, as well."

Sean laughed. "Tell me about it," he agreed.

Caputti smiled. "I also hear that you have someone else to keep you busy these days. Congratulations. I'm impressed."

"You do hear everything, don't you?" Sean noted.

Caputti gave a modest shrug. "People talk, and I listen. If I recall, you're a pretty good listener yourself."

"I've had my moments," Sean allowed.

"I was surprised you never opened up your own agency after what happened with your department," Caputti continued.

"Well," Sean said, "in the beginning, when I got kicked out, I was going to. But I kept putting it off, and after a while I realized I didn't want to do that anymore."

"Except to help your daughters," Caputti clarified.

Sean took a sip of his espresso. It was excellent. "Yes, except to help them. And," he went on, "when something puzzles me."

"You don't like to be puzzled?" Caputti asked.

Sean shook his head. "No. It annoys me, and I'm too old to be annoyed."

"Except by your girlfriend," Caputti said.

Sean laughed again and took another sip of his espresso. "They can do that, can't they?"

"Indeed, they can," Caputti said. "But at our age we're smart enough to do what they want. Makes life"—he hesitated for a moment—"more pleasant." Then he finished his espresso and changed the subject. "So, what can I do for you?"

"I have some questions."

"What makes you think I can answer them?" Caputti asked.

Sean spread his hands out. "You said it yourself. You hear things."

"And I do owe you," Caputti said after nodding to a man walking by the table. Sean had helped Caputti out with his youngest daughter a couple of years ago, when she'd been going down a bad road.

"I wasn't going to say that," Sean replied. And he hadn't intended to.

"You don't have to. What do you want to know?"

Sean picked up his teaspoon and balanced it across his espresso cup. "Let's start with Andy Dupont, shall we?"

Caputti made a disgusted noise. "Totally out of control. I'd be surprised if he's around much longer."

"How so?"

"You know what happens when someone fails to show the proper respect in this business."

Indeed, Sean did. "That bad?"

Caputti grimaced. "He thinks he's Al Capone."

"And his father can't do anything?"

"Believe me, his father has tried," Caputti said. "I've even tried, after his father asked me to have a talk with him."

"And?"

Caputti's eyes grew hard. "I won't repeat what he said to me. The only reason nothing's happened to him is out of respect to his father."

"So, Andy runs a gambling operation," Sean asked, making sure his facts were accurate.

"A small one in the scheme of things. Not really worth

bothering about." Caputti poured Sean another shot of Jameson and filled his own glass, as well. "Which might be his saving grace. Literally."

Sean picked up the drink and knocked it back as he reflected that it was a good thing he wasn't driving today. "Let's say, hypothetically speaking, that someone was late paying Andy back."

"I take it you're referring to Ralph Abrams," Caputti asked after he'd downed his shot.

Sean gave a small nod of admiration. "You *do* know everything."

"Word gets around."

"So it would seem," Sean said. "Did you happen to hear how much Ralph was into him for?"

"Somewhere between fifteen and twenty large, but I could be wrong."

"And if Ralph couldn't pay it back?" Sean asked, even though he was pretty sure he knew what the answer would be.

Caputti steepled his fingers together. "I'm told Andy's an old-fashioned kind of guy."

Sean raised an eyebrow. "Ah."

"He has people," Caputti said.

"We're not talking social secretary here, I assume," Sean replied, thinking of Libby and Bernie's description of Andy's friends.

"I've been told that sometimes his people engage in more . . . strenuous physical activities than managing his calendar," Caputti said.

"Activities that could cause physical harm?"

"Among other things. But I'm an old guy. I just know what I hear." Caputti's foot started to jiggle up and down. "But if I were Ralph and those guys showed up at my door and I had an aunt with lots of cash, I'd ask her for some, and if she didn't give it to me, I'd be really pissed."

Sean leaned forward. "You know this for a fact?"

"No. I'm just . . ." Caputti waved his hand in the air. "How you say . . . ? Hypothesizing . . ."

"You're saying Ralph killed his aunt out of anger?"

Caputti shrugged. "Sure. Why not? It's possible."

"Anything is possible." Sean paused for a moment. Then he said, "You're not trying to point me in another direction, are you?"

Caputti laughed. "Why would I do that?"

"Because of this." And Sean reached into his pants pocket and took out the pieces of paper he'd taken from Susie's legal pad, smoothed them out with the edge of his hand, and passed them on to Caputti.

Caputti looked at the papers, then looked up at Sean. "What am I looking for here?"

Sean pointed to Caputti's name in the middle of the page. "Your name. It's circled."

Caputti reached over, took the reading glasses that were sitting on the table, and put them on. He read his name on the page. "Fancy that," he said, then slipping the glasses off and putting them back where they had been. "And your point is what?"

Sean lifted an eyebrow. "You knew her."

"Since when is that a crime?"

"I'm not saying it is."

"Of course I knew her, Sean. Why wouldn't I? It's a small town," Caputti protested.

"And you two met at the local library and just happened to hit it off?"

"In a way. We met at the fund-raiser for the new high school football field."

"That was very civic minded of you," Sean commented as he folded his arms across his chest and watched Caputti fiddle with his watch.

"I like to contribute to the community when I can," Caputti said.

"Very commendable," Sean said. "Come on," he said after a minute had gone by. "Why is your name on this pad?"

"Because Susie was inviting me to tea."

"Seriously," Sean urged. "This isn't an official inquiry. I'm just trying to help out my girls and put some of the pieces together for them. Keep them out of Lucy's way."

Caputti relented. "I don't suppose there's any harm in telling you. I lent her some money. She wanted to buy the paper on a couple of her neighbors' houses."

"Surely, she must have had the money for that?"

"She said her money was tied up. I didn't ask. It was none of my business." Caputti paused for a minute before continuing. "She was a spiteful woman. Taking someone's house away because they said something bad about your cats. The house you've grown up in." He shook his head. "Who would do something like that?"

"Evidently, she would," Sean replied.

"That was a rhetorical question," Caputti observed.

"I know," Sean said. "I was just emphasizing the point."

Satisfied, Caputti continued. "She was just one of those people who couldn't let anything go. You got on the wrong side of her and"—Caputti snapped his fingers—"she'd go for your throat. I'd rather deal with someone like Andy Dupont. At least you know what you got there. Susie would smile to your face, stab you in the back, and twist the blade till it came out the other side. She was a mean, mean lady."

"And yet you did business with her," Sean pointed out.

"Money is money. I wouldn't have if I'd known that someone was going to kill her," Caputti added.

"You lost money?" Sean asked.

"Well, you don't make money from a corpse," Caputti

replied, pointing out the obvious. "Unless, of course, you're an undertaker. There's a definite downside to doing things off the books," he reflected.

"I suppose there is." This was not a problem that Sean anticipated having. He looked at his watch. It was time to go home.

Chapter 26

When Sean left the club and went to call a cab, he realized two things: he'd forgotten his phone and his wallet at home. This was not good. Now, some people would have gone back inside and used Caputti's phone to call a taxi, then paid for it when they got back to their flat. Some people. But Sean wasn't one of them. That would have been an admission that he was losing his marbles. Instead, he decided to walk a couple of miles and hitch the rest of the way.

Why not? he reasoned. It was a perfect day. Low seventies. A light breeze. Sunshine. In short, a good day to be outside. Anyway, he might not get a chance to do this again. Who knew how long the MS remission he was in would last? According to his doctor, he could go back to having to use a cane at any time. He should take advantage of this opportunity while he could.

Sean felt pleased with himself as he strolled along Ash Road. He listened to the birds singing, noticed the wildflowers growing along the road, and considered what he had learned about Susie Katz. It amazed him that she had needed to borrow money from Caputti, but he supposed that when you got to that level of wealth, you had an easy come, easy go kind of attitude when it came to cash. Or at least she had.

He was wondering how you could lose that much money when he saw the unmistakable profile of A Little Taste of Heaven's van in the distance. *Oh no*, he thought as it came toward him. This was not good. This was not good at all. He let out a groan. His first thought was to run, but there was no place to go. The road was a straight shot. His second thought was to hide, but there was no place to hide, either, so he puffed out his chest and braced for the inevitable. He knew that Libby would not be pleased. Which turned out to be an understatement.

"I can't believe you were going to walk the whole way," Libby said after her dad had gotten in the van.

Sean could see that his daughter was quivering with suppressed emotion. If he was smart, he would just say sorry. But he didn't. Instead, he said, "I was going to hitch when I got tired," words he regretted as soon as they had left his mouth, given the look on his daughter's face. Talk about making a bad situation worse.

"Hitch?" Libby squeaked, almost going off the road. "Hitch?"

"It would have been fine," Sean countered.

"No, it wouldn't have been," Libby replied. "You could have gotten hurt. You could have been killed."

"Let's not exaggerate," Sean retorted. "I used to hitch all the time back in the day."

"But this isn't back in the day." Libby took two deep breaths to get hold of herself. When her dad did this kind of stuff, it made her crazy. That was why she'd sent Marvin with him in the first place.

Sean turned to her. "Listen, I just wanted to see if I

could walk a couple of miles. Is that so hard to understand?"

"What if something had happened?" Libby asked.

"But it didn't."

"But it could have."

"And a comet could plow into the earth and destroy it."

"Come on, Dad," Libby said, playing her trump card.
"Be fair. I have enough to worry about without worrying
about you, as well."

"Sorry," Sean said, now properly chastened. Then he
muttered under his breath, "Guilt, thy name is woman." It
was an ability his wife had had and his daughters had in-
herited.

"What did you say?" Libby asked.

"Nothing. I didn't say anything," Sean hastily responded.

Libby gave him her patented "I don't believe you" glance.

"I was trying to help," Sean explained.

"Helping would have been talking to Marie," Libby
told him, still unable to let things go.

"Fine." Insulted, Sean turned his head away and crossed
his arms over his chest.

"Don't sulk," Libby said.

"I'm not sulking," Sean shot back as he gazed at the
scenery going by. If Libby wanted to be that way, it was
okay by him.

Libby decided she had gone too far, and she forced herself
to apologize, even though in her heart of hearts, she thought
she was right. "Did you find anything out?" Libby asked,
throwing a peace offering to her dad.

"As a matter of fact, I did," Sean said.

"Are you going to tell me?" Libby asked.

"I suppose," Sean answered grudgingly, though he was
dying to. Then he waited for Libby to coax it out of him.
Five minutes later, he judged she'd coaxed enough, and he

told her what he'd discovered by talking to Andy Dupont and Caputti, as well as his conclusions from seeing the murder scene.

"Interesting," Libby said.

"Interesting?" Sean was miffed. "I think it's a little bit more than interesting," he replied.

"You're right. It is," Libby agreed.

They had ridden a couple of minutes in silence when another thought occurred to Sean.

"How did you know where I'd be?" he asked Libby, even though he had a pretty good idea what her answer would be.

Libby responded promptly. "ESP."

"Right. Marvin told you, didn't he?" Sean said as they neared the shop.

"Kinda."

"Define *kinda.*"

"Okay. He did. He was worried about you."

Sean snorted.

"Well, he was," Libby protested.

Sean didn't reply. He was too busy thinking about whether or not he should reveal the Snickers bar wrappers to Libby.

"And don't you dare say anything to him," Libby warned.

"Who, me?" He decided the Snickers bar wrappers revelation would probably backfire.

Libby put on her "I mean business" face. "I mean it, Dad."

Sean pointed to himself. "I'd never do anything of the kind."

Now it was Libby's turn to snort. "He just has your best interests at heart."

Sean knew this, but it didn't help. He was still pissed.

He opened his mouth to make a snotty comment, but then his survival skills took over and he shut up, as it occurred to him that he'd already made enough trouble for himself. He didn't say anything for the last two blocks of the drive home.

"Ah, the prodigal traveler returns," Bernie quipped as Sean descended from the van. She'd seen him from the store window and come out to lend her moral support in the face of her sister's disapproval.

"I suppose you're upset with me, too," Sean said, grimacing.

Bernie laughed. "Not at all."

Sean brightened. "Good girl." Having one of his daughters mad at him was bad; two was worse, even if he was right.

"Do you know what he was going to do?" Libby demanded of Bernie as she walked over to where her sister was standing.

"Take a rocket to the moon? Rob a bank?"

Libby didn't crack a smile. "He was going to hitch a ride," she told Bernie.

Bernie shrugged. "So what?"

Libby put her hands on her hips. "What do you mean, so what?"

"Exactly what I said," Bernie told her sister. "It's not as if we're living in the Southeast Bronx, for heaven's sake. Longely is a pretty safe place. You know what the trouble with you is, Libby?" Bernie continued. "You worry too much."

"Well, excuse me for being concerned when I saw Dad's wallet and phone on the dresser after Marvin called," Libby sputtered. "Excuse me for caring."

"It would have been fine," Sean insisted, now heartily sorry that he'd started this whole mess.

Bernie patted him on the shoulder. "I'm sure it would have been."

"That isn't the point, Bernie," Libby objected. "The point is—"

Bernie interrupted her sister. "You know what? Let's eat. We can discuss this later."

"More food, less drama" was her motto.

"Yes, let's," Sean agreed enthusiastically, happy for a distraction. Also, he was hungry.

Libby agreed as well, albeit reluctantly.

Chapter 27

Bernie looked around the room and smiled. She'd made the right decision. Everyone looked happier. How could you not be when you were dining on poached salmon with dill sauce; new potatoes; and a tomato, cucumber, and avocado salad sprinkled with Maldon sea salt flakes and roasted pine nuts? It was a meal that said summer was coming. A meal that spoke to the heart.

"I guess I was hungry," Libby admitted as she bit into a new potato. The combination of the crisp roasted skin, creamy inside, melting butter, and sparkling salt never failed to satisfy.

"Me too," Sean said as he fed a small piece of salmon to the cat, then ate the rest of it himself. Copper River salmon. Nothing could beat it, and this piece was poached to perfection, a difficult feat to achieve. *Sometimes*, he thought, *you can't beat the classics*. They'd endured for a reason.

"I hear you had a nice chat with your old friend," Bernie said, beginning the conversation about her dad's afternoon adventures.

"He's not my friend," Sean protested.

"Acquaintance, then," Libby said. She'd never liked the man. She didn't like what he represented. Her mom had called him a wolf in sheep's clothing. Actually, she'd called him a lot worse than that. For some reason, though, her dad had always liked Caputti.

"Anything interesting come out of the conversation?" Bernie asked Sean.

"I think so," Sean said. And he told her what he'd told Libby.

"I find the fact that Susie Katz needed to borrow money interesting," Bernie observed when her dad was through talking.

"It is," Sean said. He waved his fork in the air, then speared a piece of avocado. "But, on the other hand, she wasn't exactly without funds. After all, she put enough money in trust to support the running of her house, pay Grace and Ralph, and keep the cats in caviar—so to speak. Not to mention pay you. She did have money for the party. A lot of money."

"True," Libby said as she tasted the salad. It was good. Not great, but good. Some fresh corn and ground black pepper might be enough to make it superlative. "If I had to guess, I'd bet," she said after she'd swallowed, "that Susie put the bulk of her money in some sort of untouchable trust and then borrowed from everyone. And they lent it to her because they thought she had money to pay them back."

"Which she had no intention of doing," Bernie said.

"That's why she was rich," Libby said. "Always use other people's money if you can. I read that in one of those 'how to get rich' books."

Bernie sighed. "I wish we could pull that off."

"Me too," Libby agreed.

"I could see where that kind of thing would really piss

people off," Sean observed. "But that's really not germane to why Susie was murdered. In this case, the motive was personal."

"Exactly," Bernie said. "I mean, think about it. Who did Susie invite to the wedding? People who hated her. Why did they hate her? They all had run-ins with her over cats. Allison tried to set Susie's cats free at the cat show, Marie complained to the CFA's powers that be about the lineage of Susie's cats, cats Susie had spent thousands and thousands of dollars on, while Charlene went to the zoning board to complain about the number of cats Susie had in her house and asked that they be removed."

"Don't forget, she was going to take Charlene's and Marie's houses, as well," Sean reminded them. "On the other hand, we're not sure about the timeline for that, so let's leave that out of the equation for the moment."

"Agreed. Let's discuss Grace and Ralph instead," Libby suggested.

"Ralph's easy," Bernie replied. "He had gambling debts, he was being threatened with bodily harm, and his aunt, I'm assuming, could have helped him out and wouldn't."

Libby ate her last salad leaf. "And Grace?"

Bernie remembered the look on Grace's face when she'd shown them the dress Susie had made her wear. "Maybe she was tired of being Susie's trained seal. After all, with Susie dead, she gets her freedom."

"Not exactly," Libby said. "She still has the cats."

"But she likes the cats," Bernie reminded her sister. "And she gets the house and money to run it and no one to tell her what to do."

Libby nodded. What Bernie had said was true.

"And as long as we're talking about people, what about Mrs. Van Trumpet?" Sean asked, continuing the conversation. "After all, she was there, and you said you can't account for her whereabouts between the time Susie opened the box of mice and Susie's death."

"I think she got in her car and went home," Bernie said. Sean sought to clarify. "Think or know?"

"Think," Bernie replied.

"Her car was gone when you went into the house?"

"I think so, but I'm not sure," Bernie confessed. "I don't remember." She turned to her sister. "Do you remember?"

Libby shook her head. "No. I didn't look. I was just thinking of getting the cats back in the house before they got out of their carriages." She ate the last piece of her salmon and thought about dessert. She was almost positive they still had a third of a peach pie left downstairs. "But why would she want to kill Susie?" she asked, taking up the conversational thread again. "Of everyone there, she has the weakest reason. She was getting paid to perform a service. She didn't have a relationship with her."

"Are you sure?" Sean asked.

Libby looked sheepish. "I'm pretty sure."

"But?" Sean prodded.

"I'm not positive."

"Exactly," Sean said, and he sat back in his chair, satisfied that he'd made his point. "What do we know about her?"

"Aside from the obvious," Libby replied, "not much."

Bernie got up. "Let's see what I can find out online," she said, and she went to get her laptop.

"And I'm going to bring up the last of the peach pie," Libby announced.

Sean rubbed his hands together and sighed in contentment. Libby's peach pie was his favorite, but then so was her strawberry-rhubarb, blueberry, apple, and pumpkin. In his opinion, pie was the perfect end to a meal. Or the perfect snack. Or breakfast.

An hour later, every last crumb of the peach pie had

been eaten, the coffee had been drunk, and Bernie had read everything online that she could about Gertrude Van Trumpet. There wasn't much there. No Web site, which surprised Bernie. Just ten articles, all of them laudatory, but not one of them mentioned a way to get in touch with Mrs. Van Trumpet. Next, Bernie had tried several online phone books, but she wasn't listed there, either.

"That's weird," Libby said. "You'd think she'd want to make it easy to get ahold of her."

"Maybe she's so exclusive that you need a personal introduction," Bernie said, hypothesizing. "Like with Goyard bags. You can't buy them online. You have to go to a store. That's how they keep their cachet. Limited access."

"Well, Susie had to get the number from somewhere," Libby observed.

"Perhaps it's on Susie's Rolodex," Sean suggested.

"Rolodex? What's a Rolodex?" Bernie asked.

Sean shook his head. God, did he feel old at times like these. He explained.

"Do people still have those?" Bernie asked in a faintly condescending tone.

"There was life before Google, you know," Sean snapped. "People actually had to know things back then."

Bernie apologized. "You think Susie had one?"

"I know she did," Sean told her. "I saw it in her desk drawer."

"And that Van Trumpet's phone number is there?" Bernie asked.

Sean shrugged. "There's only one way to find out. Call Grace and ask her."

Libby did. Grace answered on the fourth ring, and Libby explained what she wanted.

"No problem," Grace told her. "Hold on. I'll check right now."

She came back on the line a couple of minutes later with Mrs. Van Trumpet's address and phone number. Sean couldn't help smirking as Libby wrote the information down on the back of an old envelope. *One for the old guys*, he thought.

"I think you should go see her," Sean said.

"Definitely," Libby agreed. Over the years, she'd found that in person always worked best. "She lives in Great Hill."

Bernie raised an eyebrow. Somehow, she'd expected her to live someplace swankier. "Interesting."

"Not what I would have expected," Libby noted.

"Not at all," Bernie said as she collected the dishes to bring downstairs. At least, she thought, Great Hill wasn't that far away.

"And while you do that," Sean said, "I'm going to do a little more poking around and see what I can come up with."

"Just be careful, Dad," Libby said.

"I'm always careful," Sean huffed. Then he turned on the TV. As far as he was concerned, there had been enough discussion about his abilities for one night.

Chapter 28

Day four . . .

Contrary to its name, Great Hill was built on a stretch of flatland situated two miles in from the Hudson River. Maybe there'd been a big hill there once upon a time, but that had been a long time ago. Now the only hill in town was a gentle rise as you came off the highway onto Main Street.

The place had come into existence seventy years ago. It had been populated, and still was, by the people who worked for the rich folk in the surrounding area. If the town had a claim to fame, it was that the place was instantly forgettable. It wasn't cute; it wasn't awful; it wasn't great. It simply was.

You could drive through there and not remember anything about it when you drove out, basically because there was nothing to remember. Bernie had always thought that that had been the town's salvation, because while the other townships around it had fallen prey to housing hysteria as people who were priced out of New York City moved to Westchester, Great Hill had been skipped. Housing prices had grown at a snail's pace. So far at least.

"It won't be long before this place is discovered," Libby predicted as Bernie looked for the street they had to turn onto.

"You said that last year," Bernie pointed out. "But I haven't seen an espresso bar or a farm-to-table restaurant yet."

"But you will. It's only a matter of time."

"Everything is just a matter of time." But what Libby had said was true. These days people were snapping up anything that was available, even if it was a two-hour commute into the city. Not for the first time, Bernie thought about how lucky she was to be living upstairs from where she worked.

"There," Libby said, pointing to a sign that said Elm Street.

Bernie nodded and turned in. The street had an unloved feel to it. As if the people who lived there slept and ate there and nothing more. The houses looked as if they'd been built in the early fifties by one developer, because they all looked the same. Small colonials with three-step porches leading up to an entranceway painted white, with dark green trim. All the houses had postage-stamp front yards ringed with white picket fences. A few of the houses had foundation plantings, but most didn't.

"Maybe the cat marriage business isn't as good as we thought it was," Libby commented as she looked for the number of Mrs. Van Trumpet's house.

"Either that or Mrs. Van Trumpet is very frugal," Bernie replied as she spied the place she and Libby were looking for. She pulled over and parked. "Maybe we should have called," she said, referring to the fact that there was no car in the driveway. But then, she reflected, if they had done that, they would have lost the element of surprise.

"Her vehicle could be in the garage," Libby remarked,

although the garage was so small, it would be difficult to fit in anything besides a really tiny compact car.

"Let's find out, shall we?" Bernie replied as she and Libby exited their van.

When they got up to the doorway, Libby rang the bell. They could hear it chiming inside, but no one answered.

"Try again," Bernie said to Libby. "Maybe she's in the bathroom."

Another minute went by. No one came to the door. Libby rang the bell again.

"Definitely not in," Libby said after she'd walked down the porch steps and peered into the garage. It was empty.

Bernie was rummaging around in her bag for a pen and a piece of paper so she could leave a note when an elderly woman wearing a plaid cotton housecoat and felt slippers came out of the house next to Mrs. Van Trumpet's and began slowly walking over to where the sisters were standing.

"Are you looking for Gladys?" she asked. Her voice had a slight tremor to it.

"No," Libby answered. "We're looking for a Gertrude Van Trumpet."

The neighbor frowned and shook her head. "Then I'm afraid you have the wrong house. Gladys Trainer lives here."

"Are you sure?" Bernie asked.

"I'm positive," the neighbor said. "I've lived next to her for the past ten years."

Bernie thanked her. She was apologizing for any inconvenience she and her sister might have caused when something occurred to her. "Excuse me," she asked the neighbor, "but what does Gladys look like?"

The woman peered at her suspiciously and pulled her housecoat closer to her chest. "Why do you want to know?"

Bernie improvised. "You see, she won a raffle from our

store, A Little Taste of Heaven, for a peach pie, but I'm having a hard time deciphering the writing on the ticket." Bernie smiled. "So is my sister. Isn't that right, Libby?"

Libby startled. She hadn't expected to participate in the conversation. "Oh yes. Absolutely."

"I just wanted to make sure I had the right address before I dropped off the pie," Bernie continued.

"Gladys likes pie," the neighbor said. She loosened her grip on her housecoat.

A good sign, Libby thought. This time it was her turn to smile. "Everyone likes pie."

Her suspicions laid to rest, the woman told Libby and Bernie what they wanted to know.

"She's really short. Black hair. Dark eyes—"

Bernie interrupted. "How short?"

"Short, short." The woman demonstrated by bringing her hand to her shoulder.

"And her hair is black?" Libby asked.

"That's what I said," the neighbor replied.

Libby frowned. Mrs. Van Trumpet's hair had definitely not been black at the wedding. But maybe she'd dyed it since then. Or she'd been wearing a wig at the wedding.

"Like I just told you," the neighbor continued, "you have the wrong house, and Gladys wouldn't be there, anyway. She's working down at the auto parts store over on Randall Road. Maybe the address you want is Elm Avenue. That's over on the other side of town. It's easy to get confused."

The sisters thanked her and left.

"So, what do you think?" Bernie asked Libby when they were back in the van.

"I think we should check out the auto parts store."

"I think so, too," Bernie agreed as she consulted her phone. There was only one auto parts store listed in Great Hill, and it was named Auto Parts.

Five minutes later, they'd found the place. Located in a small strip mall, the store was wedged between a hardware store and a tanning salon.

"Imaginative," Libby said, pointing to the neon sign in the window that said AUTO PARTS.

"Sometimes, direct is best," Bernie noted as she maneuvered the van into a parking spot. She had just turned off the motor when Libby pointed to a woman coming out of the auto parts store.

"Look," she said. "Is that who I think it is?"

Bernie studied the woman. She was as short as Gertrude Van Trumpet, but that was where the similarities ended. Her hair was cut pixie style, and it was black, just like the neighbor had said. Her clothes were different, too. Gladys was wearing flats, tight-fitting jeans, and a T-shirt. She even moved differently.

"I believe it is," Bernie said. She clicked her tongue against her front teeth. Seeing Gertrude Van Trumpet in her present incarnation made Bernie think that she'd seen her somewhere else in a different context. A very different context. She just couldn't remember where. It would come to her, though. Of that, she was sure. It always did. "Let's find out, shall we?"

The sisters got out of their van and hurried across the parking lot. Gertrude or Gladys was just reaching for the door handle of her vehicle when Bernie and Libby intercepted her.

Now that they were closer, Bernie and Libby could see the resemblance to Gertrude Van Trumpet. It was true the hair was different, as were the eye color and the clothes, but this woman's height and build were the same, as were the shape of her head and the tilt of her nose.

"Hi, Gertrude," Bernie said. "Nice to see you again."

"You've made a mistake," Gertrude stated, daring them to think otherwise. "My name is Gladys Trainer."

"Not when you were officiating at Boris and Natasha's wedding, it wasn't," Libby observed.

"I don't know what you're talking about," Gertrude said, but Bernie could hear the notes of resignation in her voice.

Bernie laughed. "Seriously? There's no point in playing it this way."

Gertrude bit her lip. The sisters watched her decide what to do. Finally, she shrugged and gave it up. "So what if I am?" she demanded. "I didn't do anything wrong."

"That's what we're here to talk to you about," Libby told her.

Gertrude looked up at her. "Why should I talk to you? I don't want to, and you can't make me."

Bernie smiled sweetly. "This is true. But I ask you to consider this. If you don't talk to us, I'm going to take pictures of you and post them on the Internet."

"So what?" Gertrude asked, but Bernie could see from the slight twitch starting in Gertrude's right eye that the threat had upset her. "Do whatever you want. Why would I care?"

"Maybe you won't," Bernie said. "Maybe I'm wrong. I just figured you have a lucrative side business going and you wouldn't want to see it go down the toilet. These days branding counts, and for you, I suspect, it means everything. Gertrude Van Trumpet. Gladys Trainer." Bernie moved her hands up and down as if she were weighing something. "Big difference here."

"On the other hand," Libby added, "if you want to chat, our lips, as they say, are sealed about your real identity."

Gertrude didn't say anything.

Bernie pointed to her watch. "Hey, Gertrude—or should I say Gladys?—time's a-wasting. What's it going to be? Decide."

"I . . . ," Gertrude began. Then she stopped talking and contemplated the situation she was in. When it came down to it, she realized she really didn't have much choice. "Okay," she said. "There's a diner ten blocks over. You can follow me there."

"Good decision," Libby told her.

"Does the place have a name?" Bernie asked, in the unlikely event they got separated.

Gertrude shook her head. "Nope. There's just a neon sign that says DINER in the window."

"Figures," Bernie muttered as she made for the van. "I've seen her somewhere before," Bernie said to her sister as she hopped in.

"Yeah. At the cat wedding."

"No. Somewhere else," Bernie said as she put her key in the ignition, turned the van on, and followed Gertrude's vehicle out of the parking lot.

Chapter 29

In keeping with the rest of the town, the diner was a place you could go by a hundred times and not notice. Located at the intersection of Concord and Stanton, it looked like a hundred other places of its type. The booths along the window were faded, the tables and chairs that made up the rest of the furnishings looked as if they'd been around for as long as the town had, the tiles on the blue-and-white linoleum floor were cracked with age, and the travel posters on the walls were covered with a thin layer of grease.

There were five people in the diner when Gladys Trainer, as Bernie and Libby had come to think of Gertrude, and the sisters walked in. Everyone nodded at Gladys, and she nodded back as she walked to the rear and grabbed a booth. Libby and Bernie slid into the seat across from her. A moment later, the waitress, an overweight middle-aged woman with bleached blond hair that looked like straw, gold hoop earrings that were pulling down her earlobes, and a large tattoo on her arm that read JOHN, I WILL ALWAYS LOVE YOU, came by to take their order.

"The usual?" she asked Gladys, tapping her pencil on

her ordering pad. Gladys nodded, and the waitress turned to Libby and Bernie. "And you?"

"Just coffee," Libby said.

The waitress pointed to the sign posted in front of the cash register. FIVE-DOLLAR MINIMUM UNTIL SIX O'CLOCK.

"What happens after six?" Libby asked.

"We close," the waitress told her.

"Makes sense," Bernie commented. She wanted to ask the waitress if she still loved John, but she ordered two coffees and two cheese Danish for herself and her sister instead. She didn't expect much in the food and coffee department, and she wasn't disappointed. The coffee was weak, and the Danish were stale. Bernie took a bite of hers and pushed it to the center of the table. *Not worth the calories*, she thought.

"Just out of curiosity," Libby said after the waitress had plunked their orders down on the table and gone back to her magazine, "do you do a good business marrying cats?"

"Good enough," Gladys replied. She poured some sugar into her coffee and stirred it in with a teaspoon. "Cat people are nuts."

"We've noticed," Libby said. She took a sip of her coffee and pushed her mug away. It tasted like dishwater. "And yet you're working at an auto parts store and living in Great Hill," she observed. "You can't be doing that well."

Gladys shrugged. "Well enough."

"Are you hiding out here?" Bernie joked.

Gladys smiled for the first time. "Exactly. No one ever visits this place. There's no reason to—"

Libby interrupted. "How long have you been doing it for?" she asked.

"Marrying cats?" Gladys thought for a minute. "Going on ten years now."

"How do people find you?" Bernie asked.

Gladys put the teaspoon down and ran her index finger around the rim of her cup. "I'm strictly word of mouth," Gladys replied. "Adds to the cachet."

"See?" Bernie said to Libby. "Told you. These days, when you can find anything on the Internet, people think not finding it makes it special."

Gladys took a bite of her sandwich, chewed, and swallowed. "I didn't have anything to do with Susie's death," she announced after she'd taken her second bite. "I assume that's what you want to talk to me about."

"So you say," Libby said.

"Yes, I do," Gladys replied.

"Where were you after Susie went into her house?" Bernie asked her. "Because I didn't see you outside, looking for the cats."

"That's because I wasn't. I went home," Gladys said.

"Why?" Libby asked.

Gladys gave her an incredulous look. "What do you mean, why? My job was done. There was no reason to stick around and look for the bloody Russian blues."

"And you can prove that?" Libby asked.

"Actually, I can," Gladys said. "Not that it's any of your business."

"Unfortunately, it is." And Libby explained why.

Gladys sniggered. "I'm sorry I missed it. Allison getting punched." She shook her head. "It must have been quite the scene."

"You don't sound exactly heartbroken about Susie's death," Bernie observed.

Gladys finished the first half of her sandwich and went

on to the second. "Of course I am," she said in a completely unconvincing tone. "I'm very upset."

Bernie snorted. "I can see you're devastated beyond belief."

Gladys looked up. "What? You don't believe me?" she demanded.

"No, I don't," Bernie answered. "No one liked her. In fact, everyone she invited to that wedding except for us"— Bernie pointed at her sister and then at herself—"hated her. That's why she invited them in the first place. Why should you be different than them?"

"Simple. Because like you, I performed a service." And with that, Gladys finished the rest of her sandwich, wiped her hands on a napkin, then balled it up and threw it on the table, after which she finished her coffee. "If we're through here . . . ," she said.

"Not quite," Libby told her.

"I told you what you want to know," Gladys protested.

Bernie rested her elbows on the table and leaned forward. "Just a few more questions."

"Fine," Gladys said, even though it clearly wasn't, a fact she demonstrated by drumming her fingers on the table.

"You got paid before the ceremony?" Bernie asked.

"After," Gladys answered quickly, too quickly, in Bernie's estimation.

"So, you're out your fee?" Bernie asked.

Gladys shrugged again, spread her fingers apart, and studied her nails. They were pearlescent. Bernie liked the way the light shone on them. "It happens."

Libby studied Gladys for a moment. The twitch was back. "I'd want to collect my money," Libby said.

"Me too," Bernie said. "In fact, I'd probably follow Susie back to her house and ask for my money."

"Well, I'm not you. I went home," Gladys told her.

"Did you?" Libby challenged. "Maybe you did, or maybe you didn't."

"Ask Grace. She'll tell you. My car wasn't in the driveway."

"So what?" Libby said. "You could have gotten in your car, driven off, changed your mind, turned around, come back, and parked around the other side of Susie's house and gone in," Libby pointed out.

"Definitely," Bernie said. "I could see you asking for your money and Susie telling you she wouldn't pay you. She would do something like that. Maybe even blaming you for the mice—"

"I had nothing to do with the mice . . . ," Gladys said, interrupting.

Bernie held up a hand. "I didn't say you did. I said that's what Susie would have said. And then you got angry—and why wouldn't you?—and one thing led to another, and you picked up the letter opener and stabbed her." Bernie turned to her sister. "What do you think, Libby?"

"Sounds like a possibility," Libby said as Bernie looked at her phone.

Gladys turned to Libby. "You don't know anything," she told her. "You're just making this up on the fly."

"Then enlighten me," Libby urged as she picked a little of the cheese out of the center of her Danish and ate it. Then she ate a little more. She couldn't help it. She was hungry, and cheese Danish were one of her favorite things. Even when they were old and stale.

"If you must know, I was doing the wedding for free," Gladys huffed. "So, so much for that theory," she added a triumphant note in her voice.

"And why would you do that?" Libby asked.

Gladys smiled. "Because I'm a nice person."

Libby snorted. "Surely, you can come up with something better than that."

"I think I know why," Bernie answered, and she pushed her cell phone across the table. "I thought you looked familiar," Bernie said to Gladys as she pointed to the screen on her phone. "She was blackmailing you, wasn't she? That's why you weren't charging her. You were there, like everyone else, because Susie was doing a power trip on you."

"Don't be ridiculous," Gladys blustered, pushing the phone back to Bernie. "Where do you get this stuff from? Just because it's on the Internet doesn't mean it's true."

"In this case it does," Bernie said.

"Let me," Libby said, and she leaned across the table and grabbed Bernie's phone. She whistled as she read. "Nice," she said when she was done. "Bedford Hills Correctional Facility. Not bad. Manslaughter. No wonder you use a different name."

"I don't run cons anymore," Gladys said quietly. "I didn't mean to do it then. Things just got out of hand."

"Like with Susie," Libby said.

"No," Gladys said in a loud voice. "Not with Susie."

Everyone in the diner turned around and stared.

"Sorry," Gladys said, pasting a smile on her face. "I just got carried away."

The rest of the customers nodded, smiled back, and returned to what they had been doing before.

Gladys continued. "We were running a scam, and Nola decided to run off with the profits, and I tracked her down. . . ." Gladys shrugged. "She fell down the stairs and broke her neck."

"You pushed her down the stairs," Bernie said.

Gladys gazed into her cup. "I didn't mean to. I just wanted my money."

The three women sat in silence for a moment. Then Bernie said, "How did you come to marry cats?"

Gladys smiled. "I saw a cat-marrying ceremony on Facebook and thought, *I can do that*, and Gertrude Van Trumpet was born. I have almost enough saved to move out of here." The waitress came and refilled Gladys's cup. Gladys added two more packs of sugar and took a sip before continuing. "I think Allison must have told Susie about me. That's the only explanation I can come up with that explains how Susie knew. She called me up out of the blue and told me I had to do this or else. . . ."

"Or else what?" Libby asked.

"That she'd out me. If that happened, my business would disappear. Hell, no one will hire an ex-con to mow their lawns, let alone do what I do."

Neither Libby nor Bernie disagreed, because they knew what Gladys was saying was true.

"How did Allison know?" Bernie asked.

"We were in a halfway house down in Yonkers together after I got released," Gladys answered. She straightened up. "Now, if you want someone that hated Susie, I'd talk to Allison."

"We're planning on it," Libby said.

"Allison lost everything because of her," Gladys remarked. "Her job, her house, her boyfriend. And you know the worst thing of all?"

"No," Libby said. "What's the worst thing of all?"

"Susie wouldn't let it go. Whenever Allison got a job, Susie found out and went in and got her fired. She must have had a private detective or something following her." Gladys drained the last of her coffee from her cup, slid out of the booth, and stood up. "She really was a horrible human being," she pronounced. "Susie, not Allison."

"I figured," Libby said.

"Whoever killed her did everyone a huge favor," Gladys said. Then she walked away.

Bernie and Libby watched her go.

"What do you think?" Bernie asked Libby as the diner door shut behind Gladys.

"I think she could have done it," Libby said. "But then so could have Allison."

"So could have Charlene and Marie, for that matter," Bernie replied. "Everyone had the motive and the opportunity."

"And the means," Libby added, thinking of the letter opener lying on Susie's desk. "Don't forget that."

"And therein lies our problem," Bernie said as she signaled the waitress for their bill. Her phone rang while the waitress was getting it. Bernie answered. It was Lucy, Longely's stalwart chief of police, wanting an update on the progress she and her sister were making, so Bernie gave him one.

"You lied," Libby told Bernie when she was done.

"I didn't lie," Bernie replied. "I exaggerated."

"You said we're making progress."

"Speaking to people is making progress," Bernie pointed out. "Anyway, what else am I going to tell him?"

"Good point," Libby said. She watched as Bernie paid the bill. "So, he doesn't have a clue, either?"

"Apparently not," Bernie replied as she got up to go. "Otherwise, he wouldn't be bugging us."

Libby got up, too. "This is not good."

"No, it isn't," Bernie agreed. Part of her didn't believe Lucy's threat to put her and her sister in jail, but the other part of her thought he would do it in a heartbeat. What would happen to her dad? What would happen to the shop? What would happen to her feet if she couldn't get a pedicure?

"What now?" Libby asked Bernie, interrupting her thoughts.

"We work faster," Bernie said as she and her sister headed for the door. "A lot faster."

Chapter 30

Bernie and Libby had planned to do some errands on their way back to A Little Taste of Heaven, but in light of the conversation Bernie had just had with Lucy, they decided that sampling a new brand of olive oil, looking at coolers, and picking out paint swatches for the shop walls could wait for another day.

Instead, Bernie and Libby decided to take a detour and stop at what the police, if they'd been asked, would have referred to as Allison's last known address, hoping that she would be home. The house Allison was staying in was really more of a shack. A rental on the outskirts of Longely, it was situated behind a UPS store, and if you didn't know where the house was, you'd walk right by it, because it was located at the end of a narrow, unmarked path, a path that the landlord had ceased maintaining years ago.

But Bernie and Libby had had a friend in high school who had lived there for a brief amount of time, and they'd visited. It had been the sisters' first encounter with a wood-burning stove and an outhouse, and they had come away from their visit enchanted, anxious to convert their house to a similar configuration.

Libby was laughing, remembering the horrified look on her mother's face when she'd begged her mother to install an outhouse in the backyard, as she and Bernie started down the path. It was narrower than Libby remembered. Sumac, box elders, and maples had taken over, cutting off the sunlight. Bernie had taken a few steps when she felt her Manolos start to sink. The ground was muddy from last night's rain, and because there was no sun, the ground hadn't dried out.

"Damn," she said, taking her sandals off. She wasn't about to ruin a five-hundred-dollar pair of shoes, even though she'd paid only two hundred for them. Then she remembered she had an old pair of sneakers in the van. "Be right back," she told Libby and trotted off.

Unfortunately, her sneakers weren't there. She recalled she'd put them back in her closet. But then she spotted Libby's old loafers on the floor, along with a couple of used coffee cups and yesterday's paper. Bernie debated for a New York minute before slipping them on her feet.

She knew Libby would be pissed because of the underwear incident—how was she to know that that had been the last pair of Libby's clean underpants?—but what were the options? Go barefoot or come back here some other time. Neither of those would work. On her feet those loafers would go. Libby would just have to deal with it.

"Hey," Libby cried when Bernie came back. "Are those my shoes you're wearing?"

"Well, they ain't mine," Bernie replied, looking down at the scuffed loafers with worn-down heels. In normal times, she wouldn't be caught dead in loafers, let alone shoes in this condition.

"You could have asked."

"Sorry," Bernie said. Then she lied. "I thought it would be fine."

Libby drew herself up and crossed her arms over her chest. "Well, it's not."

Bernie snorted. "Getting a little grumpy, are we? Forgot to eat your daily allotment of chocolate?"

"I'm not grumpy."

"Then what would you call it?" asked Bernie, who believed that the best defense was a good offense.

"I would call it my being tired of your borrowing my stuff without asking," Libby told her.

"I already said I was sorry about the underpants. Anyway, this is only the second thing I've borrowed this month," Bernie retorted.

"That's not true," Libby replied. "What about my blue sweater?"

"I didn't borrow it. I donated it."

"You what?" Libby asked, aghast. She'd been looking for that sweater for the past three weeks.

"I said I donated it," Bernie repeated, emphasizing each word.

"You didn't."

"I did."

"But I loved that sweater," Libby wailed.

"That sweater wasn't fit to be seen in public," Bernie told her. "It had holes under the arms, and the collar was ripped. Even Goodwill wouldn't take it. I gave it to the fabric consortium."

"I had that sweater since my senior year in high school. Orion gave it to me," Libby told her. Orion was her old boyfriend.

"Exactly," Bernie replied. "It was time to let it go."

Libby jabbed a finger in her direction. "How would you feel if I got rid of some of your things?" she demanded.

"I take care of my things," Bernie told her. "I put them away in the closet."

Libby put her hands on her hips. "And you're saying I don't?"

"That's exactly what I'm saying." Bernie pointed to the shoes on her feet. "These have been on the floor of the van for the past six months."

"Maybe I wanted them there," Libby told her. "Did you think of that? And if they weren't there, you'd have to wear your precious Manolos. You should be thanking me for my foresight!"

One for you, Bernie thought, but she didn't say that. Instead, she changed the subject and pointed to the path that led to the house. "Do you want to do this or not?"

"Do it," Libby said grudgingly.

"Okay. Then let's get going."

"Fine," Libby said, and she turned and reentered the path.

Libby squinted because it was dim on the path, the light filtering uncertainly through the canopy of leaves above them. The ground was slippery, as well, and Libby had to concentrate on avoiding the tree roots and the thorns on the black raspberry bushes that snaked their way across the path, not to mention the thick poison ivy vines that wound themselves up the trunks of some of the trees. She shuddered while looking at them, because she was violently allergic.

For a minute, the only thing Libby and Bernie heard were the chirps of the birds and the rustle of the squirrels jumping from tree branch to tree branch. Then, after a couple of minutes had gone by, Bernie extended an olive branch and spoke.

"I wouldn't want to come through here at night to get home," she observed. "Especially if I'd had too much to drink."

"I wouldn't want to walk through here, period," Libby said. "Allison must be really broke to be living here."

"How much do you think she's paying?" Bernie asked.

"Got me," Libby said as she rounded the bend and 305 Laurel came into view. The five cats that had been lounging in front of the house scampered away. "But whatever it is, it's too much," Libby added, taking in the house standing in the clearing. "Do you think this place looked this bad when we were here?"

"No, but it was a long time ago," Bernie allowed.

"Fifteen years," Libby noted.

"Scary how fast time goes," Bernie said.

The house had always been a higgledy-piggledy affair. That was part of its charm. It was cobbled together from wooden pallets and random pilfered building materials, and Bernie had always thought it looked like the old man's crooked little house in the nursery rhyme, what with the gingerbread tracery on the eaves, the window boxes hanging from the window sashes, and the faded light brown cedar shingles on the upper part of the house. It was a tiny place, probably no bigger than seven hundred square feet of living space. When Bernie and Libby had been there last, the place had had a slight lean to it. Now the lean wasn't so slight. It was a definite tilt.

"The place looks as if it's going to fall down," Bernie observed, noticing the tiles missing from the roof and the lopsided door.

"All it would take is one big puff from the big, bad wolf," Libby reflected. Then she pointed to the chimney, a metal pipe attached to the house with bands of steel, which was leaning to the left. "Remind me not to stand under that," she said as she walked around three metal bowls full of dried cat food and a large metal bowl full of water. "I wonder how many cats Allison has."

"A lot," Bernie answered, taking a guess, as she spied a white one with a black spot on its nose peeking out from around a corner of the house. Bernie thought it was coming out to see them, but then Libby called out Allison's name and the cat scurried away.

Allison didn't answer. Libby tried again. The result was the same.

Libby looked at Bernie, and Bernie looked at Libby.

"It seems a shame to have come all this way...," Libby said, her voice trailing off.

Bernie indicated the door with her chin. "I don't see a lock, do you?"

"Nice to know some things never change," Libby said as she placed her hand on the door and pushed. Nothing happened. She pushed harder. This time the door swung open with a loud protesting groan. It had always had a tendency to stick, but since the house had settled, the door was more recalcitrant than it had been before.

Libby stepped inside, and Bernie followed. Since they'd last been here, the kitchen floor had developed a precipitous slope to the left and some of its tiles had rotted out, probably from a leak in the roof, and from where Libby was standing, she could see the floor had begun to separate from the walls.

"I'm surprised this place hasn't been condemned," Bernie commented. Nevertheless, the place still had a modicum of charm to it, Bernie decided, what with its light yellow enamel wood-burning stove, fabric-decorated walls, and mismatched kitchen cabinets. Then she pointed to the five-gallon jugs of water lining the wall and said, "Not having running water would make me crazy. I could do without the electricity, but I definitely couldn't do without the plumbing."

"I wonder why no one put a lock on the door," Libby mused as she took stock of the place, inhaling the smoky campfire smell that lingered in the air.

"Why bother," Bernie replied, "when you can go through the window if you want to get in?"

"Anyway, who would want to be here in the first place?" Libby said.

"I don't think *want* is the correct verb in Allison's case. I think *has to be* is," Bernie responded. "You know," she continued, "if I were Allison and I had had a job and a decent place to live and Susie did this to me, I'd want to kill her, too."

"Well, Susie definitely didn't know when to stop," Libby observed. "Which I suppose is why someone stopped her," she noted as she hugged herself and rubbed her arms. She was getting goose bumps. "It must be twenty degrees colder in here," she complained.

"It's the trees," Bernie noted as she went over to a Formica table sitting in a far corner of the room and began looking through the stack of mail on the table. "I'd hate to be here in the winter."

"Me too," Libby agreed, thinking of how cold it probably got and all the wood you'd have to burn to keep this place warm. Then she said, "Maybe we should wait outside," because she was having second thoughts about what they were doing.

Bernie looked up for a minute from the mail. "Why?" she asked.

"Well, in case Allison comes back . . ."

"We'll apologize," Bernie told her.

"I suppose," Libby said doubtfully. "What are we looking for, anyway?" she asked.

"I have no idea," Bernie said cheerfully. So far, the mail on the table consisted of flyers, old magazines, cutout vegan recipes, and the only thing of interest, a brochure about the next cat show. "I wonder if she's planning some sort of protest," Bernie said as she held up the brochure. The date the show was going to be held on and the address had been circled in red.

Libby looked up from the kitchen cabinet she'd started

going through. A cursory glance had revealed that the first two cabinets were filled with bags of cat food and cat treats, while the third cabinet contained a few cans of baked beans, a couple of packages of Oreos, and some ramen noodles. "When is the show?"

"End of the week," Bernie said. "I mean, why else circle it like that if you aren't planning on doing something? It's not as if she has show cats, and she's certainly not going there as a spectator."

"Given what happened to Allison the last time she tried something like that, I'd have to say she's certainly committed to her cause," Libby remarked. She'd just closed the third cabinet door when she heard a pop, followed by a whistling sound. A pillow on the sofa near her exploded in a shower of feathers. She was staring at it when there was another pop and a second pillow blew up.

For a moment, Libby stood there frozen, unable to make sense of what was happening. "What the hell?" she muttered, not knowing what to think. It sounded like fireworks, but the pillows wouldn't be exploding if it were. Then there was a third pop, and Libby understood. "Someone is shooting at us," she cried as she hit the floor. "Call the police."

"Are you sure?" Bernie asked. She hadn't seen the pillows.

"No. I'm joking," Libby said. "For heaven's sake, get down!"

Chapter 31

A few seconds later, Bernie saw a mug explode on what passed for the kitchen counter—two sawhorses and a couple of planks. "Holy moly," she said. "You're right."

"Of course I'm right," Libby told her as Bernie followed Libby down to the floor. "You think I'd say something like that for laughs?"

Bernie didn't reply. She was too busy getting her phone out of her tote and dialing 911. Unfortunately, there was no service where they were. Libby was not pleased when Bernie told her.

" 'It'll be fine,' you said," Libby told her, imitating her sister's voice. " 'Don't worry about a thing,' you said. 'No problem,' you said."

"You agreed," Bernie said from under the shelter of the table. "In fact, you were the one who suggested it."

Libby slithered closer to the sofa, figuring it was the bulkiest thing in the room. "But then, if you remember, I changed my mind," she told her.

Another bullet hit the table where Bernie had been standing a few minutes ago. She watched as envelopes and flyers fluttered to the floor. "At least whoever is doing this is a bad shot," she noted.

"And that's supposed to make me feel better?" Libby demanded.

"I'm trying to be optimistic here. You know, see the glass half full and all the rest of that nonsense."

Libby stretched her leg out. She was getting a cramp. Then she rubbed her elbow. She'd knocked it on the edge of the wooden cabinet on the way down. "Who the hell is doing this, anyway?"

"Damned if I know," Bernie replied. She took a deep breath and started belly crawling to the window. She cursed silently, hoping there wasn't something on the floor that was going to permanently stain her vintage Pucci wraparound dress, which was one of her favorite dresses—not that she was shallow or anything.

"What are you doing?" Libby demanded.

"I'm going to pull down the window shade so we'll be less of a target," Bernie explained.

"There is no window shade."

"I know," Bernie replied. She'd just looked up. "I realize that."

Libby turned over on her back and studied the water marks on the ceiling as she rubbed her left thigh. From what she could see, there were a fair number of leaks. "Maybe whoever is shooting at us thinks we're Allison," she suggested.

"Neither of us looks anything like Allison," Bernie objected.

"Maybe they don't know what Allison looks like," Libby countered.

"How could they not know that?" Bernie asked.

Libby hazarded a guess. "Because they haven't seen her."

Bernie snorted. "Then why would they be shooting at her?" When Libby didn't answer, Bernie said, "Are you saying someone hired a hit man to go after her? Because that's the only explanation I can think of for the scenario you're suggesting."

"No. That's not what I'm saying." Then the implications of what her sister was proposing hit Libby. "You're saying that if they're not shooting at Allison . . ."

"They're shooting at us," Bernie said, finishing Libby's sentence for her. "Give the girl a gold star."

"You're making me feel better and better."

"As your little sister, that's my job."

"Great." At which point it occurred to Libby that it might be a good idea to get between the sofa and the wall. That way if the shooter came in, they wouldn't see her. Hopefully. "Why would somebody do that?" she asked as she tried to wiggle her way into the space.

"Make you feel better?"

"No. Shoot at us," Libby cried in exasperation. The space was too narrow. She definitely needed to lose that twenty pounds she'd been talking about shedding.

"We'll know when we find them," Bernie responded.

"If it's all the same to you, I'd rather not go looking," Libby said. Then she realized the shooting had stopped. She cautiously lifted her head up. Silence, except for the birds. "Maybe whoever is doing this has given up."

"One can only hope," Bernie said. She'd had the same thought.

"Maybe they got bored."

"Or maybe they think we're dead," Bernie said.

"Maybe you should be quiet," Libby said.

"Maybe I should," Bernie agreed, thinking that if whoever was shooting at them thought he'd hit them, quiet was the way to go.

The same idea had occurred to Libby, so she and her sister stayed where they were for another five minutes. Just to be on the safe side.

"That was exciting," Libby said as she got up and dusted off her pants. They were full of hair. Cat hair, she guessed. Evidently, the cats came inside.

"Wasn't it, though?" Bernie agreed as she checked her dress. Aside from the cat hair, it seemed okay. That was the good thing about patterns. They hid dirt. Maybe things were looking up, after all, she thought as she went to the door and cautiously peered out.

"Do you see anything?" Libby asked.

Bernie shook her head. She tapped her fingers against her thigh. Where had the shooter gone? That was the question. He or she could have gone down the path when she and her sister were lying on the floor. Or he or she could still be in the woods. Waiting for them to come out. Or waiting for Allison to come in. *What to do?*

"What do you think?" Libby asked Bernie. "Should we stay put or go?"

Bernie was just about to say, "Go," when she thought she heard something. She put her finger to her lips. Libby cocked her head and raised an eyebrow. Bernie pointed in the direction of the woods and then carefully tiptoed back to Libby and whispered in her ear, telling her what she wanted to do.

"I don't know," Libby whispered back.

"What else do you suggest?" Bernie asked.

Libby shook her head. She didn't have a suggestion.

"Okay, then," Bernie said. She went over to the Formica table, grabbed some of the papers on it, and went over to the window facing out on the other side of the clearing. Then she carefully picked the broken pieces of glass out of the window frame. When she had gotten as much of the glass out as she could, she went and got the butcher knife that was sitting on the kitchen counter and then took the blanket off Allison's bed, placed it over the wooden window frame she'd cleared of glass, and climbed out, careful to hold the knife well away from her. As she dropped into the long grass and weeds, all she could think about were the ticks. *Please, God, let there not be any here*, she prayed as she made her way toward the path.

She took two steps and stopped and listened. She heard the rustle of branches up ahead. Then she heard a meow. She let out the breath she didn't know she'd been holding. It was the cats. That was what she'd heard in the house. Cats. She thought about turning back, but then she thought about what her dad would say, and she decided to walk a little bit farther.

It was tough going. The grass was high, and it hid rocks and low-growing brambles and sticky things that Bernie didn't know the names of. After a couple of minutes of that, she was ready to turn around and go back when she spotted something in a clearing she could see through the trees. It was Allison, and she was crouched down and talking to three cats in low, dulcet tones.

Bernie hurried forward. As she came into the clearing, she called Allison's name.

"Thank God you're all right," she added when Allison turned and looked at her. "You won't believe what happened."

Then she stopped talking, because out of the corner of her eye, Bernie had noticed something.

There was a rifle propped up against an oak tree.

Chapter 32

Jeez, talk about not getting the picture, Bernie thought as she dropped the knife she'd been holding and ran for the rifle. Allison sprang up and did the same thing, but Bernie was slightly closer and a little bit faster. She managed to get to the rifle a millisecond before Allison did.

"Now what?" Bernie said, pointing the rifle at Allison.

Allison put her hands in the air and took two steps back. "You're being ridiculous," she told Bernie.

"Me being ridiculous?" Bernie cried, her voice quivering with outrage. "You shot at us." She waved Allison's rifle in the air. "I can't believe you shot at us. You could have killed us. Thank God you're such a lousy shot, because otherwise we'd be dead."

"I—" Allison began, but Bernie cut her off.

"Don't you lie to me," Bernie yelled. "Don't you tell me you didn't do it, because I can smell the powder. This rifle has been fired recently."

Allison put her hands out in a calming gesture. "Let's not overreact."

"Overreact?" Bernie repeated, outrage fighting with disbelief. "What are you? Nuts?"

"It was an accident."

"Accident?" Bernie said, repeating the word. "You had an accident more than four times. Once maybe, but four times? No, I don't think so."

"Bernie, please. Just lower the rifle and give me a chance to explain," Allison pleaded.

Bernie took a step back. "I'll lower it after you explain. How's that?"

Allison tossed her hair. "Fine. Do what you want. But I think I should tell you that the rifle doesn't have any shells in it."

"Then why were you going for it?" Bernie demanded.

"Because you startled me," Allison explained.

Bernie wasn't sure if what Allison was saying about the rifle not being loaded was true or not. She really knew very little about firearms when it came down to it, but she sure wasn't going to tell Allison that. Instead, she said, "I think I'll be the judge of that. Now talk."

"I'm trying," Allison said. "You keep interrupting."

Which wasn't true, but Bernie didn't say that. Instead, she grunted and gestured for Allison to continue.

"I was going to say I was sorry," Allison told her.

"I don't think sorry cuts it in this case."

"I thought you were Marie."

"Marie?" In her amazement, Bernie lowered the rifle, realized what she had done, brought it up again, and then put it back down. Her arm was getting tired of holding it, anyway, and even with the evidence in hand, she was having trouble believing Allison had shot at her and her sister. "Marie," she repeated.

Allison nodded. "That's right."

Bernie yanked her dress back in place with her free hand. This was definitely not the kind of thing one wore to this kind of event, but then, who knew the day would turn out to involve being shot at and crawling across the floor? "Why were you shooting at Marie? If you were."

"Because she's trying to kill me."

Bernie blinked. *This is just becoming weirder and weirder*, she thought as a white-and-black cat came over and began rubbing its head against Bernie's feet. The cats had vanished into the undergrowth when she'd come crashing through, but now they were back, along with a couple more.

"That's Klepto," Allison informed her as the cat sauntered over to Allison and lay on her feet.

"And why would Marie be doing that?" Bernie asked Allison.

"Because I have proof that she killed Susie."

"Really?" Bernie said, the disbelief in her voice palpable.

"Yes, really," Allison told Bernie.

"And how do you know that? Did she sidle up and tell you?"

"In a manner of speaking." Allison bent down, picked up Klepto, and began rubbing his ears. He started to purr. "I overheard her. She and Susie were arguing in the grocery store. They were in the cookie aisle, and I was at the endcap, near the bread. Actually, they were pretty loud. Marie told Susie she was going to kill her for what she had done, and Susie laughed and told her to go ahead and try."

"I think we call that a figure of speech," Libby commented.

Allison shook her head vigorously. "Not in this case. Susie laughed again and told Marie she should have taken better care of her finances."

"And then?" Bernie said, prodding.

"And then," Allison replied, "Marie told Susie she was going to dance on her body and spit on her grave."

"Colorful," Bernie commented. "How did Susie respond?"

"She said, 'Good luck with that.' Then she said that nothing was going to stop her from turning Marie's house into a pile of rubble and that Marie deserved everything that was coming to her, up to and including being black-listed from all future cat shows."

Well, that information certainly changed things a bit, Bernie thought. If Allison was telling the truth—and that was a big if—Marie had known about Susie's plans for her house before the wedding. Had she gone there with the intention of killing Susie? Had Charlene known, as well? And what about the cat shows? Why had Susie made that threat?

"Then what happened?" Bernie asked as Allison put Klepto down, picked up a ginger tabby that had crawled out from under the bushes, and began to pet her.

"Nothing. Susie walked away," Allison replied.

"I take it you didn't tell the police this," Bernie stated.

Allison nodded. "No, I didn't."

"Why not?" Bernie asked.

Instead of answering, Allison put the ginger tabby down and surveyed two more cats that had appeared. "I know. It's dinnertime," she told them. Then she turned and looked at Bernie. "Obviously, because I don't want to have anything to do with the cops. I figure the farther away I stay from them, the better."

"Or maybe you didn't tell the police, because what you're saying isn't true," Bernie suggested.

"Oh. It's true, all right," Allison declared. "You'd better believe it. I was just afraid that if I came forward, the police would blame me."

"I see," Bernie said. "Can I ask why Marie wants to kill you now?"

Allison wrinkled her brow. "What do you mean?"

"Exactly what I said. Why now?"

Allison rolled her eyes. "Duh. Because she obviously knows that I know what she did."

"And how did she find that out? Did you tell her?"

"Of course not," Allison protested.

"Then how does she know?"

Allison stuck out her chin. "I don't have the foggiest. And now, if we're done here, I have cats to feed," Allison said, indicating the six by her feet.

"We're not done yet," Bernie told her and raised the rifle she was holding. Her arms were feeling rested. "Now, why don't you tell me how Marie knows that you know? Guess, if you have to."

Allison remained silent and began playing with the gold chain with a heart on it that was hanging around her neck.

"I'm waiting," Bernie said.

"Well," Allison began, drawing out the word *well*, after another minute had gone by, "it occurs to me I might have asked her for a little loan."

"Loan?" Bernie repeated. *Now*, she thought, *we're getting someplace.*

"Yes, loan. I told Marie I'd pay her back, but maybe she took it the wrong way." Allison made a "Can you believe it?" expression with her mouth. "Maybe she thought I was extorting her or something."

"Imagine that," Bernie retorted. "Who would have thought? I am shocked that the idea even occurred to her."

Allison straightened her shoulders. "There's no need for sarcasm," she replied. Then she went on the offensive before Bernie could say something else. "Anyway, you shouldn't have gone into my house without permission."

"The door was open," Bernie pointed out.

"The door is always open. I can't lock it," Allison said.

"So, that makes it okay to shoot at someone?"

"It does in Texas."

"But we're not in Texas, are we?" Bernie pointed out. She was about to say, "Or Florida, either," when she heard a noise. So did Allison.

They both turned in the direction of the snapping twigs and rustling leaves. A few seconds later, they heard Libby calling her sister's name.

"Bernie, where are you?"

"Over here," Bernie called back.

"Are you okay?" Libby shouted.

"I'm fine," Bernie replied.

Libby came crashing through the undergrowth a minute later. She stopped when she saw Bernie and Allison, and her eyes widened as she took in the rifle in Bernie's hand.

"What's going on here?" she demanded.

Bernie explained as Libby absentmindedly rubbed the elbow she'd banged on the kitchen cabinet when she hit the floor. It still hurt.

"I can't believe you did that," Libby said to Allison when her sister was done.

Allison frowned. She looked, Libby reflected, more annoyed than anything else. "Hey, Libby," she said. "I already said I was sorry. It was a mistake. Haven't you ever made a mistake?"

"Not like that I haven't," Libby told her.

"Listen," Allison replied, pointing down at the ground. "You . . ."

Libby held up her hand. "I don't want to hear it. Your apology is not accepted."

"I just—"

"No. Seriously," Libby told her. "It isn't."

"Fine."

"Nothing you say is going to make what you did better," Libby said, ramming the point home.

Allison shrugged. "Okay." She started to laugh and covered her mouth with her hand to hide it.

Libby put her hands on her hips. She was getting angrier than she was before. "What's so funny?" she demanded.

Allison took her hand away from her mouth and said, "I just wanted to tell you you're stepping in poison ivy."

Libby looked down. She was standing in it up to her ankles. "Oh, my God," she shrieked. Could the day get any worse?

Chapter 33

"Stop scratching," Bernie scolded Libby. It was eight o'clock that night, and Bernie, her sister, and Marvin were sitting at the bar at RJ's, nursing their beers.

"I'm trying," Libby said as she leaned down and scratched some more.

"You're just making it worse," Marvin observed.

"I know, but I can't help myself," Libby admitted as she continued scratching.

"It'll be fine if you leave it alone," Bernie said as she ate a pretzel. "It's all in your head."

"It's not in my head. It's on my ankles," Libby protested.

Bernie took a sip of her wheat beer, put the glass back on the counter, ate the orange slice that came with it, and spoke. "Listen," she said to Libby, "you washed with jewelweed soap and took a Benadryl. You'll be fine." She'd been saying the same thing to her sister for the past four hours, to no effect.

"At least an hour . . ."

"Half an hour," Bernie said.

"Passed between the time I stepped in the poison ivy and the time we got home," Libby continued. "I think that's too much time."

"No it isn't," Bernie told her for the twentieth time.

"Are you sure?" Libby asked.

"I'm pretty sure."

"But not completely sure," Libby noted. She turned to Marvin. "What do you think?"

Marvin shook his head and took a gulp of his summer ale. He wasn't getting involved in this if he could help it. "I don't know."

"See?" Bernie said.

"See yourself," Libby responded. "I looked it up on Google. . . ."

Bernie rolled her eyes. "Well, if you found it on the Internet, it must be true."

Brandon intervened in the conversation before Libby could answer. "So how come you stepped in poison ivy?" he asked Libby as he took the dish of pretzels in front of the sisters and refilled it. RJ's was busy tonight, and this was the first time there'd been enough of a lull for him to ask Libby and Bernie what had happened this afternoon.

Libby frowned at the memory. "I was tracking Bernie through the woods. I was afraid she'd gotten shot or knifed or something."

"Don't be ridiculous," Bernie told her.

"I'm not," Libby cried. "I was terrified when you didn't come back. I thought I'd find you lying somewhere."

"So now this is my fault?" Bernie demanded.

"Wow." Brandon held up his hands. "Ladies, both of you need to calm down," he told Bernie and Libby. "I just want to know what happened, without a side of bickering please."

"It's been a long day," Libby admitted.

"And I guess neither of us is in the best of moods," Bernie allowed.

"That's an understatement," Brandon said as he got himself a drink of water.

"And Lucy was waiting for us when we got back to the shop," Bernie said.

"What was he doing there?" Marvin asked.

"He'd come to gloat," Libby explained. "Because, evidently, calling wasn't enough." Libby took a sip of her beer. "This has not been a good day," she reiterated. "Way too much drama for my taste." Then she put her glass down and began to talk.

When she was through, Brandon looked at Libby and said, "You do know Allison's a crack shot, don't you?"

"How would I know that?" Libby protested.

At the same time Bernie said, "You're kidding me."

"No, I'm not," Brandon replied. "She belongs to the Longely Rod and Gun Club. Correction. Did belong to it. She got thrown out after she got arrested."

"They threw her out because she got arrested?" Libby asked.

"No," Brandon replied. "They threw her out because Susie insisted on it."

Bernie tilted her head and looked at Brandon. "And you know this how?"

"The same way I know everything," Brandon told her. "People tell me."

"Are you sure?" Bernie asked.

Instead of answering, Brandon turned and called down the bar to a portly middle-aged man wearing a baseball hat, a white polo shirt, and plaid Bermuda shorts. "Hey, Mike," he cried. "Tell these ladies about Allison Hardy."

Mike looked away from the TV on the wall. "What about her?"

"She can shoot, can't she?"

"She sure can," Mike said and went back to watching the Yankees.

"Well?" Bernie asked. "Can she shoot well?"

"Very well," Mike answered, this time without turning his head away from the TV. "She's an excellent shot."

"And there you have it, folks," Brandon said before he went to wait on another customer.

Libby took another sip of her beer and put it down. "What do you think that means?" she asked, turning to Marvin and Bernie.

"It means she could have shot you if she wanted," Marvin said, pointing out the obvious.

"Well, this certainly puts my poison ivy in perspective," Libby said.

"Obviously, she wanted to get you out of there," Brandon said, having temporarily discharged himself of his waiterly duties. "There must have been something in there that she didn't want you to see."

"I can't think of what," Libby said after she'd gone over everything in the house in her mind.

"Neither can I," Bernie said. She'd been doing the same thing as her sister. "There wasn't very much there."

"Well, then, maybe she was just pissed you were in her space, and she decided to teach you a lesson," Brandon suggested.

"I guess it's possible," Bernie said. It seemed like a pretty extreme step to her, but then Allison was a pretty extreme kind of person.

Marvin ate a pretzel. "There is another possibility," he said slowly.

Bernie, Libby, and Brandon turned toward him and waited.

"She could have done it to add validity to her story," Marvin said.

"*Validity*. That's a nice word," Brandon said. "You back to using the *Word of the Day Calendar*?"

"Yeah," Marvin said, putting on his tough-guy face. "You got a problem with that?"

Brandon laughed, grabbed a handful of pretzels out of the dish in front of Marvin, and started throwing them in his mouth. "Is that your toughest tough-guy face?"

"Ignore him," Libby said as she patted Marvin's hand. "He's just jealous."

Brandon hit his chest with his fist. "You got me," he cried before moving off to wait on another customer.

"So, what do you think?" Marvin asked Libby.

"About your word?" Libby replied.

"No. About my idea," Marvin spluttered.

"It's possible," Bernie said, jumping into the conversation. "Unlikely but possible, but then, that statement applies to everything about this case."

"What a mess," Libby said.

"Indeed, it is," Bernie agreed. "Too bad Dad didn't talk to Marie," she noted. She finished off the last of her wheat beer. "Now we have to."

"Unfortunately," Libby said.

"I wonder what she'll have to say for herself," Bernie mused.

Libby frowned. "The same as everyone else, I warrant. That Susie was a bad person, that she had done her wrong, that in spite of this, she did nothing to harm Susie, that her hands are clean . . ."

"And so on and so forth," Bernie said. Half of her wanted to stay at RJ's, but the other half remembered Lucy's grin earlier in the day as he asked her if they'd discovered anything else since the last time they'd spoken, and she knew they had to go. "Okay," she said, standing up. "Let's get this show on the road."

"To where?" Libby asked.

"To talk to Marie, of course."

"Of course." Libby pointed at the clock on the wall. "It's late."

Bernie disputed her sister's assertion. "It's nine thirty. Nine thirty isn't late."

"For some people, it is."

"I guess we'll find out if Marie is one of those people or not."

"She'll be annoyed if she's settled in for the evening," Libby pointed out.

"She'll be annoyed if we come tomorrow morning," Bernie said as she started feeling around in her tote for her car keys.

"But she'll be more annoyed if we come now," Libby replied. "I know I would be."

"She'll be annoyed whenever we come," Bernie told her sister, "because she's not going to want to talk to us."

Libby didn't have a comeback, because what her sister had said was true.

"Aha," Bernie said a minute later, having located the keys. She turned to Libby as she held them up. "Yes? No?"

Libby sighed. "I guess," she said as, unable to help herself, she bent down and scratched her ankle again. They were going to have to do this sometime. She supposed now was as good a time as any.

Chapter 34

Marie Summer lived one-quarter mile away from Susie. A dimly lit winding road went through the Pines, connecting all the houses, and although the landscaping gave the illusion of the houses being far apart from one another, they really weren't. Probably not more than a ten-minute walk.

As Bernie drove down the road, Libby considered the implications of that fact: both Charlene and Marie could have walked home, returned to Susie's house, and killed her in the requisite time. Libby sighed. The idea gave her no joy. It seemed as if the deeper she and Bernie delved into the situation, the farther away from a solution they got.

Marie's house, like the houses surrounding it, was a wood and brick midcentury colonial surrounded by a rolling lawn, with a large weeping willow in front and a spacious yard in back. Unlike Susie's home, it was practically indistinguishable from its neighbors. There were no large neon cats greeting you as you drove in, no cat pictures on the white shutters, nothing jarring, nothing that hadn't been there fifty years ago. The house was probably just the way her parents had left it, Bernie couldn't help thinking as she turned into the driveway.

An old-fashioned streetlamp cast a gentle glow on the road, illuminating a mailbox with a cute picture of a log cabin painted on it; the path up to the house, lined with bedded petunias, impatiens, and fairy lights; and the arborvitae hiding the house's foundation.

When Bernie got closer, she noticed the house wasn't as perfect as it appeared from the distance. She spotted alligatored paint on the wood on the second story, chinks of missing mortar between the first-story red bricks, and grapevines and deadly nightshade winding their way over the arborvitae.

"It is a lot of house to maintain," Libby noted, echoing her sister's thoughts, as they neared the garage. She pointed to two vehicles parked in front of the garage. "Evidently, Marie has a visitor."

Bernie frowned. "That's just ducky." Now they'd have to come back. More time wasted. She was about to turn the van around when the front door of Marie's house opened. A man came out, strolled down the three steps that led from the porch, and headed for the Civic.

"Isn't that Travis, the groundskeeper from Susie's estate?" Libby asked as they drew closer.

Bernie nodded. "I believe you are correct," she said as she brought the van to a stop next to the passenger side of the Civic. Then she rolled down the window. "Hey, Travis," she called.

Travis looked over, smiled, tipped his hat, and said, "Have a good evening, ladies." Then he got in his vehicle and drove away.

"I wonder what he was doing here?" Libby asked as she watched him take a left onto Ash Road, his taillights disappearing behind a neighbor's privet hedge.

"Maybe Marie will tell us," Bernie replied as she and Libby got out of their vehicle. They marched up to Marie's front door, and Libby rang the bell.

Marie flung the storm door open before the chimes had stopped. "Travis," she said, smiling. Then she saw who was standing in front of her, and her expression changed from happy to disappointed to hostile in two seconds. "Oh. You," she said, emphasizing the word *you*.

She was wearing an off-the-shoulder light blue knit sundress and white sandals with kitten heels. Her cheeks were flushed, and her hair was slightly mussed, and Bernie reflected that she looked as if, to use her mother's words, she had just been entertaining a gentleman caller, really entertaining him.

"What do you two want?" she demanded, folding her arms across her chest.

"World peace," Bernie answered.

"Definitely world peace," Libby said, seconding this.

"You two are a couple of real comedians, aren't you?" Marie observed.

"We like to think so," Bernie replied. "We like to think we bring a little bit of joy into everyone's day."

"Well, maybe you should take another think," Marie told her.

"I must say you're not being the gracious, welcoming hostess I heard you were," Bernie replied.

"I'm not trying to be," Marie informed her as she glowered at the sisters.

"You could have fooled me," Libby said as she started scratching her wrist, realized what she was doing, and stopped. *Please, God, don't let the poison ivy be there, too,* she prayed before she asked Marie another question. "What was Travis doing here, if you don't mind my asking?"

"He was helping me with my sink, if you must know, and I do mind your asking. Now, if we're all done here, it's late and I want to go to bed."

"I thought you already had," Bernie said.

"That's it," Marie declared. "I don't need to be insulted in my own house."

"I wasn't insulting you," Bernie replied. "I was complimenting you."

Marie pointed to the road. "Leave. Leave before I call the cops." She began to close the storm door, but Bernie was faster.

Good job, Bernie told herself as she stepped into a small vestibule with a tiled floor. *Nothing like antagonizing the person you're trying to interview, I always say*, Bernie thought as she noticed the door to the house looked old and worn and needed to be replaced. She could hear meowing coming from behind it.

"Sorry," Bernie told Marie. "I was out of line."

"Yes, you were," Marie agreed, looking slightly, the operative word being *slightly*, less put out.

"My sister has no filter," Libby explained, indicating Bernie with her chin. "She says whatever comes into her head."

"Evidently," Marie agreed.

"Think how I feel, having to live with her," Libby said to Marie, who smiled at the comment.

"Hey," Bernie cried. "That's not very nice."

Libby ignored her sister and concentrated on Marie. "So how do you know Travis?" Libby asked, making small talk.

"He used to work for a lawn service that I hired." Marie gave out the information like she was parting with her Social Security number. "Why do you want to know?"

"Because my sister and I are looking for a plumber," Libby lied. "Is he any good?"

"Good enough," Marie said. She made a big deal of holding her arm up and studying the face of her watch. "Now, it's late, and I'm getting ready to turn in."

"Fair enough," Bernie said, taking up the conversational baton. "That's not why we came here, anyway."

"Do I look like I care?" Marie asked, reverting to hostile mode.

"Actually, you kinda do," Bernie replied.

"It was a rhetorical question," Marie spit out. She turned to Libby. "Your sister is an extremely annoying person."

"Believe me, I sympathize," Libby said.

"Marie, don't you want to know why we're here?" Bernie persisted.

"To ask me for a recommendation for a plumber?"

"Seriously, Marie, you might want to hear this," Libby told her. "It's important."

"I doubt that," Marie answered.

"Well, we're going to tell you, anyway," Bernie said, "because that's the kind of people we are."

Marie held up her hand. "Thanks, but no thanks," she said.

"Allison had some interesting things to say," Bernie continued.

Marie snorted. "That nutjob? Let me guess." She frowned. An expression of disgust crossed her face. "She was probably going on about how cruel I am to keep my cats indoors. How they need to be outside in the fresh air."

"Actually," Bernie said, "she accused you of murdering Susie and then trying to kill her."

Marie laughed. "Get serious."

"We are," Libby said.

"This is your big news?" Marie put air quotes around the word *news*. "This is what you came to tell me?"

"Indeed, it is," Bernie confirmed, motioning to herself and her sister.

"You could have saved yourself the trip," Marie scoffed.

"Really?" Libby asked. She, too, could hear cats mewing behind the door. She wondered if Marie had as many cats as Susie had had.

"Yes, really," Marie snapped.

Bernie raised an eyebrow. "So, we're supposed to ignore what Allison said?"

"Yes," Marie replied. "You are. I can't believe you'd take the word of a convicted felon, someone who's been in jail, someone who is a pathological liar."

Bernie shrugged. "I don't know about the liar part, but just because someone's been in jail doesn't mean they're not telling the truth."

Marie put her hands underneath her breasts and yanked her sisters up. This, Bernie reflected, was why she didn't wear strapless dresses unless they had a built-in foundation.

"How many cats do you have?" Libby asked Marie.

"Eight, unlike someone else I could name," Marie said. She shook her head. "Talk about gall. Allison really has some nerve."

"Then why did she say what she did?" Libby wanted to know.

Marie gave them a "How dumb are you?" look. "So she could lift the suspicion off herself, of course."

"Of course," Libby echoed.

"I'm serious," Marie told her. "Think about it. After all, it was Susie who had Allison arrested, Susie who was responsible for her being fired from her job, Susie who was following her around like some avenging angel."

"On the other hand," Bernie said, "Susie was going to take your house. Plus, there's that whole cat title thing. Let's not forget that."

"So," Libby added, "that's why we figure you'd like to tell your side of the story to us."

"Well, I wouldn't," Marie told Libby and Bernie.

"There's no 'my side of the story' to tell. I've already given my statement to the police, and that's quite enough, thank you." She put her hand over her heart. "I can't bear talking about it. Just seeing Susie like that." Marie shook her head, indicating she was overcome by emotion.

Bernie couldn't help it. She snorted. By now the mewing had become louder and more insistent.

Marie glared at her. Then she did a half pivot and faced the door. "I'm coming," Marie said to the cats. She turned back to Bernie. "My kiddos need me," she explained before turning back to the door.

Bernie watched as Marie turned the doorknob and opened the door a crack. Literally, a crack. But evidently, it was enough. Two Russian blues managed to squeeze through the opening.

"Oh no," Marie cried as she slammed the door shut before any of the other cats could get out. "Get them," she yelled at Bernie as the cats brushed against Bernie's ankles. Bernie bent down and tried to grab them, but by then, the cats were already out the storm door and racing down the steps.

"Sadie, Stanley," Marie yelled as she ran down the steps after them. "Come back."

But the cats didn't come back. They didn't even stop. They kept on going.

"I have tuna," Marie cried, and she made a clicking noise with her tongue.

The cats weren't impressed. They ran faster.

"Damn," Marie cursed as she went after them.

"Oh dear," Bernie said as the cats and Marie rounded the house and disappeared.

Libby sighed. "I think our conversation is over."

"It was over before," Bernie pointed out.

"Yeah. But now it's over, over," Libby said.

Somehow, Bernie had pictured a different outcome. "This is not turning out well."

"You think?" Libby said, instead of saying what she really wanted to say, which was, "I told you so."

"Of course, this might have an upside," Bernie said as she twisted the doorknob. "Or not. It looks as if this is the kind of door that locks automatically."

Libby stifled a yawn. The drink she'd had at RJ's was catching up with her. "Time to go home," she announced as she started down the steps.

"I suppose," Bernie said as she followed her sister. She was just about to get into the van when an idea occurred to her. She held up her hand. "Give me a sec."

"What now?" Libby asked.

Bernie pointed to the attached garage's door. "It's manual," she noted.

"So what?"

"So, that means that unless it's locked, I can open it."

"And you want to do that why?" Libby asked in exasperation.

"Because I want to see what's inside."

"There's nothing inside that's going to be of any possible interest to us," Libby said.

"You don't know that."

"I think it's a pretty fair assumption. Let's go home."

"It'll take me two seconds."

"Bernie, Marie will be back any minute. What are you going to say to her when she sees you in there? 'Gee, thought I'd take a tour of your garage and see what you've done with the decor?' I mean, it's not as if she's not going to notice."

"I'll put the door down," Bernie said as she walked over to the garage door. "She won't see a thing."

"You're going to get us arrested," Libby complained as

she watched her sister take a step forward, plant both her feet firmly on the ground, bend down, grab the door handle with both hands, and yank upward. The garage door let out a groan and rose.

"Don't be so negative," Bernie told Libby before she took a couple of steps inside.

As she surveyed the interior, the phrase "A place for everything and everything in its place" crossed her mind. The inside of the garage was meticulous. The garden hose was neatly coiled around its holder; the lawn mower sat in the far left-hand corner, next to two large bags of fertilizer, a couple of bags of sphagnum moss, and a bag of rose food, while snow shovels, spades, hoes, and rakes hung from pegs on the wall. The two shelves in the back of the garage were neatly filled with gardening implements, cartons of mason jars, boxes of toilet tissue and paper towels, and boxes of cat food. But there was a smell in there, a smell Bernie couldn't place. And then she saw its source.

"Libby," she cried, turning to face the van. "You lose big-time."

Chapter 35

"Good God," Libby said as she stared at what lay in front of her.

"You were wrong," Bernie told her.

"Apparently, I was."

"There's no apparently about it."

"Fine," Libby told her. "I was wrong. I admit it. Happy?"

"Very." Bernie grinned. "I told you."

"Don't gloat," her sister grumped. She hated being wrong. Especially this wrong. "It's rude."

"I'm trying not to," Bernie said as she and her sister went back to staring at the cages over in the right-hand corner of the garage.

"And not succeeding very well, I might add," Libby noted as she took a step forward to get a better look. "Does this mean what I think it means?"

"I can't think of any other thing it could mean," Bernie replied.

"But why keep them?" Libby mused as she continued to stare at the cages. "Given the circumstances, it seems like a stupid thing to do."

"I can't even begin to speculate," Bernie said. She noted that the four yellow plastic cages were connected to each other with lighter yellow plastic pipes. Each cage contained a bowl of food, a water bowl, cedar shavings, a little house, and field mice.

Bernie counted twenty mice in all, but given the size of the cages, she bet there'd been more before. The mice had been sleeping when Bernie opened the garage door, but the noise and the light had woken them up. Now they were milling around, sniffing, their attention directed at Bernie and Libby.

"I bet they're waiting to be fed," Bernie said, and she started to look around for their food. She'd just spotted it on the top shelf on the back wall when Libby tapped her on the shoulder and called her name.

Bernie turned around to see Marie standing behind her. "No kitties?" Bernie asked, saying the first thing that came into her head.

"They're in the house. More to the point, what are you doing in here?" Marie demanded.

"We were looking for your kitties, too," Bernie lied. "We thought we heard meowing coming from the garage, and we knew you would want us to investigate."

"They ran the other way," Marie said.

"We thought they doubled back," Libby said, coming to her sister's defense. "Cats do that. But in this case, I can see that we were wrong."

Marie glared at her. "A likely story," she told Libby as she dabbed at a scratch on her arm. Her eyes narrowed. "You're trespassing. I'm going to call the police. I'm going to call them right now."

"Are you sure you want to do that?" Libby asked.

"And why wouldn't I?" Marie asked.

Bernie pointed to the cages full of mice. "That's why."

Marie did a good approximation of shock. "Those aren't mine. I never saw those mice in my life."

"Maybe you saw them in your past one? This is your

garage, isn't it?" Libby asked. When Marie didn't answer, Libby added, "So how could you have never seen them?"

Marie took her braid and moved it from her shoulder to her back before replying. Then she said, "I never saw them, because I never go in here. I park my car outside because the door is too heavy to lift all the time." A fact Bernie could attest to. The door did weigh a ton, and she would do the same thing in Marie's place. "And the lock is broken," Marie said. "Anyone, and I do mean anyone, can come in."

Bernie gestured to her sister and herself. "Like us?"

"Yes, like you," Marie said. "I'm being framed," Marie declared. "Someone is setting me up. Like you two."

"And why would we do that?" Libby asked.

"To get yourselves off the hook," Marie replied.

Bernie made a rude noise and tucked a strand of hair back behind her ear. "Oh, please, spare me. Can't you come up with something better? You're embarrassing me."

"It's true," Marie insisted. Her chin began to quiver. She wiped her hands on her jeans. "It is. Talk to Allison. She's probably the one behind this."

Bernie gestured to the mouse food on the shelf in the back. "What you're saying is that Allison sneaks in here every day and feeds and waters the mice and cleans their cages? Is that what you're saying? And you've never noticed?"

"She does it when I am out of the house," Marie told her.

Bernie laughed. "Seriously?"

Marie stuck her chin out. "Okay, so maybe they are mine. Maybe I just like them and I can't keep them in the house, because of the cats."

"You expect us to believe that?" Libby asked.

"Why not?" Marie countered. "Some people like snakes. I like mice. In any case, you can't prove that these mice are the ones that were at the wedding."

"Not those exact ones," Bernie replied. "But they look a lot like the mice at Boris and Natasha's wedding, not to mention the ones that were so thoughtfully dropped off at our shop."

Marie shrugged her shoulders. "Mice are mice."

"No. They're not," Bernie said. "Each one has a unique DNA profile. All we have to do is compare the profiles of the mice that were present at the wedding and at our shop and the profiles of these mice"—Bernie pointed to the mice in the cages—"and we'll have our killer."

"That's ridiculous," Marie said. "How do you expect me to believe something like that?"

"Because it's true," Bernie lied. She reached for her phone. "I thought you might want to explain, but, hey, if you don't want to, that's okay, too. I'll just call the cops, and you can talk to them. I think this is about the time you get in touch with your lawyer."

Marie looked from Bernie to Libby and back again. "Okay. Okay," she said. "So, I was the one who sent the mice. I did it. I admit it. But I didn't kill Susie." Marie reached up and began massaging her neck with her right hand. "I was with Charlene. We went to her house and had a glass of wine to celebrate. Two glasses, actually. We killed the bottle."

"So, Charlene knew what you were going to do?" Libby asked.

"Not only did she know," Marie said, "she was the one who suggested it."

"Really?" Bernie said as she folded her arms across her chest.

"Yes, really," Marie replied. "She wasn't serious, but once she suggested it, I couldn't resist. Considering what Susie was doing to us, considering that she was making us attend that stupid wedding, I thought this was the least I could do. A kind of 'punishment fitting the crime' kind of thing."

"And did Charlene think it was a good idea to send a little package to our shop, too?" Libby demanded.

"Yeah, she did," Marie said.

"And you went along with it?" Libby asked.

Marie shrugged. "I told Charlene not to, but she insisted."

"Why?" Bernie asked. "What was the rationale?"

"She figured it would make you think of Allison."

Bernie shook her head. She didn't get it. "For what reason?"

"Allison let a whole bunch of mice out at a cat show in Florida two years ago," Marie explained.

"That's news to us," Libby said, pointing to herself and her sister.

"Charlene thought you knew," Marie told her.

"Who delivered the packages?" Bernie asked, changing the subject.

"Charlene's nephew. But he didn't know what was in the boxes," Marie swore. "He was just doing Charlene a favor."

"Nice aunt," Bernie observed. "Nothing like making your nephew an accessory to a crime."

Chapter 36

"Do you believe Marie?" Libby asked Bernie as they got back in the van.

"About not killing Susie? I don't disbelieve her, but then I don't believe her, either. I think I'm on the fence," Bernie told her sister as she inserted the key in Mathilda's ignition and turned it.

"No. About the mice. About raising them as pets."

"Absolutely not. I think she got the idea and then acquired the mice."

"From Baker's Supply?"

Bernie nodded while she listened to the engine cough and shudder. She had been doing some research online and had found that Baker's sold animals, including deer mice, to labs.

"Come on, Mathilda. You can do it," Bernie coaxed, while Libby crossed her fingers and said a prayer to the car gods. Bernie gave the engine a little more gas. The engine spluttered. Bernie silently cursed as she turned the engine off, counted to sixty, and tried again. This time the engine caught.

"We need a new battery," Bernie observed as she pulled out of the driveway onto Victor Street. "Or a new starter."

"Or a new van," Libby said. "Maybe we should take Andy up on his deal."

"When hell freezes over," Bernie said, remembering her first car and the way it had caught on fire. The only good thing about it was that she hadn't been in it when it happened.

"You certainly carry a grudge," Libby remarked.

"Let's just say I have a long memory," Bernie told her sister as she turned left onto Eclipse Avenue. Charlene's house was a little less than seven minutes away—if you knew where you were going. Bernie had a general idea, but the roads were confusing in the dark, winding this way and that to create a maze, and for some reason, Bernie's GPS was off-line, which didn't help matters.

"Just because something happened once doesn't mean it's going to happen again," Libby said as she looked out the window and tried to figure out which road they needed to take to get them to Charlene's house.

"Fool me once, shame on . . ."

"You. Fool me twice, shame on me," Libby said, finishing her sister's sentence for her. "I know. I know. We're never going to get a new van, are we?" she asked.

"Not until Jose tells us to," Bernie answered. Jose was their mechanic. "He thinks Mathilda can make it to two hundred thousand."

"Well, when we break down in the middle of no-where . . ."

Bernie laughed. "In the middle of a raging blizzard . . ."

"Don't say I didn't warn you," Libby replied.

"I won't have to," Bernie told her. "You'll say it for me."

"Cute," Libby said, and since there was no point in continuing the van discussion, she went back to concentrating on which street they should turn onto. "I hate these kind of developments," she groused. "It's like they design these roads like this on purpose."

"They do," Bernie said.

"Why?" Libby asked as she bent down and scratched her ankle.

"To keep the riffraff out, obviously."

Libby scratched some more. "That's us, all right." Then she leaned forward and squinted, trying to read the street sign they'd just gone by, but she couldn't. Bernie was going too fast. "Slow down," she said. "We're going to miss the turnoff."

"I'm going only ten miles an hour," Bernie informed her.

"Then go five." Libby started to scratch and balled her hands into fists to stop herself. "You do know that Marie has probably called Charlene by now to tell her we're coming," Libby said to distract herself from the itching.

"You're right," Bernie allowed. "We should have taken Marie with us."

Libby bent over. She couldn't resist. "And how would we do that?" she asked as she gave in to the urge. She groaned with pleasure.

"Tie her up and throw her in the van, of course."

"Of course, Bernie. Why not? What's a little kidnapping in the scheme of things?"

"My thoughts exactly," Bernie told her. "And for heaven's sake, stop scratching. You'll spread the poison ivy everywhere."

"I know, I know," Libby said. "It just feels so good." She saw the sign for Summit Street coming up. "Turn left here," she told Bernie. "Two blocks and I think we're there."

"It's not that long a walk—maybe twenty minutes—if you know where you're going and you don't go around in circles," Bernie observed as she put on a little speed.

No one was out. As they drove down the road, Bernie could see some of the houses were lit up like stages, while other houses were dark, all lights off. Presumably, the occupants were in bed. Bernie thought Charlene would most likely be up. Even if she was an "early to bed" kind of gal, Marie's phone call would have woken her. Libby was right about that. Why wouldn't Marie call? If Bernie were in her position, she would.

"The walk from Marie's to Charlene's is just a little longer than the walk to Susie's and back," Libby noted as she spotted a doe watching them from the side of the road.

"Marie could be telling the truth," Bernie mused. "Maybe she and Charlene just wanted to disrupt the wedding."

"It's also entirely possible that one or both of them returned to Susie's house and got into a fight with Susie and stabbed her," Libby said.

Bernie didn't answer. She was too busy reading the numbers off the houses—at least the ones that were visible. Some weren't. She was doing the math in her head and had just figured out that Charlene's house was three houses down on the left-hand side of the road when she heard a noise. Libby heard it, too. They both looked in the same direction. A garage door was going up, flooding the house's driveway with light. A moment later, a car backed out.

Libby elbowed Bernie in the ribs and pointed. "I think that's Charlene in the driver's seat."

"I do believe you're right," Bernie said. She pulled over to the side of the road, stopped the van, and turned off the lights. "Especially since that's Charlene's house."

Libby leaned forward so she could get a better view. "I wonder where she's going at this time of night. She doesn't strike me as the kind of woman who's going off to a club."

"Or meeting up with a hot date at the bar," Bernie added as she watched Charlene make a left and drive down the street in the opposite direction from where they were parked. "Although we could be wrong."

"Or she could be going to the grocery store to get a pint of ice cream."

"She could," Bernie agreed, thinking about the cinnamon ice cream she'd made this morning and hoping there would be some left when she got home. "But you can't deny the timing. She leaves after Marie calls her."

Libby corrected her. "Presumably calls her. We don't know that Marie did. It could be a coincidence."

"And the ice in the Artic isn't melting."

"You mean it is?" Libby said. Then another possibility occurred to her. "Or maybe Charlene developed a sudden desire to go to the Bahamas."

"Maybe, but then she'd be carrying a suitcase," Bernie commented as she watched Charlene's vehicle get farther down the road. "Let's find out, shall we?" Bernie said, and she started the van up but didn't turn the lights on. If they didn't follow her now, they'd lose her.

Once under way, Bernie was careful to keep well behind Charlene. Bernie had thought that driving without lights would be difficult, but it turned out to be surprisingly easy because the headlights of Charlene's car provided enough guidance for her to stay on the road. Now the dark was their ally. In the daylight, Charlene would have spotted the van—it would have been hard not to, especially since the shop's name was painted on Mathilda's side—but the blackness cloaked it.

"Do you think Charlene knows we're behind her?" Libby asked as she watched Charlene exit the development a couple of minutes later and turn left on Victor, then go down another block and turn right onto Reunion Avenue.

Bernie shook her head. "She's certainly not driving as if she does." Then she fell silent again and slowed down even more. There were vehicles on Reunion, and Bernie had to turn on her lights so she wouldn't get in an accident with one of the other cars.

Three miles later, Charlene turned into a small strip mall that housed a pizza place, a tanning salon, a Thai restaurant, a dentist's office, and a high-end used clothing store. "Maybe Charlene's going to get takeout," Bernie suggested, killing her lights again as she followed her in.

"I hear Thai East is pretty good," Libby said, thinking that she could do with some pad thai right around now and then wondering if they could do a riff on the dish this fall using sweet potatoes instead of noodles.

"So do I. We should try it sometime," Bernie told her as she tried to figure out where to park.

There was a clump of trees at the entrance to the strip mall, and Bernie decided to stop behind it. It was the best she could do under the circumstances. Hopefully, the trees would allow Bernie and Libby to see and not be seen by Charlene. Bernie half expected Charlene to go into one of the restaurants, but she didn't. Instead, she drove to the far end of the mall. Then she parked her vehicle and got out. She was carrying something, but Bernie and Libby couldn't see what it was. Only that it was on the small side. Bernie whipped out her phone and started filming. The sisters watched as Charlene walked over to a Dumpster, lifted up the top, and threw whatever she was carrying into it.

"Interesting," Libby said as Charlene got back in her car, started it up, and sped out of the lot.

"Very interesting," Bernie agreed, looking at the video she'd made. It wasn't crystal clear, but it was good enough.

Chapter 37

"The question is—" Bernie began, but Libby interrupted her before Bernie had a chance to finish her sentence.

"I'm not doing it," she declared, anticipating her sister's request.

"Not doing what?" Bernie asked, as if she didn't know.

Libby pointed to the Dumpster they were now parked in front of. As soon as Charlene had driven away, Bernie had driven over to it. "Obviously, climbing in there to retrieve whatever Charlene got rid of." Libby shuddered. "I don't want to think about what's in there."

"Garbage."

Libby glared at her.

"Don't you want to know what Charlene threw out?" Bernie wheedled. "Aren't you curious?"

"Not as curious as you are." Libby scratched her wrist. My God, was the poison ivy spreading to her arms, too?

Bernie raised an eyebrow. "It has to be something pretty important if she came all the way here to throw it out. Otherwise, she would have tossed it at home."

"Fine," Libby said, conceding defeat. "So, maybe you're right. I am curious. It is something important. I just think you should be the one going Dumpster diving. After all, you were the one who suggested it."

"You know I would if I could," Bernie cooed, having anticipated this. "But I can't."

"And why not?" Libby asked.

"It would be a waste of money."

Libby cocked an eyebrow. "How do you get that?"

Bernie pointed to Libby and then pointed to herself. "Look at you and then look at me."

"So?" Libby didn't get where her sister was going.

"So, I'm wearing a Stella McCartney dress and a vintage Prada sweater, and you are wearing old sneakers, khaki shorts that should have been thrown out two years ago, and a weird color brown T-shirt. That's why."

Libby drew herself up. "It's not weird. It's purply brown."

"It's ugly," Bernie informed her.

"I like this shirt," Libby exclaimed, plucking at it. "What's wrong with this shirt?"

"Aside from the color, everything," Bernie told her.

"What's your point?" Libby demanded.

"My point," Bernie explained to her, "is that my clothes are worth considerably more than yours."

"If that's what's holding you back, Bernie, you know what? I have a suggestion. Take your clothes off and dive in."

"Okay. I will," Bernie promptly answered. As Libby watched, her sister took off her sweater and handed it to her. Then she began unbuttoning her dress. "Of course, Brandon got me my panties and bra, and I wouldn't want to get those dirty, either," she mused, "so I guess those will have to go, as well."

"Stop," Libby cried, horrified.

"Why?" Bernie smiled sweetly. "I'm just following your suggestion. Here." Bernie took off her shoes and handed them to Libby. "I wouldn't want to ruin my Manolos."

"But what if someone comes out?" Libby demanded. She was pretty sure that Bernie was kidding, but she wasn't positive. She could see her sister carrying out her threat. Bernie did take things to the extreme.

Bernie shrugged. "Then they'll see me naked. So what?"

Libby put both hands up in a gesture of surrender as she pictured the scene. It wasn't worth it, she decided. She didn't even want to think about what her father would say. "Okay. You win. But you owe me for this. You owe me big."

"I was willing—"

"Don't even bother saying it," Libby said, cutting her sister off, wanting to get it over with. She asked Bernie to move Mathilda closer to the Dumpster to make it easier to get in. Once Bernie did, both sisters got out of the van and Libby climbed onto the hood.

"Very graceful," Bernie commented as she watched her sister bend over, grip the edge of the Dumpster and half step, half fall into the metal container.

"Then you do it," Libby snapped as she righted herself. She'd stepped on something she didn't want to speculate about. "This is disgusting," she said.

"Oh, come on," Bernie replied, trying to jolly her along. "It's not that bad."

"It's bad enough," Libby told her. But Bernie was right, not that Libby was going to say that. It was pretty bad, but it wasn't "hold your nose and try not to throw up" terrible.

Despite the smell of rotten vegetables and the yucky stuff on the walls of the Dumpster, the origin of which

Libby refused to speculate on, most of the garbage was contained in black plastic bags. In addition, the Dumpster must have been emptied recently, meaning it was less than half full, which was a godsend.

"I don't see anything," Libby said as she looked around.

Bernie peeked over the edge. "I bet whatever Charlene threw in fell between the cracks and went down to the bottom," she said, speculating.

Libby groaned. This certainly gave new meaning to the term *Dumpster diving*. She began lifting up the garbage bags on the right side and piling them on top of each other on the left side. Fortunately, most of them were light. When she finished, she studied the Dumpster floor.

"Find anything?" Bernie asked as Libby looked.

"Nope." That is, outside of rotten lettuce leaves, moldy slices of pizza, a sprinkling of white cheese that had turned green, and eggshells. "If Charlene got rid of something, I'm not seeing it. Maybe we're wrong. Maybe we imagined the whole thing."

"No. We didn't. It has to be down there. Maybe a little light would help." Bernie took out her phone, activated its flashlight, and handed it to Libby.

Libby played the light around the Dumpster. She didn't see anything on the floor. She moved one of the bags and heard a squeak and jumped.

"I think I hear a rat," she said.

"It's probably a mouse," Bernie said, trying to reassure her.

"No. It's probably a rat, and I'm going to die from the bubonic plague," Libby said as she kept looking.

"No one dies from the plague anymore," Bernie replied. "They have antibiotics for that."

"I'll be the first," Libby told her, moving another bag. This one had some sort of slimy stuff on it, and she wiped the stuff from her hands onto her shorts. Then she moved a couple more bags. Two round metal containers slid down to the Dumpster floor, along with something that looked like a plaque of some kind or other.

"I think I found what Charlene got rid of," Libby said, picking the items up. She was just about to hand them to Bernie when Bernie heard a noise, someone whistling.

"Duck down," she whispered to Libby. "I think someone's coming."

"You're kidding me, right?"

"Shush." Bernie put her finger to her lips. "Keep it down, and no, unfortunately, I'm not."

The whistling grew louder. Now Libby could hear it, too. A moment later, a middle-aged Asian man wearing khaki slacks, a short-sleeved white shirt, and dark shoes rounded the corner. He was carrying a large bag of garbage in either hand. When he saw Bernie and the van, he came to a dead stop.

"What are you doing?" he asked Bernie. Then he read the sign on the van and said in a louder voice, "Trying to get rid of your garbage?"

"Don't be silly," she told him, deciding that he was the owner of the Thai restaurant. She recognized him from Sam's Club.

"I'm not paying the haulage fees to have you use this Dumpster," he told her angrily, pointing at the logo on the side of the van.

"We have our own service, thank you very much," Bernie snapped back. But she could understand why he was annoyed. She used the same company, and they were not cheap. None of the trash removal companies were.

The owner's frown deepened. It was obvious he didn't believe her. "I have a good mind to call the police," he told her.

The last thing we need, Bernie thought as she gestured to herself. "Call the company and check." She sighed. "Look," she continued, "would I be wearing this if I was throwing garbage in your Dumpster?"

"Why wouldn't you?" the owner asked, unimpressed with Bernie's argument.

Obviously, a man with no fashion sense, Bernie decided.

She was just about to explain her statement when the owner said, "Okay. If you're telling the truth, then what are you doing here?"

Bernie explained. She waved her hands in the air, doing her best damsel in distress imitation. "I thought someone was following me, so I slipped in here to lose him."

The owner nodded and tossed the garbage bags in the Dumpster. "I see," he said as he reached over and closed the top. Bernie flinched at the thud. "I don't know why everyone can't remember to shut this thing," he continued. "How hard is it?" he asked Bernie.

"We have that problem, too," Bernie replied, trying not to think about what Libby was feeling right now. Especially since Libby didn't like closed-in spaces.

The owner turned to go, but then he turned back and faced Bernie. "There's no one out there now," he remarked.

"Thanks," Bernie told him.

The owner nodded.

"I guess I should be going," Bernie said.

"I guess you should," the owner replied, and he planted his feet on the ground and crossed his arms over his chest.

Clearly, Bernie thought, he wasn't going to leave before she did.

"Have a good evening," she said to him as she got into the van. She started Mathilda up.

Libby is going to kill me, she decided as she put the van in drive and motored out of the parking lot. But there was nothing she could do about the situation now. As she exited, she could see the restaurant owner in the rearview mirror. Now he was standing in front of Thai East, smoking a cigarette and watching to make sure that she left. She took the first right that presented itself and went down Veil Road. Chesterton Street was the next right, and she turned onto it.

Now she was in the Hidden Valley development, a development that was newer and considerably cheaper than the one Marie's and Charlene's houses were in. The houses here were smaller and closer together, the lawns were edged with white pavers and dotted with ceramic gnomes, and the cars in the driveways were Kias and Hyundais instead of BMWs and Infinitis. Kids' bikes littered the driveways, and there was an abundance of portable basketball hoops set back near the garages. Two of the houses Bernie went by had small RVs parked in front of them.

Normally, the street would have been crowded with kids and parents, but it was late, and everyone was in for the night. Bernie went up a couple more houses and parked on the side of the road in front of a brick colonial that had a FOR SALE sign out front and no vehicles in the driveway. As a precaution, though, she took out an old phone—since Libby had hers—and pretended to talk on it in case someone was in the house and called the police because they wanted to know what she was doing there. But no one came.

It seemed to take forever, but finally five minutes was up and Bernie made a U-turn and drove back to the strip mall. This time, she drove in from the other side of the mall, taking care not to cross in front of the Thai restaurant. Then she pulled up next to the Dumpster, parked, and got out.

"He's gone," Bernie whispered as she lifted up the Dumpster top.

Libby popped up like a jack-in-the-box. "You certainly took your bloody time getting back here," she snarled as she glared at her sister.

Bernie decided that if looks could kill, she'd be dead. "I couldn't help it. I had to make sure the guy was gone."

"I thought I'd die in there."

"Let's not exaggerate," Bernie told her sister. Then she was sorry she did, because a statement like that didn't help matters.

"You didn't have garbage bags thrown on your head." Libby picked up a speck of white on her shirt and held it up. "Oh, my God," she screamed. "It's a maggot."

"It's a grain of rice," Bernie said.

Libby took a second look. Her sister was right.

"Here," Bernie said, and she reached over and brushed some more grains of rice from Libby's hair and shoulders. "Let me help."

Libby was not placated. "What if I'd been attacked by rats? What if I'd suffocated to death?"

"But you weren't, and you didn't," Bernie told her.

"But I could have been," Libby replied.

Bernie sighed. "Can I see what you found?"

"All I can say is I hope it was worth it," Libby said as she handed the items to her sister.

Bernie studied them. "Let's go see what Charlene has to say about this, shall we?"

"Yes, let's," Libby agreed, and then she said, "Oh, by the way, Lucy called while I was in the Dumpster."

Bernie's stomach flip-flopped. "What did he want?"

"To see how we were doing."

"And what did you tell him?"

"That we were doing great. He said he'd drop by our flat later to hear about our progress."

"Wonderful," Bernie said.

Chapter 38

Bernie looked at Libby. She was rubbing the scrape on her leg she'd gotten from climbing out of the Dumpster. Getting in had been easy. Getting out had been a lot harder. Libby wasn't strong enough to pull herself out, and Bernie didn't have enough upper-body strength to make up the difference.

In the end, Libby had had to pile the garbage bags on top of each other so she could use them to scramble out. Just in time, too. As they left the strip mall, Bernie saw the owner of Thai East in the van's rearview mirror. He was coming out of the restaurant with another two bags of garbage in his hands.

"Well, that was close," Bernie observed as Libby got a tissue out of the glove compartment and blotted the scrape on her leg.

"I should probably get a tetanus shot," she said.

Bernie had the good sense not to say anything.

Libby looked at her watch. It was covered with slime. "I loved this watch," she said mournfully.

"It'll be fine," Bernie said.

"Yeah. But every time I look at it, I'll think about being in that Dumpster."

"I'll get you a new one," Bernie told her.

"I've had it forever," Libby moaned, trying for maximum guilt.

"You bought it last year in Chinatown. I was with you."

Libby couldn't think of an answer, so she just grunted and moved away from the window. It had started to drizzle, and she didn't want to get wet.

"I don't suppose we could close the windows," Libby said.

"Not unless you want the smell of garbage in the van," Bernie said. "You should burn those clothes when we get home," she added.

Libby moved a tad closer.

"Stop it," Bernie said as she inched farther away.

"Stop what?" Libby asked, all pretend innocence. She was enjoying watching her sister squirm. "I'm not doing anything."

Bernie snorted. "Stop trying to stink me out."

Libby didn't say anything, because it was true. They arrived at Charlene's house ten minutes later. It was a little after twelve. All the houses on the street were dark except for Charlene's.

"No big surprise there," Bernie observed as she parked at the end of Charlene's driveway. Then she got an umbrella out from behind the driver's seat and stepped out of the van. Libby joined her, and they marched up the driveway and climbed the five steps that led to the house.

Bernie leaned over and rang the bell. When no one answered, she rang again, this time keeping her thumb on the button. A moment later, the door swung open.

"What are you doing here?" Charlene demanded. "Do you know what time it is?"

"Indeed, we do," Bernie said. "I believe it's a little past the witching hour."

Then Libby took a step forward, and Charlene took a step back, flinching at the smell coming off Libby. "Here." Libby held out the two tins and the plaque she'd found in the Dumpster. "We thought you'd want these back."

Charlene swallowed. Twice. "I don't know what you're talking about," she said, looking at what was in Libby's hands, then looking away.

"You shouldn't play cards," Bernie told her. "You don't do a poker face very well."

"It's simple," Libby explained. "We saw you throwing out these things in the Dumpster near Thai East, and we're being good neighbors and returning them to you."

"You must have the wrong person," Charlene blustered.

"I don't think so," Bernie said. "We have you on video."

Charlene swallowed again. "I don't believe you."

Bernie showed her.

Charlene bit her lip as she watched. "That could be anyone," she said in a shaky voice after the video was over.

"I don't think so." Bernie pointed to the T-shirt Charlene was wearing in the video. "I saw you wearing that T-shirt a couple of weeks ago at the supermarket."

"Lots of people have that shirt," Charlene protested.

"Yeah," Libby said. "A shirt with BIRDSEED BY BOBBY on it is definitely a big seller. I bet they carry it in all the department stores these days. It's a cult thing."

"You should learn to mind your own business," Charlene snapped. She started to close the door, but before she could, Bernie stuck her foot in the doorway.

"Unfortunately, that's not an option," she told Charlene.

"You just couldn't see the caviar go to waste, could you?" Libby added. "So you took the unopened tins out of the cooler. I can understand that. Really, I can. But the plaque? Come on. Why that? Then Marie called you, and you panicked. A really dumb move, if you ask me. If you'd left the stuff in your house, we wouldn't be having this conversation."

Libby and Bernie could see Charlene's jaw set, could see self-righteous anger settling in and taking hold. Charlene stood up straight and looked Bernie and Libby in the eye. "She owed that caviar to me," she told them.

"Really?" Bernie said.

"Yes, really." The anger in Charlene's voice was palpable. "She owed it to me for everything she's done."

"And I suppose Susie owed you the plaque, as well?" Libby asked.

Charlene shook her head. "No. But Susie owed Marie the plaque. She deserved it. Her cat would have won the show if Susie hadn't paid off one of the judges."

"You mean Dana?" Libby asked.

Charlene nodded. "Yes. That's exactly who I mean."

Libby smiled a gotcha smile. "Really? Because we talked to Dana, and she denies your accusation."

"Well, Dana's a big fat liar," Charlene spat back.

Bernie tilted the umbrella to keep the rain off her back. "I would have thought disrupting the wedding would have been enough for you and Marie. But I guess it wasn't enough. I guess you had to kill Susie. Which one of you stabbed her? The first person to confess usually gets a better deal."

"Wow." Charlene put her hands out. "Slow down. Neither of us killed her. We would have liked to, but we didn't."

"Someone did," Libby observed.

"It wasn't us," Charlene said. "The mice were a joke. Just a joke."

"Not a very funny one," Libby said.

Bernie changed the subject. "When did you take the plaque?" Bernie asked Charlene.

"After Marie left Susie's house. I thought it would be nice for her to have."

Libby frowned. "Okay," Libby said. "Run this by us again, because I'm not getting it."

"Getting what?" Charlene asked.

"The timeline," Bernie said.

"It's simple," Charlene said. "We went back to the house."

"After the cats got out," Bernie replied.

Charlene nodded.

"We didn't see you," Libby objected.

"That's because we doubled back through the tent," Charlene explained. "By that time," she added, "you and your sister were out in the meadow."

"Why'd you go back?" Bernie asked.

"Because Marie and I wanted to tell Susie what we'd done. But she was in the bathroom."

"How did you know?" Bernie demanded.

"Because we could hear the water running through the pipes. We figured she'd gone upstairs to take a shower."

Libby leaned down and scratched her ankle. "Then why didn't you and Marie wait for her to come down?"

"Marie got cold feet. She decided telling Susie wasn't the best idea, and she left, but I stayed." Charlene pointed to herself. "I was going to tell Susie and not mention Marie's name. I really wanted to see the look on her face when she found out that I was responsible for what had happened. But then I started thinking, and the more I thought about what Susie would do when she found out what I'd done, the more I thought that maybe Marie was right, after all. So I left, too."

Libby stopped scratching and straightened up. "After you took the plaque?"

Charlene nodded.

"But before Susie came down?" Libby asked.

"Yes," Charlene answered. "Before Susie came down."

"And yet," Bernie said, "when Susie was stabbed, she was wearing the same clothes she had on at the wedding. I don't know about you, but after taking a shower, I usually change into clean clothes."

Charlene shrugged. "Maybe she wasn't like you. Or maybe she heard someone come in after I'd left, and just grabbed what was on the bathroom floor and put it on so she could see who was there."

"So you say," Bernie told her.

"I do." Charlene smirked at Bernie. "Unless you can prove different."

"What about the plaque?" Libby asked, jumping into the conversation and switching subjects. "Tell me again when you took it."

"I already told you. When I was waiting for Susie to come down, of course."

"Of course," Libby echoed.

Charlene ignored the sarcasm. "I was petting the cats in Susie's study, and I saw the plaque sitting there on the shelf, and I got really angry, because Marie should have won the show. It wasn't right. I grabbed it to give to her, and I walked out the door."

"And Susie was alive when you left?" Libby asked.

"That's what I said," Charlene snapped. "How many times do I have to repeat myself?"

"Tell me once more how you knew that," Bernie said.

Charlene sighed the sigh of the put upon. "Like I said, because I could hear the water running. Are we done?"

Bernie crossed her arms over her chest. "Indulge my sister and me for a few more minutes. Tell us, what did you do then?"

"Duh. I put the caviar and the plaque in my car and went down to get a drink with Marie. Then we came back up to Susie's house."

"And yet you kept the plaque," Libby noted. "You didn't give it to Marie. Why was that?"

Charlene shrugged her shoulders. "I forgot about it. With everything that was happening. I don't know. I just didn't. I guess I wasn't thinking."

"Why did you and Marie go back to Susie's house?" Libby asked Charlene.

"It would have looked funny if we hadn't, wouldn't it have? We didn't want to give Susie a reason to suspect us."

"Nice story," Bernie noted.

"It's the truth and you can't prove otherwise," she told Bernie.

Which was true. Not something that Bernie wanted to admit. Instead, she changed the subject. "Why did you send a package of mice to us?"

"Yes. Why?" Libby asked. "What did we ever do to you?"

"It was Marie's idea," Charlene told them. "You'll have to ask her."

"Funny, but she said it was yours," Bernie said.

"Well, she's lying," Charlene told her.

Bernie adjusted the umbrella. "Is she?"

"Yes, she is," Charlene declared. "I know what you're doing. You're trying to make us turn on each other. I watch TV. I've seen *Law & Order*."

"Which makes you an expert," Libby said.

"Expert enough," Charlene shot back.

"And yet your nephew is the one who delivered the packages. Both packages," Libby pointed out.

"That doesn't prove anything," Charlene insisted.

"It proves that you're heavily involved," Bernie told her.

"Not just involved, but heavily involved," Charlene mocked. "Wow. Now I'm really worried."

"Let us help you," Bernie said, having decided to ignore the sarcasm and try another tactic.

Charlene gave her a "How dumb do you think I am?" look.

Bernie slogged on. "Seriously," she said. "Right now, it looks as if you're going to jail. Murder two." Bernie shook her head sadly. "That's a long time to spend in jail. Maybe if we spoke to your nephew, he could tell us something that would help us prove your innocence."

Charlene started to laugh.

"What's so funny?" Bernie asked.

"You," Charlene told her. "Nice try, but no cigar."

"What does that even mean?" Libby asked.

"It means I'm tired of playing your stupid 'I think I'm a detective' game. It means you can go to hell," Charlene told her. Then she slammed the door.

Bernie got her foot out of the doorway just in the nick of time. "Well, that didn't go well," she noted.

"At least we kept our promise to Susie about finding out who sent the mice," Libby observed as she and Bernie headed for the van. "Too bad we still don't know who killed her."

"But we will, Libby. We will."

As they got to the bottom of the driveway, the sky let loose with a torrent of rain. It came down in sheets, working its way into the sisters' hair and running down into their eyes and ears. Then, just as suddenly as it came, the storm departed, leaving the sisters soaking wet, Bernie's umbrella having given up the ghost against the onslaught.

"I guess I don't have to take a shower now, Bernie," Libby kidded as she wrung the water out of her shirt.

"Oh no, Libby. You do. You definitely do," Bernie said as she reached up and brushed some more rice and a couple of snow peas that she'd missed out of Libby's hair.

Chapter 39

Day five . . .

The rain had woken Sean up at five in the morning, and it gave no sign of letting up. It hit the windowpanes as he studied one of the sheets of paper he'd ripped off the legal pad he'd found on top of Susie's desk. When he was done, he leaned back in his chair, put the page down, looked out the window, and sighed. It had been a wet spring. He just hoped it wasn't like this in the summer.

Sean watched the water running down the street in streams, the streams carrying leaves and twigs along, forming little lakes around the storm drains, and eddying around the curbs. If it kept up like this, Sean wondered if the street would flood, something that hadn't happened since the city fixed the drainage system twenty years ago. Before that, there'd been water in the basement. He sure hoped that wasn't going to happen again.

Main Street was deserted. Except for the mailman scurrying along, Sean didn't see anyone else out. Even Mrs. McDonald had run out with her corgi and run back in as soon as Edna had done her business. They'd been having a lot of these kinds of days recently, Sean reflected. Too many. The painters couldn't paint, and the farmers couldn't plant. The strawberry festival had been rained out, as had the ice cream social by the library, and Libby and Bernie had been complaining about a drop in their business. People didn't want to park down the block and run into the shop. And who could blame them?

Sean remembered the days when he'd been out in this kind of weather, when he got called to every accident in the area. Snow was bad, but rain was worse. Once you got wet, you were wet for the whole day. That was the good thing about being retired, he supposed. He wasn't on a schedule.

With that thought in mind, he extracted another page from under Cindy and tried once again to find some clue, some hint of who had killed Susie in her scribblings. And failed. He'd been looking at those pages on and off ever since he'd gotten them. But the result was always the same. Nothing stood out. Nothing struck him. And yet his gut told him the answer he was looking for was in the pages. Somewhere. If he could only see it.

"What do you think, Cindy?" he asked the cat.

Cindy swished her tail and meowed. Sean supposed it was as good an answer as any. He was about to ask her what she meant when he heard footsteps on the stairs. Ah. Breakfast was about to arrive. He smiled and put the papers aside. Maybe after he'd eaten, an answer would suggest itself. And in the meantime, he and his daughters had other things to discuss. A moment later, Bernie and Libby arrived, bearing trays loaded with food. Sean grinned and rubbed his hands together in anticipation. Judging by what he was seeing, he had a good meal in store.

Sam poured a little more coffee into his cup from the French roast sitting on the coffee table, added a small amount of cream, two cubes of raw sugar, and stirred. He watched the cream turn the coffee a light tan. Then he took a sip and savored the bittersweet taste, after which he ate a piece of the fried duck egg sitting on the blue-and-white china plate that Libby had set before him.

"What do you think?" Libby asked as she sat down to her breakfast, which was the same as her dad's.

Sean took another bite and chewed carefully. "I think the duck eggs taste the same as chicken eggs. If you hadn't told me, I wouldn't be able to tell the difference."

"That's what I said, too," Bernie replied as she took her seat near the coffee table and tasted her egg. She and Libby were discussing serving duck eggs in the shop.

"I think it would be a neat novelty item," Libby said. "Something new to try. People like new."

"Some people," Sean observed.

"Young people," Libby said and laughed.

"True," Sean said, and he laughed, too. "What's the difference between the two kinds of eggs, then?" he asked Libby. As he waited for the reply, he took a bite of the blueberry, arugula, goat cheese, and toasted walnut salad and followed that up with a bit of toasted, buttered brioche. As he did, he reflected that he was a lucky man to have daughters who liked to cook and bake.

Libby answered. "Well, the duck eggs last longer because their shells are thicker, they're larger, they have bigger yolks, more omega-three, and a higher cholesterol count. Also, they're supposed to make a fluffier omelet."

"They're also more expensive," Bernie added. "A lot more expensive."

Libby waved her fork in the air. "Not in this case, though. Not for us."

"The Codys have a flock," Bernie explained to her dad. "And they want to build up their business, so they're giving us a deal."

"A very good deal," Libby said.

"In that case, by all means, go ahead and serve them," Sean said. "What are you going to do with them?"

"For starters, I'm thinking roasted asparagus with a fried duck egg on toast, with strips of speck, for an upscale breakfast sandwich," Libby said.

Sean raised an eyebrow. "Speck?" He'd never heard of it.

"It's an Italian bacon-tasting cold cut. Kind of like prosciutto."

"Sounds good," Sean commented.

"It is good," Libby agreed. "The only problem is the fried egg part might be tricky. Especially in the morning, when everyone wants to get in and get out quickly. I'll have to see if I can figure it out." Then she pointed at the papers Sean had put aside. "Are those Susie's?" she asked.

Sean nodded. "I keep hoping something's going to pop out at me."

"I take it nothing has popped," Bernie observed.

"You take it correctly." And Sean took another bite of brioche.

"Maybe there's nothing there to pop out," Bernie said.

Sean ate a bit more of his egg. It did taste a little different from a hen's egg, he decided. The duck egg was a little richer. Especially the yolk. "I think I like these, after all," he said. Then he pointed to the papers with his fork. "I just have this feeling there's something there, but maybe you're right. Maybe my feeling is wrong. Maybe I've lost my ability to sniff things out."

"Let me see them again," Bernie said, reaching out her hand.

Sean passed the pages to her. "Be my guest."

Bernie put the pages on the coffee table, between herself and Libby, so they could both study them while they ate. Sean watched his daughters and ate his breakfast, pausing now and then to give tidbits to Cindy, who seemed to like the brioche as much as she liked the egg.

"So, what do you think?" he asked his daughters after five minutes had gone by.

Bernie swallowed the last of her salad before answering. "The same thing I thought when you showed me the pages the first time. I think this is Susie's to-do list for the party, plus her tasks for the day. She said she was an obsessive list maker, and evidently, she was right." Bernie tapped the yellow papers with one of her fingernails. "Here she's calling the roofer, here she's calling the oven repair guy, and here she's made a note to herself to take care of the deeds to some of her properties. Unless these notes are a code for something else, this is pretty straightforward."

Sean sighed. "Agreed. Libby, what do you think?"

"If there's anything on these pages that would be helpful to our investigation, I'm not seeing it, either," Libby concurred after she'd finished her egg. "I wish there was, but I don't think there is." Libby gestured to the numerous cats Susie had doodled on the pages. Some had hats, some had collars, a couple were wearing tiaras, others were wearing bow ties, and one had a lace dress on.

"Susie was really obsessed with Boris and Natasha's wedding, wasn't she?" Sean noted as he put the pages back where they had been. Then he finished his coffee, sat back in his chair, rubbed Cindy's ears, and waited for Libby and Bernie to tell him what had happened with Lucy.

Sean had been up last night when Bernie and Libby came in looking like drowned rats and smelling like a garbage dump, so he'd heard most of the details of their evening's adventures. What he was waiting to hear was what Lucy had said to them when he'd appeared at A Little Taste of Heaven at seven o'clock this morning.

For a few minutes, no one spoke. The only sounds in the room were the sounds of rain hitting the windowpane, the hum of the customers downstairs, and the tick of the clock on the wall. Then Libby began.

"Let's just say that Lucy wasn't impressed with the plaque and the caviar tins as evidence," Libby told her dad before she took another bite of her brioche.

"He's not going to arrest Charlene and Marie, I take it?" Sean asked.

Bernie shook her head and finished the last of her egg. "No. He's still talking about arresting us."

"He won't," Sean reassured them.

"Well, he's certainly talking as if he will," Bernie said.

"Did you show him the video, Bernie?" Sean asked.

"Yeah, I did, and he wasn't impressed, Dad. Far from."

"What did he say, exactly?"

"He said that Charlene having the caviar and the plaque doesn't prove that she killed Susie. Except he didn't say it as politely."

"I can only imagine," Sean said. "Unfortunately, Lucy's correct. It doesn't."

"It does put her at the scene, though," Libby said.

"But she was already at the scene," Bernie objected. "What it doesn't do is put her hand on the knife."

"Letter opener," Libby said, correcting her.

"Whatever," Bernie snapped. "We're going to have to face the fact that Charlene's story might be true. Given the circumstances, I might have taken the caviar, as well. And even if it isn't true, even if she's lying, it doesn't matter, because we can't prove anything different. We're no closer to finding out who killed Susie than we were before."

"What now?" Sean asked, looking from one daughter to the other. "What's your plan?"

"Good question," Bernie said.

"We don't have one," Libby admitted. "We're just running around in circles like a chicken without a head." She turned to her father. "What would you do, Dad?"

Sean replied promptly. "Who haven't you spoken to yet?"

Libby and Bernie both thought for a moment. Then they both said at the same time, "Charlene's nephew."

"Then I'd try to find him and hear what he has to say. Maybe he has something to contribute, and even if he doesn't"—Sean shrugged—"at least you'll have tried. What do you know about him?"

"Not much," Bernie replied. "We don't even know his first name."

"Makes finding him a little challenging," Sean observed.

"Yes, it does," Bernie agreed. She thought for a moment. Then it came to her. "I do believe it's time to wake up Brandon," Bernie said. "If anyone would know, Brandon would. After all, everyone goes to RJ's."

"Let's hope so," Sean said as his daughters went downstairs to start their day. He reached over, picked up the *TV Guide*, and thumbed through it. Two of his favorite movies were on this afternoon. *Excellent*, he thought as he sat back in his chair and began the day's crossword puzzle.

Chapter 40

Bernie came armed for her encounter with Brandon. She'd filled a tote with a large thermos of coffee with cream; a sausage, egg, and avocado sandwich on a toasted, buttered piece of sourdough bread; a pint of freshly made fruit salad with mint and rosemary; and a half of a blueberry pie. Then, after making a quick stop at the bank, Bernie had driven over to Brandon's flat and banged on his door.

She would have used the bell except it wasn't working. It hadn't since Brandon moved in, and it didn't look as if that was going to change in the near future. When Brandon didn't answer, Bernie banged on the door again.

She was lifting her arm to knock on the door for the third time, when it swung open. "Third times the charm," she muttered to herself. A tired-looking Brandon was standing in the doorway in his boxers and T-shirt, rubbing his eyes.

"What's the matter?" Brandon asked, stifling a yawn. "What's wrong?"

"Nothing's wrong," Bernie said as she walked by him

into the kitchen and put the food she'd brought down on the kitchen table.

Brandon trailed behind her. "Then what are you doing here?" he demanded, yawning again. "Do you know what time it is?"

"As a matter of fact, I do. I have a question for you."

"Good for you," Brandon growled, now pissed. "I'm going back to bed. I didn't get to sleep until five."

"You really need to find a normal job with normal hours," Bernie told him as he headed for his bedroom.

"Thanks." For emphasis, Brandon slammed his bedroom door.

Given the circumstances, that had probably not been the best thing to say, Bernie reflected as she got the coffee out of her tote, poured it into one of Brandon's mugs, added a generous amount of sugar, took out the egg and sausage sandwich, and carried the coffee and the sandwich into the bedroom.

"Go away," Brandon said as Bernie approached the bed. "I'm not talking to you." And to make his point, he pulled the covers over his head.

"I have coffee and your favorite breakfast sandwich," Bernie sang. "And I brought some fresh fruit salad and a half of a blueberry pie, as well."

"When was it made?" Brandon asked, his voice muffled by the covers.

"The pie?"

"Yes. The pie."

"This morning," Bernie told him.

"All right." Brandon pulled the covers back and sat up. Bernie handed him the coffee and the sandwich. "Couldn't this have waited?" he asked after he'd drained the mug.

"I wouldn't be here if it could." Bernie took Brandon's

mug from him, went into the kitchen to refill it, and brought it back.

"What do you want to know?" he asked, taking a sip.

"The name of Charlene's nephew and where he lives."

Brandon wrinkled his nose. "Who?"

"Charlene's nephew. His last name is Eberhart."

Brandon shook his head. "It doesn't ring any bells. Describe him to me."

Bernie did. "He's about six feet tall. Skinny. Close-cut cropped hair. Brown eyes. Brown hair. He was wearing jeans and a T-shirt with a picture of the Brooklyn Bridge on it."

"You'll have to do better than that," Brandon said right before he tore into the sandwich Bernie had brought.

"He has a tattoo around his wrist. A really bad tattoo of Mickey Mouse. It looks as if he tried to get it removed, but someone didn't finish the job."

"Oh, him," Brandon said. "That's Ricky."

Bernie cocked her head. "Ricky?"

"Yeah. Why the look?"

"It's just an old-fashioned name."

"Maybe his parents are old-fashioned people."

"Maybe," Bernie said. "Do you know where I can find him?"

Brandon shook his head. "I know he does errands for Andy Dupont on occasion."

"Great," Bernie muttered.

"I expect payment," Brandon said.

"I brought you half a pie."

Brandon leered and twirled an imaginary mustache. "That's not exactly what I had in mind."

Bernie grinned. "I figured."

Bernie pulled up to Andy Dupont's father's car lot an hour and a half later. She parked Mathilda and used the rearview mirror to put on some lipstick and make sure all her shirt buttons were buttoned before she got out of the van. Then she walked to the trailer and opened the door.

Andy Dupont stopped playing *Call of Duty*, took his feet off the desk, and put them down on the floor when Bernie stepped inside.

"Come to trade in your van?" he asked her.

Bernie shook her head and closed the door behind her. The bell jingled again.

"Then what?" Andy wanted to know.

"I'm looking for Ricky, Ricky Eberhart."

"Don't know him," Andy Dupont told her, his eyes drifting back to his game.

"Brandon says you do. He said Ricky works for you sometimes."

Andy shrugged his shoulders and held out his hands, palms up. "What can I say? Your boyfriend is wrong."

"Not about this kind of stuff."

Andy shrugged. "He is this time."

Bernie persisted. "The guy I'm trying to find has a tattoo of Mickey Mouse on his wrist, a bad tattoo."

Andy laughed. "Oh. You mean Speedo."

Bernie wrinkled her nose. "Speedo?"

"Yeah. That's what we call him."

"Why? Because Ricky wears Speedos?"

"No. Because he's so damn slow. Does this have to do with the Susie thing?" Andy asked.

Bernie walked over, perched herself on the edge of Andy's desk, leaned over, and glanced at the papers on it. "Will my answer make a difference?"

"Not really," Andy said. He picked up the papers Bernie was looking at, opened a desk drawer, put them inside it, and then closed the drawer, slamming it shut for emphasis, after which he picked up his gaming console. "He's not working for me anymore."

"How come?"

"Let's say we had a difference of opinion."

Bernie tugged at her skirt hem. "Over what?"

"How much money was in the till."

"I see. Do you know where I can find him?"

"The hospital."

Bernie raised an eyebrow. "Seriously?"

Andy smiled. "Nah. I'm kidding. He just took a quick trip to the ER."

Bernie smiled back. "That was generous of you."

Andy blew on the knuckles of his right hand and rubbed them on his chest. "I told you, I'm a sweetie pie."

"That's not exactly the word I would use." Bernie shifted her weight and leaned forward a little. "So, Andy, are you telling me you don't know where Ricky . . ."

"Speedo . . ."

"Speedo is?"

"Not at all, Bernie. Far from. The last I heard, he was bunking in with Fred."

"Fred who?"

"Fred 'the Hand' Alberti."

"The one who used to run the strip club down in Piedmont before it got busted?"

"Yes. That one."

"And do you happen to know where Fred is living?" Bernie asked, wondering if this conversation could go any slower.

"As a matter of·fact, I do," Andy Dupont replied. "He lives in the run-down house next to the cement factory."

Bernie knew the one. The cement factory had ceased operation, but the house had remained. "That's quite the comedown," she observed as she stood up.

Andy Dupont snorted. "He's lucky he's not in a shallow grave after what he did."

"Can I ask why you're being so helpful?" Bernie asked.

"Because he deserves whatever he's got coming to him," Andy replied, turning his attention back to his video game.

He didn't look up as Bernie left. The sounds of the game followed her out the door.

Chapter 41

The house Andy Dupont had mentioned had always given Bernie the willies. It had been built by the owner of the cement factory so that he could keep an eye on his property, but it had been abandoned a long time ago, consigned to a slow, inexorable decline.

Located on a one-way dead-end street on the edge of town, the house and the cement factory were the only structures for a square block. The two-story house was dark green with white trim, the green paint made lighter by the fine layer of concrete dust that seemed to have permanently settled on it. The place looked deserted, with its two upstairs windows boarded up with plywood, the mailbox that leaned to the left, the garage that was in the process of toppling over, the blue tarp that covered half of the roof, and the moldering telephone directories on the doorstep.

Bernie passed by the place when she went to and from the farmers' market. Sometimes there were cars in the driveway, and sometimes there weren't. Sometimes she saw lights in there; sometimes she didn't. Squatters, she figured. Now she could put a name to two of them.

She arrived at the house after leaving the car lot. Three turkey buzzards perched on the roof flew off when they heard Mathilda coming. Bernie parked out on the street, because it made her feel better, and walked to the house, avoiding what had once been a flagstone walkway and was now a jumble of heaved-up pavers and weeds. She knew she was being ridiculous, but she called Libby and told her where she was—just in case something happened—before she got to the door.

When she got there, she looked for a bell, but there wasn't any, so she knocked. The door was a hollow-core one, and she could feel the flimsiness against her knuckles. A moment later Fred Alberti answered.

"What do you want?" he asked through the closed door.

"To speak to Ricky."

"Who?"

"Speedo."

"Yeah." Alberti's voice was gruff. "Well, he's not talking to anyone right now."

"He'll want to talk to me."

"And why is that?" Alberti demanded.

Why was that? Bernie asked herself. *Good question*, she thought.

"Hey. You going to answer or what?" Fred Alberti asked when Bernie didn't reply immediately. "I got better things to do than stand around all day."

"Tell him I'll give him fifty bucks to answer a couple of questions," Bernie replied after a momentary pause. After all, it was Susie's money she was spending.

"Wait here," Alberti said. "I'll get him. The bum owes me twenty."

While Bernie waited, she watched the buzzards resume their perches. Then a fourth one landed, and a fifth one was about to when Alberti opened the door and pushed Speedo, aka Ricky, aka Charlene's nephew, out onto the stoop.

"Here he is," he said to Bernie. "And you," he said, turning to Ricky, "better tell this lady what she wants to know." Then he closed the door, leaving Ricky standing there with a beer in one hand and a joint in the other. The smell of weed wafted through the air, reminding Bernie of her younger days.

"What?" he demanded as Bernie took in the black eye and the cast on his left hand.

"Did Andy do that to you?" Bernie asked.

"Is that one of the questions?"

"No, it isn't."

"It'll cost you an extra fifty to find out."

"I don't care that much," Bernie told him.

"Then what do you want to know?" Ricky asked.

Bernie told him.

"Let me see the money first," Ricky said.

Bernie got out five ten-dollar bills and showed them to him. Ricky took a gulp of beer, crumpled up the can, threw it on the ground, and reached for the money.

"Not yet." Bernie pulled her hand back. "After you answer my questions," she told him. "Did Marie or Charlene ask you to deliver the mice?"

Ricky shrugged. "They were both there."

"Yeah. But which one asked you?"

As Ricky took a hit off his joint, the door to the house opened, and Alberti emerged.

"Answer her," he growled at Ricky.

He must have been listening at the door, Bernie decided.

"Give me a moment," Ricky whined. "I'm thinking."

Bernie didn't make the obvious comment.

"My aunt," Ricky said after another minute had gone by.
"You're sure?" Bernie asked.

"Kinda. Like I said, they were both there."

Bernie frowned. This was leading nowhere. "How stoned were you?"

Ricky grinned. "Really stoned. Really, really stoned. I was smoking some good stuff."

Alberti stepped forward. "Speedo answered your questions," Alberti said to Bernie. "Now give him his money."

"He didn't really," Bernie objected.

Alberti glared at her. Bernie thought about arguing with him, then decided against it. There didn't seem to be much point, what with Ricky's power of recollection being what it was. One of the turkey buzzards sitting on the roof probably remembered more than Ricky did.

"Fine," Bernie said, holding out the money, but before Ricky could take it, Alberti grabbed it.

"Hey," Ricky protested. "You said you were just going to take twenty."

"I changed my mind," Alberti told him as he pocketed the tens. "Sue me." Then he walked back inside the house.

Ricky looked as if he was going to cry. Then he brightened and leaned toward Bernie. His breath, a combination of beer, weed, and tobacco, washed over her. "Hey," he whispered. "You got a twenty?"

"That depends," Bernie said.

"Will you give it to me if I tell you something?" Ricky asked in a voice full of hope.

"Like what?"

"Like something important?"

Bernie nodded. She wasn't expecting much, but she felt sorry for the guy. She decided he was going to be her good deed for the day.

Ricky blinked and took another hit off his joint. "But you can't tell anyone it came from me."

"I promise," Bernie said as she watched Ricky snuff the joint out with his fingers and carefully put the roach in his T-shirt pocket.

"You gotta swear," Ricky told her when he was done. "'Cause they're going to be pissed."

"Who?"

"Everyone."

"Not exactly informative, but fair enough." Bernie held up her hand. "I swear. Satisfied?"

Ricky nodded. Then he looked at the house and looked back. "He's probably watching," Ricky said.

"It wouldn't surprise me," Bernie agreed, figuring Ricky meant Alberti.

"Can you give me a lift to Nice N Easy?" Ricky asked.

"I can do that," Bernie told him. The convenience store was five blocks away.

"Good," Ricky said, and he walked over to Mathilda and got in the passenger side. "I'm gonna go back to school and get my GED," he told Bernie as she started the van up.

She nodded. "Sounds like a good idea." As Bernie pulled into the road, the turkey buzzards on the roof rose in the air, wheeled around, and resettled themselves. Their eyes followed the van until it turned the corner.

Ricky looked at his fingers and picked at a cuticle. For a moment, the only sound in the van was that of the van's tires crunching over the gravel lying on the street. Then he started to talk. The words came out in a rush. "See, after I delivered the package, I came back because I was feeling a little . . . off . . . and I wanted to light up, but it . . ."

"Your joint?" Bernie said, guessing.

"Yeah. Must have slipped out of my pocket—I have this hole—when I was delivering the package, so I went back to find it."

"Then why didn't I see you?" Bernie asked, glancing at Ricky.

" 'Cause you and your sister were running around down near where the trees were," Ricky explained. "And, by the way, I'm sorry. I didn't know what was in the package. I really didn't," Ricky added for emphasis. "If I had, I wouldn't have done it. That lady . . ."

"Susie Katz?" Bernie asked for the sake of clarity.

"Yeah. Her. She never done nothin' to me." Ricky's eyes narrowed. "And Charlene didn't pay me, like she said she was going to. She keeps telling me she has to get money out of the bank, but she never does."

"Funny thing about that," Bernie commented.

"Next time, I'm asking for the money up front," Ricky said.

"Maybe there shouldn't be a next time," Bernie suggested.

Ricky scowled and began picking at his cuticle again.

Bernie decided to return to the matter at hand. "Is that what you wanted to tell me?" she asked.

Ricky shook his head. "No. I wanted to tell you that Ralph told me he knows who killed Susie."

"And how does he know that?"

"Because he saw it happening."

"I see." Bernie raised an eyebrow. "Funny, but he never mentioned that to me."

"Maybe he had his reasons," Ricky replied.

"Such as?" Bernie asked. They'd arrived at the Nice N Easy.

Ricky rubbed his thumb and index finger together in the universal sign for money.

Bernie stopped the van. "He's blackmailing the person?" She asked, handing Ricky twenty bucks.

He shrugged. "I guess you'll just have to ask him." Then he opened the van door and stepped outside.

Chapter 42

Sean was watching a movie on TV when Libby came up the stairs with a pot of tea and some shortbread cookies for herself and her dad. The strawberry tarts were done, the chicken was soaking in its buttermilk bath, the salads were prepped, the pickup orders were ready for pickup, and the dishes were washed, at which point Libby had decided she could use a break.

"Is that *Mr. Deeds Goes to Washington?*" she asked her dad as she set the tray down on the coffee table in front of the sofa.

Sean looked away from the TV for a minute. "No," he answered. "It's *Mr. Smith Goes to Washington* and *Mr. Deeds Goes to Town,* not the other way around. The first has James Stewart, and the second one has Gary Cooper."

"I can't tell the actors apart," Libby admitted as she poured her dad a cup of tea, put two shortbread cookies on the saucer the cup was resting on, and set the cup and saucer on the table next to Sean. Then she served herself tea and cookies as well.

"That's appalling," Sean told her. "They were two of the greatest actors of my generation. Or any generation."

He took a sip of tea. "Nice," he said appreciatively, refer-ring to both the tea and the cup and saucer. They were his wife's Rosenthal china, and she had always insisted on using them every day, a tradition his daughters had lately started following again, even if it meant washing the bone china by hand.

"It is a pretty pattern," Libby agreed as she sat down on the sofa next to Cindy. The cat hissed at her, jumped down, and stalked off. "Be that way if you want," Libby called after her.

She tasted the tea. Her mom was right, she decided. Tea did taste better when one drank it out of a bone-china teacup instead of a mug. But why? Was it perception or re-ality? While Libby was mulling the question over, she watched Cindy strut into her bedroom, jump onto her bed, give her a defiant stare, and curl up on her pillow.

"Don't bother," Sean told Libby as she started to get up to shoo Cindy off her bed. "You can't win with a cat," he noted before he went back to watching the movie. "That's why I like dogs."

"And yet we have Cindy," Libby observed, thinking of Susie's kitties and wondering how Grace and Ralph were doing with them. She took another sip of tea and a bite of her shortbread cookie. The cookie melted in her mouth, the way it was supposed to. The few crystals of sea salt she'd put in the batter dissolved on her tongue, providing a pleasant contrast with the sweetness of the sugar and the smoothness of the butter.

"Excellent," Sean said, sighing with pleasure. "This is your best version ever."

Of course, her dad said that about all her versions, but, Libby thought, it was always nice to be complimented. Then she turned her attention to the movie. For the next ten minutes, the only sounds in the room were the ticking of the clock on the wall and the sound of a dog barking at a squirrel outside. She was watching a scene concerning Mr. Deeds and the bankers when it hit her.

"Dad," she said, leaning forward and putting the teacup down. "Remember those pages that were on Susie's desk, the ones with her to-do list on them?"

Sean tore his eyes away from the screen for a minute. "You mean the ones I've been obsessing about? What about them?"

"Where are they?"

"Right where I put them." Sean gestured to the desk. "Over there. On top of the pile. Why are you asking?"

Libby got up. "I'll tell you in a minute," she said as she went over to the desk. Then she started looking.

The desk, a large rolltop saved from a 1920s train station, was piled high with junk mail, flyers, and magazines, but the pages Libby was looking for were in plain sight, lying on top of a car manual for the Chevy her dad had owned fifteen years ago.

"You could get rid of this, you know," Libby said, holding the manual up as she glanced at the pages Sean had taken from Susie's desk.

"I could," Sean said, watching to see what his daughter was up to.

Libby put the manual down. "But you won't," she answered as she studied a phrase Susie had written in the middle of the first page.

"Correct," Sean replied as Libby continued staring at the phrase. Unlike everything else on the page, Susie had underlined the phrase several times and had followed the last word with several exclamation marks.

In addition, Susie had borne down on the pen when she'd underlined the words, leaving an indentation in the paper. Libby looked at the words for a moment, running her finger along the underlining, to reassure herself that she was correct. Libby shook her head and walked over to the chair Sean was sitting in. *Amazing. It has been there all along,* Libby thought as she showed her dad the paper. They just hadn't seen what was in front of their eyes.

"I think we were wrong about this," she told him. Sean looked where Libby was pointing.

"Wrong about what?" Sean asked.

Libby told him. "I don't think the word *deeds* refers to properties. I think *deeds* refers to a last name."

Sean stared at the phrase for a moment. He read it aloud. "Get rid of deeds."

"You see what I mean?" Libby asked.

"It's possible," Sean allowed.

"I think it's more than possible," Libby retorted. "The first letter of the word is capitalized. Also, if *deeds* referred to property, the word *the* would have preceded it. Anyway, why would Susie be getting rid of property deeds? She was in the process of acquiring property."

Sean thought about all the papers he had stuffed away in his filing cabinet that he didn't need anymore. "That's easy. This was a note to herself to clean out her old files," he suggested.

"I disagree. This was her note to herself to get this person out of her life."

Sean leaned back in his chair and glanced at the TV screen again. "Who are we talking about?"

"The name's on the tip of my tongue," Libby said.

"Tell me when you remember," Sean said, then turned his attention back to the TV.

Libby ate the last cookie, even though she really didn't want it. She hated when she couldn't remember something. It made her feel as if she was losing her grip. She finished her tea, grabbed her cell, and texted Bernie the list of things she needed her to pick up. She was just about to text her about the deeds thing when a sales rep called about a new coffee system. She set up an appointment with him, then texted her sister again.

Does the name Deeds ring a bell? she wrote. **It's making me nuts. Who is he?** She'd just pressed SEND when she heard the downstairs door open and Amber calling up to her, telling her their credit card machine was off-line.

"Terrific. Just what I don't need," Libby muttered as she went down the stairs.

Usually, it was a matter of connecting and disconnecting the lines. Hopefully, that was what it was now. That was the problem with running a place like this, she thought. There was always something to take care of. If it wasn't the equipment breaking, it was the staff not showing up, and if it wasn't the staff not showing up, then it was the suppliers messing up the order. *Oh well.* As she crawled under the counter to get to the wires, she forgot about Deeds. An hour later she remembered, but by then it was almost too late.

Chapter 43

Bernie had dropped Ricky off and was pulling onto Loomis Avenue from the Nice N Easy parking lot when she got Libby's first text. She didn't read it right away, because she was making a left turn into oncoming traffic, but she did a couple of minutes later, when she stopped at the next red light.

Ah, she thought as she slipped the phone back in her tote. *More stuff to get*. Her life was one long errand. How they could go through so many napkins, straws, and sugar packets at the shop was beyond her. Plus, they were almost out of fives and tens, and she'd just gone to the bank yesterday.

Well, the errands would have to wait. She wanted to talk to Ralph first, to look him in the eye and see what his reaction was when she asked him if he knew who had killed his aunt. Then she'd talk to Libby. There was no point in getting her sister excited if this turned out to be a big fat nothing. Which it probably was, given the source of the information. With that settled, Bernie reached over and turned on the radio, tuned it to her favorite station, and then, because Libby wasn't in the van, she turned up the volume, thereby missing Libby's incoming text.

Because of a fender bender on Roth Street, it took Bernie almost half an hour to get to the old Connor estate. It wasn't a big-deal accident—someone had driven into a ditch—but people slowed down to look, which backed everything up, which meant that the drive took ten minutes longer than it should have.

"Oh my," Bernie exclaimed as she turned into the estate. Things had not improved. The pink cat was now lying facedown in the dirt, the grass was even longer than it had been the last time Bernie and Libby were there, and the weeds were taking over the flower beds.

On the drive up to the house, Bernie spotted four paper coffee cup lids and several fast-food wrappers along the side of the road, something that Susie wouldn't have tolerated if she were alive. Obviously, Travis wasn't doing his job without Susie to keep him in line, Bernie reflected, as she parked the van, got out, and walked up to the house. She could hear the cats meowing as she rang the bell.

A minute later, Grace opened the door. A Russian blue peeked its head out, and Grace quickly scooped the cat up before she could run outside. "Yes?" she said, stepping onto the porch and closing the door behind her. She appeared to have lost weight since Bernie had last seen her. Her cheekbones were sharper, her eyes had a sunken-in look, and her hair looked dull and lifeless.

"Are you okay?" Bernie asked her.

Grace averted her eyes. "I'm tired, that's all. I haven't been sleeping well."

Bernie thought there was more going on, but she didn't say that. Instead, she said, "I need to speak to your brother."

"About what?" Grace asked, a note of alarm in her voice.

"Nothing important," Bernie lied. "I'm just tying up a few loose ends."

"He's at the lodge," Grace answered, looking relieved.

"Lodge?" Bernie wasn't sure where that was.

"Where Travis lives."

"I don't know where Travis lives."

Grace pointed. "Just go to the end of the house, take a left, and keep going," Grace explained as the cat scrambled up on her shoulder and began kneading the back of her head. Grace winced.

"We didn't see it when we were here," Bernie said as Grace lifted the cat off her shoulders and hugged her to her chest.

"You can't see it from where the tent was, because it's hidden by apple trees."

Bernie nodded her thanks. Then she asked Grace if she was all right again.

"Fine," Grace answered, petting the cat she was holding. "Why shouldn't I be?"

"I don't know. You look really, really stressed."

"I am stressed," Grace admitted. "Ralph made me promise not to tell."

Bernie waited. Sometimes it was better not to say anything.

Grace leaned in toward Bernie and lowered her voice. "You have to swear not to say anything."

Bernie held up her hand. "I swear."

Grace hesitated for another moment. Then she said, "We have fleas." Bernie stopped herself from laughing. This wasn't what she was expecting. "I don't know how we got them," Grace confided, "but we do, and they're driving me crazy." She touched noses with the Russian blue she was holding. "Right, Natasha?" Natasha mewed, and Grace smiled. "She's such a dear," Grace said. "I'd be lost without the cats." Then she opened the door to Susie's house, went inside, and shut the door after her.

"Good luck," Bernie called out, and then she started walking.

On the way, she checked her phone and saw her sister's second text. **Here now. Should be easy to find out,** Bernie texted back. Then she slipped her phone back in her tote and kept walking. She'd expected some sort of path, but there wasn't one. Evidently, everyone approached the lodge from the other side of the house.

As she walked, trying—and failing—to keep her heels from sinking into the dirt, Bernie thought about Libby's latest text, about whether her sister was right or not and, if she was correct, about what that meant. It could mean a lot, or it could mean nothing, Bernie concluded as she got to the end of Susie's house, where, as instructed by Grace, she made a left and kept walking.

A couple of minutes later, she had passed Susie's house and the garage attached to it. In the distance, she could see the trees Grace had mentioned, and she picked up her pace. When she got closer, she noticed the apples ripening on the tree branches. She wondered what kind they were as she watched the clouds scudding across the sky. Maybe they were an old varietal. As she rubbed her arms, she made a note to herself to ask Grace if she and Libby could come back and pick some when they ripened.

It had suddenly turned colder, as the sun had disappeared behind a cloud. *It's going to rain soon,* Bernie decided as she threaded her way through the trees and came face-to-face with the lodge. It was a plain Jane type of building, without any landscaping to soften its lines.

When the estate had been a farm, the lodge had been the place where the farmhands had bunked. Then, when the farm had been sold off, the farmhouse razed, and the Connor house built, the bunkhouse had undergone a transformation, as well.

Now the long, low-slung building was insulated and covered in slate-blue vinyl siding. The windows were small, and the door was narrower than most doors were these days. The roof was red metal, the kind you found on commercial buildings, and an aluminum flue sprouted out of the lodge's left side, while a satellite dish perched on the roof's right side.

Bernie walked up to the door and knocked, because there was no bell. When no one answered after a minute, she called out, announcing herself. Again, there was no response. She called out for a third time. Nothing. She walked a couple of feet and looked around for signs of activity.

She didn't see anything except two squirrels chittering at one another from opposite branches of one of the apple trees. She sighed. Three possibilities. Either Grace was wrong; or she'd been lying to her; or she'd called Ralph and told him Bernie wanted to speak to him, and he'd decided to get out of town, which would explain why she hadn't asked Bernie why she wanted to speak to her brother.

Bernie stood there for a minute, tapping her fingers on her thighs, while she decided what to do next. She could leave. Or she could try the door. She tried the door. It was open. She stepped inside. After all, she reasoned, if Travis didn't want anyone in there, he would have locked the door. *Right?* And then there was Libby's text about Travis. *Time to check that out, as well.*

"Travis, Ralph. Anyone home?"

Silence reigned. The only sounds Bernie heard were faint scrabbling noises coming from upstairs. *Probably mice or squirrels in the walls,* Bernie decided. It made sense in an old building like this, she figured as she looked around the place. A large living room flowed into a dining area and from there into a kitchen. A fireplace sat on the far wall, opposite three stairs that, Bernie assumed, led to the bath and bedrooms.

The place was sparsely furnished. In the living room, there was a stained, beige wall-to-wall carpet on the floor, a leather sofa and a matching recliner, and a desk that looked like the kind you'd find at IKEA. A large TV hung on the wall opposite the sofa. It was the dominant object in the room. In the dining room, the table consisted of a large slab of wood resting on two sawhorses. It was piled high with papers and surrounded by four oak chairs.

The scrabbling continued. *Must be an infestation*, Bernie thought as she went over and looked through the papers on the dining-room table. She picked up a flyer from an auto parts store. The address label read TRAVIS DEEDS OR CURRENT OCCUPANT. Bernie reread the label just to make sure. So, Libby's hunch was correct, after all.

When Susie had written, "Get rid of deeds," on her yellow pad, she had meant to get rid of Travis Deeds, not to get rid of the deeds. But why did Susie want to do that? What had Travis Deeds done? That was the question. Bernie thought about it as she went through the rest of the pile of papers on the table. Just more flyers, unpaid and unopened bills, car magazines, old pizza boxes, and used paper plates. Basically, nothing of interest.

When she was done, Bernie snapped a picture of the label on the auto parts store flyer and sent it off to Libby. Then she walked over to the desk in the living room. There was a laptop sitting on it. She tried opening it, but it was password protected—not a big surprise—and after a few minutes of futzing around, Bernie abandoned the effort and started opening the desk drawers.

The left-hand drawer was full of computer cables, while the drawer in the middle held a couple of reams of computer paper, and the right-hand drawer held a folder labeled PETTY CASH AND ORDERS. Bernie remembered seeing it sitting on Susie's desk. It was bright pink, with a picture of Grumpy Cat on it. Hard to forget.

Bernie wondered what the folder was doing in Travis's desk as she opened it and started reading. The folder, as stated on the label, contained lists of household expenses, receipts for said items, and notations stating when Travis had been reimbursed for his expenses.

Nothing unusual in that, except that Susie had questioned half the expenses. Her comments ranged from *See me* to *Where's the receipt?* to *You have to pay more attention* to *Pennies count* to *See me immediately!* The last comment referred to a lawn mower purchase. Susie had written a further notation, as well. *Two? Double billing? Did you think I wouldn't notice?*

Okay, Bernie thought as she clicked her tongue against the roof of her mouth. *What do we have here?* Given the folder's contents, she could only surmise that Susie believed that Travis had gone from carelessness to pilfering petty cash. When she looked at the receipts again, she noticed the date on Susie's comment about the lawn mower. It was the day before the wedding. So, had Susie confronted Travis about it? Had she threatened to have him arrested if he didn't pay her back the money? Knowing Susie, that seemed like a likely possibility.

And then what happened? Bernie came up with two scenarios. In either case, Travis had spent the night stewing about it. Then one of two things had happened: either he'd decided to get the receipt back, so he snuck into the house the following day, Susie caught him rifling through her desk, and Travis panicked and stabbed her; or Travis had decided to talk to Susie and they got into a fight and he stabbed her, at which point he panicked, fled the scene, and took the folder with him.

Either way, the results were the same. Travis had killed Susie. And then there was Ralph. Had he really seen Susie being killed? Was he blackmailing Travis, like Ricky had said he was? And if that was the case, did Travis have the money for a payoff, or was he just stringing Ralph along? Had Ralph finally realized that and confronted Travis?

Bernie decided she really had to get hold of Ralph. He was the key. She'd just decided to call Grace and see if Ralph had gone back to the house when she heard the front door open. She turned as Travis stepped into the room.

Chapter 44

"Oh, hi, Travis," Bernie said, trying for casual as she pushed the folder closer to the laptop. "This is quite the place you have here."

"Really?" Travis said as he moved across the floor, the door slamming shut behind him, while his eyes went from Bernie's face to her hand and back again.

Bernie took a step away from the desk. "I was looking for Ralph. Grace said he was here, but I guess she was wrong." Bernie gave Travis her brightest smile. "The door was unlocked, so I hope you don't mind that I popped in." She nodded toward it. "I don't suppose you've seen Ralph?"

Travis folded his arms across his chest. "No, I haven't." But Bernie noticed Travis's eyes strayed to the staircase at her mention of Ralph. It was just a momentary glance, but it was enough.

"Mice," Travis explained as the scrabbling grew more insistent.

That's Ralph up there, Bernie thought as she swallowed, and then she told herself to stay cool. She had to get out of here and get help. "That's what I figured," she told Travis, trying for nonchalance. "If you see Ralph, tell him I'm looking for him." But she couldn't help herself; like Travis, she glanced upstairs at the mention of Ralph's name. *Super.* She shook her head. She could tell from the expression on Travis's face that he knew that she knew. *So much for plan A.*

"What do you want to talk to Ralph for, anyway?" Travis asked.

"Just cat stuff," Bernie replied, heading toward the door.

Travis moved in front of her. "I don't believe you," he said.

Bernie shrugged. "Have it your way, but it's the truth."

"Why were you looking through my stuff?" Travis demanded as he grabbed Bernie's wrist. "Did you think Ralph was in one of my desk drawers?"

"Ha. Ha. I wasn't looking."

Travis stuck his face in Bernie's. "So how did that folder get from the drawer to the desktop?"

"Levitation?"

Travis twisted Bernie's wrist. "Wrong answer."

"Ouch." Bernie tried to pull away, but she couldn't. Travis was too strong. His grip around her wrist was like a vise. Then he grabbed Bernie's other wrist with his left hand, spun her around, pulled both wrists behind her, and bent her arms up, forcing her to lean forward.

"What have you done with Ralph?" Bernie asked through gritted teeth. There was no point in pretending now.

Travis didn't say anything. Instead, he yanked Bernie's arms farther up, putting pressure on her shoulders.

"He was blackmailing you, wasn't he?" she managed to get out. Talking was distracting her from the pain. "But then he must have found out you don't have any money. What did he do? Threaten to go to the police? Did he see you kill Susie, or did he figure it out later, when he came across the folder? Did he bring the folder here? Did he tell you he was going to take it to the cops?"

"You just don't shut up, do you?" Travis said as he dragged Bernie toward one of the chairs by the dining-room table.

"Will you let me go if I do?"

"Funny lady," Travis said. The sound of a door slam-ming and someone moaning took Travis's attention off Bernie for a moment.

He turned to look. Then he cursed under his breath. Bernie looked, too. It was Ralph. He was staggering down the stairs. He was holding his side, and blood was leaking out from between his fingers. He took half a dozen steps and collapsed on the floor.

Momentarily distracted, Travis's grip on Bernie loos-ened. Bernie decided it was now or never. She brought her foot back and stamped down on Travis's instep with her high heel with as much force as she could muster. He screamed and let go of her. Bernie ran for the front door.

If she could reach the van, she'd have a chance. She was turning the doorknob when she felt Travis's hand on her shoulder. He yanked her back, spun her around, and punched her in the face. She saw stars. Literally.

I thought that was a metaphor, Bernie later remembered thinking before everything went black. She came to a cou-ple of minutes later. The first thing she was aware of was the throbbing in her jaw. The second thing she was aware of was that she couldn't move her hands or feet. She looked down. They were zip-tied to a chair. She heard groaning and looked over. It was Ralph. He was lying on the floor, so weakened by blood loss that all he could do was groan. Then she looked up. Travis was pacing back and forth. Finally, he stopped and came over to her.

"You want to know why I killed Susie?" he asked.

"Why not?" Bernie said, reflecting on the irony of the situation. Indeed, timing was everything. Three hours ago, she would have been delighted to find out the particulars of Susie's death, but now, not so much. *First rule of detecting: never hear a confession when you can't get away from the killer who's making it.*

"Susie was going to fire me."

"That's because you stole from her," Bernie couldn't help herself from saying.

"So what?" Travis's voice rose in indignation. "With all the money she had, she could have paid me a living wage. But she wouldn't. She was too cheap. Everything went to those damned cats."

"You could have gotten another job," Bernie pointed out.

"I didn't want another job. I like it here. I didn't even take that much. Just a little here and there. Enough to take Grace out to a nice dinner once in a while." He paused for a moment before going on. "I knew I shouldn't have tried that thing with the lawn mower, but what could I do? My car needed work."

"And a guy can't be without a vehicle," Bernie observed.

"Exactly," Travis agreed. "Susie could have bought me an Infiniti if she wanted to. I just got so mad."

"Of course you did," Bernie told him, trying a different tactic. "Anyone would have in your position. Here was this wedding going on for cats, a wedding Susie was spending thousands and thousands on, and all you wanted was enough money to fix your ride."

"That's right." Bernie could hear Travis's voice softening. "One of those cat collars would have taken care of me and . . ." Travis stopped.

"Marie," Bernie said, remembering she'd seen Travis coming out of her house. "It wasn't only about the money. It was about Marie, too, wasn't it?"

"So, what if it was?" Travis said. "Susie was wrecking Marie's life, just like she was wrecking mine and Grace's. I was doing everyone a favor. Susie got what she deserved."

"Yes, she did," Bernie agreed.

"She was a bitch," Travis said.

"Undoubtedly. You didn't mean to kill Susie. You just lost it. Anyone would have in your position. I'm sure the DA will charge you with manslaughter," Bernie lied. "Maybe you'll get house arrest. But not if you don't prove your good intentions by letting us go. Ralph needs to get to a hospital."

Travis set his jaw and crossed his arms over his chest. "I'm not spending my life in jail."

"You won't, not if Ralph is still alive. You're not a murderer," Bernie told him, despite the evidence to the contrary.

Travis chuckled. The sound sent shivers down Bernie's spine. "You know," he told her, "that's what I would have said before I killed Susie, but it turned out I was wrong."

"My sister knows where I am," Bernie countered.

"That's nice," Travis said. "When she gets here, she'll be able to collect what's left of you."

As Bernie watched, Travis went over to the stove and turned on the gas burners. Then he took her cell phone out of her tote and placed it on the counter next to the stove. "When I'm far enough away from the house, I'm going to call you and *poof.*" He sketched a cloud in the air with his hands. "It will be a tragic accident." As Travis headed toward the front door, he detoured to kick Ralph in the ribs. "That's for trying to blackmail me, you son of a bitch."

Ralph groaned.

"Hang on, Ralph," Bernie told him after Travis left. "I'm going to try to get us out of here."

"Sooner would be better than later," Ralph observed as the room spun in front of his eyes.

Looking around, Bernie spotted a kitchen knife on the table next to her. The knife was near the edge. If she could jiggle the table, maybe she could get the knife to fall off. Or, better still, to fall in her lap. Then all she'd have to do was somehow use the knife to cut one of the zip ties. *Piece of cake.* But first she had to get the knife off the table. Okay, it was a long shot, but it was better than sitting here waiting to asphyxiate. Of course, they could always blow up, but asphyxiating was the more likely possibility.

"Hurry up," Ralph urged. He began to cough. "I'm having trouble breathing," he managed to get out before he succumbed to the coughing fit.

"The joys of a well-insulated building," Bernie noted as she began rocking in the chair to get it nearer to the table. The motion moved the chair only slightly. She had to get the chair close enough to move the slab of wood that was the tabletop and knock the knife down. She'd have to do better than she was doing. She'd have to get more motion going. She rocked the chair harder. Nothing. Then she rocked it even harder.

But she misjudged and moved too far forward and tipped over. Now she was on the floor, attached to the chair, with her behind pointing toward the ceiling. This was not what she had planned. *Very dignified!* She was trying to figure out how to get on her side when the front door flew open.

"It certainly took you long enough," Bernie told Libby as she and Grace raced in.

Chapter 45

So, her gut had been right, after all, Libby thought as she saw her sister lying on the floor, with her butt pointed to the ceiling.

At first Libby had been annoyed; then she'd been worried and annoyed as lunchtime approached and Bernie still hadn't shown up or called or answered Libby's texts. But then Libby had reasoned that maybe her sister had forgotten to charge her phone battery, or she'd met someone at Costco and stopped to chat, or she was somewhere with no phone reception. There were still a few no-reception places left in Longely. Libby had told herself she shouldn't be such a worrywart, she'd told herself she was overdramatizing, she'd told herself there was a reasonable explanation, but she hadn't been able to shake off the niggling kernel of worry in her gut.

She'd been trying to decide what to do when Marvin walked into the shop for a chat, a cup of coffee, and a grilled cheese and tomato sandwich.

"I'm sure she's fine, but let's look," Marvin had suggested to Libby after she'd confided her fears to him.

"Yeah," Amber had said as she filled up the coffee grinder

with French roast. "Go look. We've got everything covered."

Libby remembered glancing around and concluding that Amber was correct, that everything was under control, before taking Marvin up on his offer. Thank heaven she had, she reflected as she caught sight of the knobs on the stove turned to high. She didn't want to consider what would have happened if she were still back at the shop.

Even now, thinking about the ten minutes she and Marvin had spent driving around before they got here gave her the chills. She'd known Bernie had a list of errands, but what she hadn't known was what order she'd done them in, so she and Marvin had started with the places that were closest. The Connor estate was their last stop.

They'd just reached the house when Grace stepped outside and flagged them down.

"Are you looking for Bernie?" she'd asked.

"Funny you should say that," Libby had replied, "because that's what I was going to ask you. Is she here?"

"She went to talk to Ralph up at the lodge, but I didn't see her come back down. I just texted her, but she hasn't answered."

The niggle of doubt Libby had been feeling turned into a full-fledged feeling of panic. Marvin and Libby exchanged looks.

"Something isn't right," Grace added, not that she needed to.

"No kidding," Libby said. Then she told Grace to get in the car. They needed to find out what was going on.

"Let's go," Grace replied after she opened the car door and jumped into the backseat. Then she leaned over and directed Marvin to the lodge.

On the way there, they passed a run-down tennis court,

a gazebo that had seen better days, and a couple of utility sheds that looked as if they were ready to collapse.

"I guess this is the side of the estate no one sees," Libby commented.

Grace nodded. "Susie said she didn't play tennis or sit outside, so why bother to repair the court or the gazebo? There was enough for Travis to take care of as it was. Which is true. Anyway, she preferred to spend her money on her cats."

Libby was about to answer, when she spotted Travis hurriedly walking toward them. He'd obviously just come out of the lodge. "Look," she said, pointing to him.

"I bet he's going to the utility shed," Grace said, guessing. "That's where he keeps his car."

But Grace was wrong. When he spotted Marvin's car, he stood there for a minute, a look of panic on his face. Then he took off running toward the apple trees.

"That can't be good," Libby observed.

"No. It certainly is not," Marvin agreed, jamming on the brakes and bringing his car to a dead stop in the middle of the road. He got out of the car. "Don't worry," he called over his shoulder. "I'll get Travis. You see about Bernie."

"And Ralph," Grace added as Marvin took off after Travis. "I bet he's in there, too."

Libby nodded as she and Grace jumped out of the car.

"Oh, my God," Grace cried as they got close to the lodge. "I think I smell gas."

Libby sniffed. The odor was faint but unmistakable. And the closer she got, the stronger the smell became. When she got to the lodge, she took a deep breath and opened the door. The fumes rushed out as she and Grace rushed in. Grace headed for her brother, while Libby turned off the gas and opened all the windows before going over to her sister's side.

"Nice position. You look like a snail," she couldn't help telling Bernie as she squatted down next to her.

"I'm glad you like it," Bernie snapped. "Now, get me out."

"You're lucky you didn't die," Libby said, and then she became serious as she turned toward Ralph. "How bad is he?" she asked Grace.

"I think he looks worse than he is," Grace responded. "But we have to get him outside."

"We all have to get outside," Libby said as she picked up the knife that was on the table, the knife Bernie had tried to get, and cut the zip ties away from Bernie's wrists and ankles.

"Thank God," Bernie said as Libby helped her up. Every muscle in her body was shrieking in pain.

Libby pointed to Bernie's jaw. "It's swollen. What happened?"

Bernie rubbed her wrists and ankles to get the circulation going. "Travis punched me."

"That wasn't very sporting," Libby observed.

"No, it certainly wasn't," Bernie agreed as she hobbled over to Ralph.

"I thought we were goners," he confessed, looking up at her.

"Naw," Bernie said, although she'd thought that, too.

Grace stood up. "I'm going to get a sheet from the bedroom," she announced. "We can use that as a stretcher."

"And I'll call nine-one-one," Bernie said as she went to get her phone.

"Are you nuts?" Libby asked, aghast. "And blow us up? Wait till we get outside."

"That's not going to happen," Bernie told her.

"The going outside part?"

"No. The blowing up part."

"Then why are there signs all over gas stations, telling you to turn off your cell before you fill up?" Libby demanded.

"Okay. It could happen," Bernie allowed. "But it's a long shot. As a rule, cells don't spark."

"There was one that caught fire," Libby pointed out. She was about to add the phrase "Better safe than sorry" when she heard a noise. She turned. Travis was standing in the open doorway, and he had a gun in his hand.

"Please don't," Bernie yelled.

Travis grinned. "But I want to."

"Travis, please put the gun down," Bernie begged. "You shoot that thing and you'll kill yourself, as well as all of us."

Travis shrugged. "That's fine by me. I'm dead, anyway." And he disengaged the safety.

Bernie and Libby watched in horror as Travis aimed the gun at the stove. They both shut their eyes and waited for the inevitable. A few seconds later there was a crash. Libby and Bernie opened their eyes. Travis was lying on the floor, and Marvin was sitting on top of him, his face red from running.

"Get the gun," Marvin managed to gasp out.

Libby ran to get the gun as Travis began to wiggle out from under Marvin.

"What are you going to do, Libby?" Travis mocked as he shook Marvin off and got to his feet. "Shoot me?"

As Travis took a step toward Libby, Marvin spied a metal doorstop in the shape of a cat by the wall. He ran over, got it, and brought it down on the back of Travis's head.

"Thank God," Libby said as Travis crumpled to the floor.

Marvin's hands were trembling. "Do you think I killed him?" he asked Libby.

"No. His chest is moving. But he's going to have a very bad headache when he wakes up," she replied. "We should leave him here," Libby added as she started to drag Travis outside.

"Yes, we should," Marvin agreed as he ran to help her.

"Thank God for Marvin," Grace said as she came down the steps, carrying a bedcover she'd found in one of the bedrooms.

"He's definitely moved to hero status in my book," Bernie noted as she and Grace maneuvered Ralph onto the bedcover. Then they dragged him out to the front yard.

By now Travis had come to, but before he did, Libby and Marvin had found zip ties in Travis's pockets, had used them to secure his wrists and ankles, and had propped him up against a tree.

"My head, my head," Travis cried as he rocked from side to side. He pointed to Marvin with his chin. "You tried to kill me."

"I was trying to get you to stop killing everyone else," Marvin explained in a shaky voice. The adrenaline surge was leaving him, and he felt so exhausted, he was having trouble standing.

"No, Marvin," Travis said. "*You* were trying to kill me, and that's what I'm going to tell the police."

"You do that, Travis," Libby snapped at him. "I'm sure they'll believe that coming from someone who killed one person and tried to kill two—no, five—others."

Grace had been kneeling over Ralph. She got up and

went over to Travis. "You almost killed my brother," she shouted at him as she kicked his leg.

"He was blackmailing me," Travis protested.

Grace kicked him again. Harder. "You are a despicable man. And to think that I actually loved you, that I thought we had something going."

Travis tried to smile through his pain. "We did. We do."

"So, Travis, does Marie think that about you and her, too?" Bernie asked. "Just curious."

Grace turned toward her. "What do you mean?"

"You mean you don't know about Marie?" Bernie asked Grace, all pretend innocence. "Libby and I saw Travis coming out of her house."

"Is that true?" Grace demanded after facing Travis.

"It wasn't a big deal," Travis told her.

"Marie looked pretty happy," Bernie observed.

"Okay," Travis conceded. "So maybe we did do it a couple of times."

Grace kicked him for the third time.

"Stop." Travis pleaded. "It wasn't like that."

"Then what was it like?" Grace asked, the words coming out through gritted teeth.

"You know I love you, baby. I was just helping her out. . . ."

Grace turned to Ralph. "Did you know about Marie?"

Ralph turned his head away.

"I'll take that as a yes. Why didn't you tell me?"

"Because I didn't think you'd believe me."

"Because you're a liar," Travis yelled at Ralph. "And you know that no one will believe anything you say." He nodded in Ralph's direction. "He's the one who killed Susie," Travis told Bernie. "All that stuff I said to you before about the stuff I did . . . I was just kidding around. I was pretending."

"Sure you were," Bernie said. She could hear sirens in the distance.

The ambulance and the police were going to be here any minute. Bernie smiled. She was going to enjoy seeing the look on Lucy's face when she told him what had happened.

Chapter 46

Six weeks later . . .

"It could be worse," Bernie said as she handed Ralph a slice of peach and apricot pie. She was referring to the ugly scars on his body that Ralph was left with after Travis had knifed him. "It's not as if you're entering a bodybuilding competition."

"It could always be worse," Ralph noted.

"Yeah," Libby told him. "You could be in prison for blackmail."

"Well, there is that," Ralph allowed.

"There certainly is," Grace said as she shooed Natasha off the table. She was still pissed at her brother for doing what he'd done.

She, Bernie, Libby, and Ralph were sitting in the dining room of the main house on the Connor estate, surrounded by Boris, Natasha, and two other cats, all of which were eyeing the bowl of whipped cream sitting next to the pie.

"Maybe we should give them some," Bernie suggested as Boris jumped on the table.

"It's not good for their stomachs," Grace said as she sat Boris on her lap. "It'll give them the runs."

"By the way, congratulations on winning," Libby said to Grace and Ralph. Boris had won best in show at a major cat show down in New York.

Grace nodded. "Susie would have been pleased."

"She would have been ecstatic," Bernie said.

"So now what?" Libby asked as she tasted the pie. She'd tried something new with it. She'd used dried apricots and fresh peaches, and it had turned out better than expected. The trick had been to give the apricots a good long soak and to add a touch of ginger to spice things up.

"I guess we carry on carrying on," Grace said. "Although we're going to change some things around. We're building a large covered outdoor area so the cats can go outside. Allison is helping."

"She must be happy about that," Libby noted.

"Oh. She definitely is," Grace agreed. "And I think the cats will be, too. She's actually very nice when you get to know her. Just a little intense."

"And we're rehoming some of the kitties," Ralph said. "The trustee said we could."

"Of course, we're doing home visits first," Grace said. "Just to make sure they go to good families." She ate a bite of pie. "This really is delicious. I wish I could bake."

"Libby and I could teach you if you want," Bernie offered as Natasha jumped up on her lap.

Grace smiled. "That would be wonderful."

Bernie couldn't help it. She dipped her finger in the whipped cream and let Natasha lick it off. "It's just a little," she said apologetically. "She's hard to resist," she added.

"I know," Grace said as Ralph gave Olga a taste.

"It's not going to kill them," Ralph said to Grace, even

though Grace hadn't said anything to him. "Speaking of kill," he said, "I can't believe that Travis said that Marie was behind the whole thing."

Bernie nodded. The story had been in the local paper. "Yeah, but not even Lucy bought it."

Grace shook her head. "The man is such a weasel."

"Just be glad he didn't name you as his accomplice," Libby said.

Grace shook her head. "I can't believe I didn't see what he was."

Bernie fed Natasha another tiny dab of cream. "Well, he's going to be in jail for a long time. My dad said he pled down to second-degree murder—that's twenty-five to life."

Grace shook her head. "Such a stupid thing to do. Why didn't he just leave?"

"Because he thought that Susie owed him," Libby said. "Because he was really angry about the way Susie treated him, and he wanted to get her back."

"I hated her, too, but I didn't kill her," Grace said. She sighed and looked sad. "I guess I need to work on making better choices in men."

"I know how you feel," Bernie said, thinking of some of her mistakes.

Grace rubbed Boris's ears. "I think I'm going to concentrate on Boris for a while."

Ralph leaned forward. "Maybe you could meet someone at my Gamblers Anonymous meeting," he suggested. "There are a lot of guys there."

"Unclear on the concept," Libby and Bernie both blurted out at the same time.

Everyone looked at each other and started laughing. Then they went back to eating the pie. Everything had turned out well, Bernie reflected. Or at least it had for the people in this room. She and her sister had solved Susie's murder with two days to spare, Ralph was attending Gamblers Anonymous, and Grace had gained back some of the weight she'd lost, a condition that Bernie suspected was related to her relationship with Travis.

Of course, things hadn't worked out so well for Travis. But then, he hadn't behaved so well, either.

Or Susie. Especially, things hadn't worked out for her. But then maybe if she'd been a little kinder, none of this would have happened at all.

Recipes

Since this book deals with a breed of cat that supposedly comes from Russia, and since my grandmother came from someplace in Russia and loved cats, I thought it would be nice to offer up two of the recipes my grandmother made, but then I realized that like many cooks of her generation, my grandmother didn't use recipes. She cooked by smell, taste, and touch. If you wanted to learn how she made something, you had to be in the kitchen with her. Sometimes even that didn't help.

Take strudel. I don't know how many times I watched my grandmother clear the kitchen table, spread out newspaper, and roll out the strudel dough until it was so thin you could read the print through it. Unfortunately, watching didn't help. I could never do it. I did learn to make beet borscht, however. We ate it cold in the summer and hot in the winter. Not only does it taste good, but the soup is a beautiful shade of red, which becomes a lovely pink when you add a dollop of sour cream.

I made my grandmother's borscht for years, and then, for some reason, I stopped making it, and when I went to find the recipe, I couldn't. So, I went on the Internet to look for the very same recipe because not only did I want to make it, but I also wanted to include it in this book. But I couldn't find it there. Finally, in a last-ditch effort, I did what I should have done to begin with. I turned to my dear friend, and a fantastic cook, Linda Kleinman. Of course, she had the recipe I was looking for. She always does, so here's Linda Kleinman's recipe for borscht. I should also add that this soup tastes best when the beets are really fresh.

LINDA KLEINMAN'S BORSCHT

6 large red beets
½ cup fresh lemon juice
¼ cup granulated sugar
1 tablespoon salt
1 Idaho potato, peeled and cubed (optional)
Sour cream, for serving (optional)

Peel the beets and grate them in a food processor. Transfer the grated beets to a large pot and add 6 to 7 cups of water. Next, add the lemon juice, sugar, and salt.

Bring the beets to a boil over medium-high heat, and then turn down the heat and simmer for 40 minutes. (If you want a soup with more substance, throw in a cubed potato, although I like it better without it.)

Taste and adjust seasonings. Serve the borscht hot or cold, with or without a dollop of sour cream.

The recipe makes four generous servings.

My grandmother also made something she called blini, which were thin pancakes she served for dessert with apricot or strawberry jam. Only they weren't actual blini, because blini are made with buckwheat flour and yeast, while hers were made with regular flour and butter. They are closer to French crepes or Hungarian *palacsinta*, which are crepes by another name, but whatever you want to call them, they are delicious and, like the borscht, easy to make.

MY GRANDMOTHER'S PANCAKES

1 cup all-purpose flour
1 teaspoon granulated sugar
¼ teaspoon salt
2 cups whole milk
3 large eggs
3 tablespoons melted sweet butter
Oil for cooking the pancakes
Good-quality apricot or strawberry jam, for serving

Sift together the dry ingredients in a medium bowl and set aside.

In a large bowl combine the milk and the eggs and then beat with a whisk. Slowly add the reserved flour mixture and beat until smooth. Then whisk in the melted butter. Cover the bowl the batter is in, and let the batter rest in the refrigerator for at least one hour, although it can stay in there for as long as twenty-four.

Lightly coat a small frying pan with oil and heat the pan over medium heat. Ladle ¼ cup of batter (or less if you want smaller pancakes) into the pan and tilt and rotate the pan immediately until the batter covers the entire bottom surface. Cook the pancake for 30 seconds, or until lightly golden brown on the bottom. Then flip the pancake and cook the other side for 15 seconds, or until lightly golden brown. Remove the pancake to a large plate and repeat the process until all the pancakes are made.

Spoon about a tablespoon of jam in the middle of each pancake, fold each one over, and serve at once.

The recipe serves four to six.